Praise for *Pushing Water*

"An extraordinary voice. A mix of Pelecanos, Leonard and Wambaugh."
>—Colin Campbell, author of the Jim Grant novels and 30-year veteran of the West Yorkshire police

"*Pushing Water* is smart, rhythmic, and relentless with a gripping narrative and a keen eye for how cops act and think."
>—Sgt. Adam Plantinga, San Francisco Police Department, 19-year police veteran and author of *400 Things Cops Know* and *Police Craft*

"Facing a flood of armed robberies—and murder—Detective Doc Dougherty and his partners never lose their professional edge or hometown humanity in *Pushing Water*. With twists that shock and detective work that rings true, King is among the best cop writers going."
>—Mark Bergin, Alexandria VA Police Department (retired) and author of *Apprehension*

PUSHiNG WATER

ALSO BY DANA KING

The Penns River Novels
Worst Enemies
Grind Joint
Resurrection Mall
Ten-Seven

The Nick Forte Mysteries
A Small Sacrifice
The Stuff That Dreams Are Made Of
The Man in the Window
A Dangerous Lesson
Bad Samaritan

Stand Alone Novels
Wild Bill

DANA KING

PUSHING WATER
A PENNS RIVER NOVEL

DOWN&OUT
BOOKS

Down & Out Books
3959 Van Dyke Road, Suite 265
Lutz, FL 33558
DownAndOutBooks.com

Cover design by Eric Beetner

ISBN: 1-64396-073-3
ISBN-13: 978-1-64396-073-9

For The Beloved Spouse, as are they all,
whether she gets the credit or not.

There is nothing more deceptive than an obvious fact.
—Sherlock Holmes

CHAPTER 1

Jacques Lelievre pushed a ten across the bar, tapped it with an index finger.

"Thanks, Larry." Don Kwiatkowski tipped his fresh beer in Jacques's direction. Under the impression Jacques's name was Larry Robinson. A reasonable mistake: that's what Jacques had told him.

"You ever hear of a guy named Elmore Leonard?" Jacques careful to keep his French Canadian accent under control.

Don swallowed. Showed thought. "He a fighter? Sounds like a fighter's name."

"Writer. I think he did some time, though. Writes a lot of books about guys who did time and knows how they think."

Don swallowed. Set the glass on the bar. "You know much about guys that did time?"

"Some."

"Got a lot of convict friends, do you?"

"Not a lot. Some."

"Where'd you get to know not a lot, but some convicts?"

Jacques sipped his drink. "Prison."

Don took his time with another swallow, cagey like. "So you're saying you're a convict. That's how you know about this Elmore guy."

"I'm not saying anything. Being a con isn't the kind of thing you brag aboot." Jacques flinched inwardly.

1

Don took a few seconds to really look at Jacques for the first time that night. "Where you from, exactly?"

"Vermont. Way the fuck up by Canada. Got tired of freezing my cock off seven months a year and moved to Florida. Got so hot there I had to change clothes three times a day. Now I drive truck and move around a lot. Get a little of everything." Jacques really had gotten tired of freezing his cock off, though it had been somewhat north of Vermont.

"What'd you do to get put in prison?"

"Does it matter?"

The pause told Jacques snap judgments weren't Don's strong suit. "Not really, I guess. No. It don't matter at all."

"That's good," Jacques said. "I'd hate to think you were close-minded."

"Not me." Don finished his beer. Looked at Jacques's Crown Royal sitting half-full on the bar. Jacques slugged it back and held up two fingers, pointed to his glass and Don's. Don said, "I'm pretty liberal when it comes to shit like that. This Elmore you mentioned. What about him?"

"He write a book about a guy who has rules for armed robbery. Makes a lot of sense."

"You know a lot about armed robbery?"

"Some."

Don welcomed his fresh beer like a cousin he hadn't seen in years. "Why're you telling me?"

Jacques pretended to think about what to say. "You're on strike from that steel mill across the river, right?"

"We ain't on strike, goddammit. We're locked out. The union's willing to work without a contract while things get settled, but those cocksuckers want givebacks. Locked us out and brought in scabs." Then, into his beer: "Cocksuckers."

"Pay's about the same, though. Locked out or on strike?"

"You just now drunk enough to break my balls, or is there a point here?"

"I'm not drunk." Jacques gave Don time to make eye contact.

"Funny thing, towns without much money usually got plenty of cash. Hard to get credit for people out of work or part-time. People who write money orders don't take checks. Payday loan places have to keep lots of cash on hand. The less money a town has, the more cash is in circulation."

"So?"

Jacques needed Don to be stupid enough, but not too stupid. Not as sure now which side of the line he fell on. "All that cash? It's not nailed down. It has to be available for people to use. That makes it available for everyone."

The lightbulb came on over Don's head. Sixty watts, tops. With a dimmer. "That time you did. Wasn't for robbery, was it?"

Jacques sipped his drink. Smiled.

Don said, "Why are you telling me?"

Jacques let the anticipation build a few seconds. "It takes two men to do it right."

Don gave a long hard look. "What makes you think I'm the kind of guy robs people?"

"What kind of guy is that? A guy who robs people. They look different? Have three eyes? Gun permanent attached to their hand? You know who armed robbers are? People who need money. You know anyone like that?"

Don's beer sat forgotten on the bar. "You didn't say nothing about armed robbery before."

"You know another way people give you money don't belong to you?" Left time for Don to speak up. "I didn't think so. The difference between an armed robber and any of these doncs around us is ambition. You think there's anyone in here don't need money?"

Don looked around at Fat Jimmy's usual clientele. "Some of these guys do all right."

Jacques snorted. "They wouldn't drink in this toilet if they had money to go anyplace else. We been talking here over an hour. You got truck payment, you got child support, you got rent. All you don't got right now is a job."

"I got a fucking job."

"I'm sorry. You got a job. What you don't got is income." Let that one lay on the bar to see if Don picked it up. "I got an idea for income. But I need another guy."

Don turned on his barstool to face Jacques, closing them off from the other drinkers. "I ain't got a problem with...taking some money. But armed robbery? That's an extra five years in this state, I think."

Jacques knew he had a partner as soon as the conversation turned to specifics. "Doesn't matter. No one is going to give you the money if they don't think you got a gun, and that's all it takes. Even you put your finger in your pocket like this— pretend gun—if they think you have a gun, the law says you do. Least that's how it is in Vermont."

"Yeah. Here, too, I think."

Jacques sipped his Crown Royal. "It's funny, when you think about it. They make a big deal about how much more serious is armed robbery, then they write the law so pretty much any robbery is one. You want to call it just robbery? Fine. I'll be armed. You do what you want."

Don's beer sat unattended, nearing room temperature. Jacques finished his drink. Let the warmth flow down his throat. Relaxed and in his element. Hoped Don asked the question before he exploded.

"How do we do it?"

"The first thing is to always be polite on the job. Say please and thank you."

CHAPTER 2

Ben "Doc" Dougherty and his brother Drew stood on Drew's back deck watching Bobby D'Alessio and five other guys with blood alcohol levels higher than the temperature play touch football. Party at Drew's house because he won this year's football pool, picking games against the spread. A dubious prize, what with having to clean up afterward and the risk of random yet potentially significant household damage. On the plus side, the champion didn't have to drive home.

The brothers drank Drew's home brew IPA. Made side bets on who'd give up on the football game first, and how bad the injury would be. "Bobby'd play quarterback for both teams if they'd let him," Drew said.

"I wouldn't put it past him to find a way anyhow." Doc took a sip. Pointed to one of the players. "He already made a mistake not picking Sisler. The man's an athlete."

"He sure looks like one, but how drunk is he?"

"You mean compared to the rest of them?"

Still twenty minutes before the Steelers and Patriots got it on for the AFC championship. The brothers watched half a dozen men in their thirties and forties make more noise than a prison riot as they slipped and slid around Drew's backyard, which had endured snow, sleet, thaws, and hard freezes over the past week.

Drew sipped beer. Said, "I hear that youth or community

5

center or whatever it is down on Fourth Avenue is supposed to open in a few days."

"Tuesday." A sincere and distinct "Fuck!" cut through the general merriment in the yard. "I think I'll make an appearance. Show the town takes an interest."

"Nice to have a job where you can come and go as you please. I got a GPS in my mail truck tells them everyplace I go. I'm not even supposed to come home for lunch and my route's not three minutes away."

"Let's see. You make more money than I do, have more time off, better benefits, and a pension. Damn right I want you working a full shift and not sneaking home to watch The View or whatever it is mailmen do when they should be working."

Drew gave his tight little smile. "I heard they were trying to get some money for that youth thing from Dan Hecker. That ever come through?"

Doc waited for an outburst to subside on the field. Spoke in a flat voice with none of his usual humor. "Danny Hecker's a piece of shit. He grabbed that preacher's religious mall for thirty cents on the dollar after the fire. Promised a riverside park, which I knew was bullshit because he'd still have to buy two more blocks to get to the river." Took a swallow. "I figured he'd at least put in some kind of shopping, since that's how it's zoned. What do we get? A liquor store, yet another vape shop, used videos, and a strip joint. The old man about shit when he heard what the council did to get that titty bar in." Their father on the zoning board.

"I'll bet." They watched the game for a while. Sean Sisler dove parallel to the ground to catch a touchdown. "Here it comes."

"Motherfucker!" Bobby's voice.

"That's five bucks, Bobby." From Tony Lutz. Bobby promised his wife not to make obscene incestuous references in public during the party. Named Tony the enforcer.

Bobby glared as if he had more to say. Settled for, "Oedipus!" Stared at Tony.

"Much better. You still owe five, though."

"Cocksucker." Tony looked ready to say something. Bobby beat him to it. "That one's free. It's just motherfucker I can't say."

"Ten bucks," Tony said.

"Mother—son of a bitch! I thought you were my friend."

"He is your friend," Drew yelled. "He's just doing what you told him to do."

Bobby hollered back up at Drew. "I thought you were my friend, too, and here you turn on me."

"If I wasn't your friend I would've ratted you out for the three motherfuckers you let slip when Val and Tony weren't around." Drew turned toward his brother. "Oops. Did I say that out loud?"

"Hey, Tony." Doc showed fingers in Tony's direction. "Three more." Tony waved acknowledgement.

"There they go, the tag team Doughertys," Bobby said. "No matter where yinz two are, the space between you is a taint."

"Come on, Bobby," someone said from the yard. "We gonna play or what?"

Drew filled Doc's half-empty cup from a pitcher on the railing. The beer ice cold in the sub-freezing evening. "Why does everyone kiss Hecker's ass like they do? He milks money out of this town like it was a cow with that dumpy casino and never sends any back."

"You seen me kiss his ass lately?"

"You know what I mean. Official people. The mayor. City council. Zoning board on that titty bar thing. Hell, even Dad won't buck him. Pisses and moans, makes speeches once in a while in meetings, but the most he'll do is abstain when it comes to a vote."

Doc rubbed his right thumb against the index finger. "What little does come back from the casino pays for campaigns and swimming pools for the mayor and the council. The zoning board serves at their pleasure. There's only so many times Dad can shit in that punch bowl, and only so big a splash he's allowed to make."

"Why doesn't he quit?"

"He likes it. Not the bullshit—he hates that—but the work. Since he retired there's only so much time he can spend in the garden or cutting the grass or working in the shop. Remember when they wanted to build a road up the top of Garver's Ferry Hill and cut down all them trees for that cell tower? Remember that map Dad had, showed most of the new coverage would be across the river? He lives for that shit."

"That was before Hecker."

Doc finished his cup. Refilled himself and topped off Drew. "Lots of things different then. Don't know if they were worse or better, or how much to blame on Hecker, but he sure as hell hasn't helped."

Drew looked at his watch. "Steeler game's ready to start." Turned toward the yard. "Hey! There's real football coming on if you can take a break from measuring each other's dicks."

"Measure this!" floated up from the yard, followed by laughter, then by a football Drew jumped to deflect before it shattered the sliding door. The players trudged into the basement to dry off.

Drew took the recliner, his right as champion and homeowner. Tony finished last this year. His job to ensure Drew always had a drink and food at hand. Everyone just about settled in when the doorbell rang. "Tony." Drew snapped his fingers. "Door." More laughter.

New England's kickoff in the air when Tony's voice came from the front of the house. "Drew! This guy says he wants the owner of this zoo to get his ass out here right now!"

Drew threw a dirty look that direction, maintained the presence of mind to hit the pause button before getting up. The rest of the party followed like ripples behind a boat.

The man at the door was late fifties, balding, red-faced, and looked as if he'd had a few himself. Seeing the six-foot-five Drew Dougherty followed by a dozen people threw him for a second. He chose to brazen it out. "This your house?"

"Yeah. Drew Dougherty. Who are you?"

"I moved into the house next door a couple of weeks ago."

"That's your name?" Semi-suppressed laughter from the partiers.

"I didn't come over here to introduce myself. I came over to tell you to keep the goddamn noise down. My wife and I are trying to watch a movie and we can't hear ourselves think, for Christ's sake."

"Sorry if things got a little rowdy. We're all inside watching the game now. That'll take care of the noise."

"It had better. Hell of a first impression this neighborhood makes on newcomers. The street's clogged with cars and grown men running around in the snow like baboons or chimpanzees or something. It stops now."

Doc, several beers into the day, tried to think if chimps and baboons lived where it snowed. Also wondered why it wasn't the new arrival's job to make a good impression. Took a second to beat himself up over his lack of etiquette awareness, a topic he'd bring up at length after this asshole left. Any doubts about the guy's assholiness erased by the memory of Drew's wife Paula taking over a whole lasagna and a tray of pizzelles a few days after Mr. and Mrs. Asshole moved in.

Drew's voice drew Doc's attention back to the here and now. It took a lot to get his brother's Irish up, but it was a magnificent sight when something did. "It stops now? Or what?"

"Or I call the police."

Doc, Sisler, and four others pulled badge holders from their pockets, flipped them open. "Yes, sir," Doc said. "Is there a problem?"

CHAPTER 3

Elmore Leonard's Third Rule of Armed Robbery was "Never call your partner by name—unless you use a made-up name." Actually Frank Ryan's Third Rule for Success and Happiness, as Elmore Leonard never robbed a bank in his life and would have been too smart to talk about it if he had. Whoever's rule it was, Don Kwiatkowski broke it less than three minutes into the robbery of the payday loan joint on Sixth Avenue. It shouldn't have been hard for Don to remember to call Jacques "Sundance." He'd picked the names.

It wasn't like Don didn't know the rules, intent as he seemed on breaking them all. He'd already told at least one person to shut the fuck up (Rule One: "Always Be Polite") and talked like a teenage girl on crank since they got there, in direct contravention of Rule Two: "Never Say More Than is Necessary." Dressed like he'd just climbed out of a ditch. So much for Rule Four.

Jacques stepped in before anything dramatic went wrong. "Everything is fine. No one is going to get hurt." Five people there, including him and Don. No reason to yell. "This place is here to give money to people. We are just going to take more than most. Now, who has the keys?"

The guy on the floor where Don had forced everyone said, "I do."

Jacques noticed the melting slush, faced him with an almost

apologetic smile. "What is your name, sir?"

"Ed Spicer."

"Brush yourself off, Ed. This floor is filthy. Butch, let the rest of these people up before their clothes are ruined."

Don didn't recognize his code name the first time. The sixty-watter went on after Jacques's second request. "Where do you want them?" Waved the shotgun he'd brought, which also appalled Jacques, who'd requested a low profile.

The job started badly. Jacques had been here before, knew to expect a manager and a teller. No one present when he cased the place was there today—he would have recognized either of them—and no one was in working positions. The only people in the building when he and Don walked in were bullshitting in the customer area. Jacques wanted to let the players sort themselves out but Don screamed—that was the only word for it—for "everyone to foot their paces on the fucking floor" and charged the shotgun, which ejected a shell because he'd already done that "getting ready" in the car. They'd have two minutes before the police showed once an alarm activated. Time not as tight with no one close to any alarms, but another customer would come in sooner or later and Don wasted twenty seconds that seemed like half an hour looking for the shell.

"Let's everybody stand in that corner over there, facing the wall." Jacques trying to move things without hurrying and any-one making a mistake. Assumed Don would make at least one more, hoped whatever it was didn't kill someone. "I'm very sorry about the floor. We had no idea it would be so dirty."

"Keep your hands where I can see them, goddamnit!" Jacques trying for Elmore Leonard while Don acted like he was in *Heat*.

"Butch." Jacques heard the edge in his voice, took care to smooth it out. "Give them a few seconds to clean up. Facing you, so you can see their hands. Then ask them to move to that corner. Anyone else comes in, escort them into the group. No one expected us, so be nice. Ed and I will get the money and we'll be on our way."

Ed so cooperative Jacques thought about asking him along on the next job. Couldn't get the money out of the drawers and safe and into the bag fast enough. Followed Jacques's instructions to a T, skipping large bills and splitting open bundles to avoid dye packs. "Please don't hurt anyone. We'll give everything that's here. I have money in my wallet if you want it."

"Take it easy, Ed. You are doing fine. We both understand it's not your money and it's insured. The people you work for should be grateful it's not you robbing them, all the more they probably pay you."

The drawer and safe empty, Jacques and Ed went back into the customer area. First thing Jacques saw was the two women standing with their noses to the wall. Don stood two meters behind them scanning the room with the shotgun like he expected the Rangers or Green Berets or whatever the Americans called their elite troops to storm in any minute. At least he hadn't shot anyone and no one else had come in.

Jacques let the money bag hang loose in one hand, gun in the other. "All right, everyone, we are leaving now. Before we go, Ed, I want you to reach into the bag and take out three ten-dollar bills." Ed gave a look like Jacques wanted him to cut his hand and stick it in a piranha tank. "It's okay. Please, I need three tens."

Ed rummaged in the bag. Withdrew three tens. "*Bon.* Thank you. Now keep one for yourself and give one to each of these lovely ladies. Please get your clothes dry cleaned with my compliments. I apologize for the inconvenience and hope nothing is ruined. Butch, it's time to go."

Now came the part that worried Jacques most: There should be a wheelman. Sixth Avenue dead this time of day and he'd done jobs without a driver before, but always alone. He never would have chosen Don under normal circumstances, but he needed cash in a hurry and didn't know anyone in Penns River. Stopped one night to get gas and saw a hotel with rooms by the week that didn't look too much like the usual SRO shithole. Decided this was as good a place as any to go to ground and wait for his package.

Stepped up next to Don as they entered the doorway. "Take your time. You run and I shoot you myself. And hide that fucking shotgun." Jacques's pistol already in his pocket.

Drove the car he'd stolen for the job a mile to the old glass house and parked it in an alley behind his own car. Looked both ways. Said to Don, "Take your time. We are not in a hurry."

"Let's go. There's no one here."

"Then there is no reason to hurry, is there?"

They got out and walked to Jacques's car. The one he'd been driving, which was no more his than the one they just got out of. Stolen from a valet lot in Buffalo with plates picked up somewhere in northern Pennsylvania or western New York. Jacques didn't know. Fucking deep dark woods was all he saw that night.

He pressed the fob. The trunk popped open. Jacques pointed inside. "Leave the shotgun."

"What if I need it?"

"What would you possibly need it for? The job's over."

"What if we get stopped?"

Jacques sighed. "Two days ago you don't like the idea of a gun at all. Now you are ready to shoot a cop. It's simple: If we get stopped, we go to jail. We are a lot less likely to get stopped if no one sees that fucking shotgun through the window. If you can fit it in your pocket, you can keep it. If not, in the trunk. You can get in with it, you want to stay close by."

Don placed the shotgun in the trunk. "Sorry. I'm new at this, remember?"

"It's okay. You'll learn. Here." Jacques tossed Don the money bag. "Keep this on the floor between your feet. I should have give it to you when we leave the job. I can't drive for shit with it on my lap."

"Shouldn't we put it in the trunk, too?"

"You want to leave it behind if we have to move in a hurry? Get in and let's go."

Near the top of Drey Street, Jacques thinking they might have filmed the chase scene from *Bullitt* here, steep as it was. Looked over and saw Don rummaging through the bag. "What the fuck are you doing?"

"I want to see how much we got."

"Rule Six! I know you know them. You told them to me last night. What is Rule Six?"

"Is that the one about junkies?"

"You have junkies on the brain. Last night you thought they were half the rules. It's only Rule Nine. Rule Six: 'Never count the take—'"

"In the car. Gotcha." Don folded over the top of the bag and let it fall between his feet.

Jacques turned left on Freeport Road, drove past the Dairy Queen and the water plant. Tried to stay quiet. Couldn't do it. "I don't want to sound like I am picking on you, but let's get it all out now and be done. What is Rule Four?"

Don's eyes rolled up and his lips moved as he recited the rules in his head. Flew through the first three, hung up on Four until Jacques turned right onto Tarentum Bridge Road. "It's something about clothes."

"What about clothes?"

"Neat or something. I forget. I got a lot on my mind today, my first armed robbery and that."

"Dress well. Never look suspicious or like a bum."

Took Don a while to realize it was his turn. "What? You don't like how I'm dressed?"

"It's very nice if you're changing the oil in your car. Okay if you clean the garage. Maybe you can look a little better next time?"

"Hold on there." Don turned in his seat to face Jacques. "I was thinking of saying something to you about that exact same thing. Did you see anyone else downtown with a tie on? Even the manager—what's his name, Ed—didn't have a tie on. You're the one stuck out. Not me."

Jacques had to admit Don had a point. "Fair enough. I won't dress quite so much next time. Could you at least wear something clean?"

Don said he could and Jacques eased the car to a stop for a red light at the corner of Stevenson and Greensburg Road. "You hungry? That Dairy Queen back there got me thinking. There's one right around the corner here. You want one of those five-buck lunches? I'll pay."

CHAPTER 4

Doc watched Chet Hensarling give a speech about how much the new community center would mean to this part of Penns River. Give the kids a place to go after school where they wouldn't get into trouble. Careful never to mention what kinds of trouble the darlings might get into. No point to it, since Penns River officially acknowledged no drugs, no gangs, no violence, no vandalism, no burglaries, robberies, or assaults. Dear God, no rapes or prostitution.

Doc swigged from a bottle of water while he rocked front to back like he'd done when standing a post. The breeze coming off the river felt good on his face. Temperature in the low forties not unpleasant for the last week of January. The Steelers getting their asses kicked took a little steam out of the festivities at Drew's house, but the serious drinking had already been done. Monday went about as well as could be hoped, now a hazy memory well behind him.

He didn't pay much attention to the speeches. He was there less to listen than to be seen. The people here knew him, remembered when he'd leave his car for hours at a time and walk the sector like an old beat cop. Penns River only about seven percent black, but ninety percent of that small fraction lived within half a mile of here. Doc knew that even in a town with as little overt racial friction as Penns River a white cop had a hurdle to clear. He talked to everyone and after a year, almost everyone talked to him. His approving eye on the community center was more important than the mayor's to these people.

Chet finished and cut the ribbon to less than tumultuous applause. Doc started for the building to check in with the organizers, stopped when he saw someone he thought he recognized. "Mr. Bickerstaff? You clean up pretty good. How've you been?"

Last time Doc saw Delonte Bickerstaff, the man was sleeping in an under construction mall. Today he was clean shaven, needed a haircut. His clothes showed wear at the seams, as did he. "Detective. You look well."

"I can't complain. What are you up to?"

"Well put. 'What are you up to?' Like you see me looking transitional and can't decide which direction I'm going."

"Transitional, maybe. General direction is definitely up. No one would look at you now and think 'vagrant.'"

"Semi-vagrant." Delonte wrapped a loose thread from his coat around a finger. Broke it off. "I sleep indoors often as not now."

"Glad to hear it. How are your other prospects?"

"I eat regular. Hot food when I want it, too."

"You working?"

"Odd jobs. Shovel snow when we get some. Haul debris. Spring comes I can get back to yard work. Whatever turns a buck."

The small crowd dispersing, not everyone as enamored as Doc with the fresh air. He and Delonte stepped closer to the building to get out of the wind. "You want something more reliable, my offer still stands. I can't promise anything right away, but I can get you put on a crew if they need someone. It's not much better than what you're doing now—hell, it's pretty much exactly what you're doing now—but it'll be regular."

"You don't want me to snitch no more?"

"I never wanted you to snitch."

"I'm sorry. I forgot. You wanted me to be a source. It's a subtle distinction."

"That's right, but seeing as how you never sourced anything for me, I might as well put you to work."

"I am working."

"I mean steady work."

"You don't think I can get steady work if I want it?"

Delonte Bickerstaff could break balls with the best of them. Doc took a deep breath and a swallow of water. Offered the bottle to Delonte, said, "You wipe the lip of that bottle and we're not friends anymore."

Delonte gave him a quick inspection. "You look pretty safe. For a cop." Took a drink. Left an inch in the bottle and handed it back.

Doc didn't wipe the rim, either. Finished the water. Capped the bottle and put it in his coat pocket. "So why don't you want it?"

"Want what?"

"Regular work. I know you're not lazy."

"You look me up? Make sure I'd be a reliable snitch-source?"

"No, sir. I did not. I figured you'd tell me anything you wanted me to know. It's been almost a year. I wasn't sure I'd ever hear from you again."

"You got to be the least nosy cop I ever met. I don't see how you can be any good at it."

"I'm as nosy as I need to be. Ask around."

They stood silent for half a minute. Not uncomfortable, neither in a hurry. Delonte broke first. "You still care why?"

"Why what?"

Delonte gave a frustrated face. Doc smiled. He wasn't bad at ball-breaking himself. "Why I don't want regular work," Delonte said.

"If you want to tell me. Not like I'm asking."

"You asked a minute ago."

"That was a minute ago."

"Now you don't care?"

"I didn't say I didn't care. You want to tell me, I'm standing right here. You don't want to tell? We'll talk about something else. I'm just enjoying the company on a nice day."

"For January."

"Well, that's when it is."

Delonte used close to minute to decide what to say. "You like me, don't you?"

Doc winked. "I must."

"You're the closest thing I have to a friend among people who assume they're sleeping indoors." Doc didn't say anything while Delonte made up his mind to go on. "You know what I used to do for a living?"

Doc shook his head. "I meant it when I said I never looked into you."

Delonte nodded twice. "Remember Second Duquesne Bank?"

"Sure. They were more of a big deal the other side of Pittsburgh, over by Ohio and West Virginia. Didn't they get bought out about ten years ago?"

"Not quite that long. I worked there. Before the sale. Vice president of consumer loans. Good job. Good at it, too. Wife. Two honor students for kids. House not too big, but nice. The bank had a good reputation, but commercial loans were slow so they transferred me to Business Development. Kept my own hours. Tickets to a suite for ball games, hockey games, concerts. Casino junkets. Great life.

"What no one knew—including me—was that I'm not a disciplined man. The consumer loan job had places I had to be and things I had to do. Biz Dev was different. Out all hours. Drinking. Showing people a good time. Not much sleep, so a man needs something to keep him going. Gets revved up and it's not like there's an off switch, so he needs something to calm him down. After a while it don't matter. Being high is enough. Speeding, nodding, whatever. Just so long as you're not straight."

That took a lot out of him. Doc gave Delonte time, said, "You're not like that anymore. I've seen a lot and if you're high, or looking to be, I should turn in my badge."

"I'm clean. Be six years in July. July twenty-sixth. I thought I hit bottom before and still found excuses to get high. Must have been a hell of a thing that happened July twenty-fifth. That and I got luckier than I ever deserved to get."

Doc arched an eyebrow. Delonte went on. "A man died. Overdosed. Scheduled for a bed in a clinic in Homewood. All set to get straightened out. Maybe it scared him. Something. Anyway, a man who should've known how to get responsibly high," laughed with derision, "fucked himself up. Left a bed open for me because I happened to apply when the first three they called didn't answer the phone, and they didn't want the bed to go empty. So here I am. Clean as the day I was born."

Doc didn't speak until it became clear Delonte had talked himself out. "I'm happy for you. How things worked out. You realize that story asks as many questions as it answers."

"Such as?"

"You're intelligent. You're willing to work hard, and you're clearly more self-disciplined than you let on if you've been straight all this time. Pardon me saying it like this, but what the fuck are you still doing on the street?"

"It's where I belong." Delonte's voice was hollow and flat, like he'd gone over this in his head a million times and was reciting more than telling. "What I said before. That was all about me. That's what junkies do, you know. Everything's about them. Us. Me. I get high because I got problems no one else has and no one else understands. What none of us wants to admit is we have those problems because we're high all the goddamn time.

"You know who really has problems? People who depended on me. People I worked with who lost their jobs because bad as Biz Dev was before, I ran that fucker into the ground. People who loved me. Mine was not a rosy marriage, even when I was straight. But my wife always held up her end. And the kids." No crack in his voice. No wavering in his tone. But he needed a break to continue. "What did they do to deserve losing their house and their friends when their degenerate drug addict old

man stopped bringing home the money for the mortgage?"
Stared over Doc's shoulder. The old glass house three quarters
of a mile down this street. Delonte was looking well past that.

"When's the last time you saw them?"

Delonte blew air through his nose in disgust. "You know
what the hell of it is? I don't remember. I can tell you the last
day I got high but I honest to God don't remember the last time
I saw my children. I think I was on the nod when my wife took
them. Left me a note said not to come looking, and I didn't.
They're well rid of me."

"You haven't seen your kids in six years?"

"Way more than that. Losing my family wasn't bottom
enough for me. I had a ways to go. I think it's been almost eight
years, but I couldn't swear to it."

Doc had no idea what to say. Looking for a way to salvage a
relatively graceful exit when Delonte continued.

"You still wondering why I don't want a job? Find a way to
get a regular place to live, sleep in a warm bed every night? It's
because for me the two things don't go together. I have more
than pocket money, I don't trust myself to resist temptation.
Right now I stay straight because I can either get high or eat. I
don't know what I'd do if I had money for both."

"Bullshit." Facts were hard to argue with. Self-pity Doc
could handle. "A junkie—not someone who chips a little but a
serious fiend—he'll do without food to get high. You're past that
and you know it. I have to wonder how a man like you resists
the temptations you're talking about with nothing to do all day."

"Walking all over these hills looking for odd jobs keeps me
plenty busy. Fit, too."

The far-off look had left Delonte. Replaced by the bantering
demeanor Doc knew well. It was Doc who wasn't in the mood
now. "Okay. You know yourself better than I ever will. Here's
my card. You decide you want a paycheck, call me."

Delonte about to reply when Doc's phone buzzed. Someone
had robbed the payday loan joint three blocks away.

21

CHAPTER 5

Sean Sisler met Doc at the door, first uniform on the scene. "Is Shimp coming?"

"You don't think I can handle a simple robbery on my own?"

Sisler ducked his head and lowered his voice. "I think one of the two women here wet her pants. She's real hinky talking to me and has that...aura about her. She might be more comfortable talking to another woman."

"What aura are you talking about? Does she smell?"

"She's wearing slacks and keeps her coat wrapped around her hips so you can't see any of her upper leg."

"What do you care about her upper leg? You're gay."

Sisler shook his head slowly. No one else in Penns River knew. Doc would never tell. Didn't mean he couldn't have a little innocent fun once in a while. "Is Shimp coming?"

"I really don't know. What else do we have here besides a woman with a weak bladder?"

Sisler laid it out for him: two employees—manager and teller—and one customer who may have wet herself. Two men in stocking masks came in with guns. One herded the women into a corner while the other took the manager in back where the safe was.

"Anyone hurt?"

"Not that they'll admit to."

Doc inventoried his witness-victims. "What's the manager's name?"

"Ed Spicer."

"He spent the most time with the crooks. I guess I'll start with him." Doc gestured toward the women. "Call and find out if Shimp is coming. If not, ask for Snyder or Burrows. Whoever's working. If this woman really did pee herself, it's probably a good idea for another woman to talk to her. I'm a little disappointed you didn't think of that yourself."

Doc stepped away and gestured for Ed Spicer before Sisler could voice an opinion. "Mr. Spicer? I need you to tell me everything that happened."

"There were two of them, with stockings over their faces. And hats."

"They had hats over their faces?"

Ed didn't appear to be sure if Doc was jagging him. "On their heads," he said. "Pulled down low."

"I figured," Doc said. No time to keep coming back and back and back to get everything straight. "I need as many details as you can give me. Lay it all out for me. Don't assume I know anything."

Ed's expression implied this would not be difficult. "They came in when Sheila and me were out front. It was bad luck for us. Sheila could've of set off the alarm if she'd been in her cage. If I'd been in my office...things would've of been different if I'd have been in my office."

"Why were both of you out of position?"

"Marcy—the one in the blue coat—brought in some baby pictures. She used to work here."

Doc made a note. What Sisler picked up on as fear could be the nervousness of a decoy confronted with actual police. Not likely—the woman had already pissed herself when Sisler arrived—but it would be good to know why she brought pictures and not the whole baby. "The two men. What did they look like?"

"I just told you they wore masks and had their hats pulled

down low. I couldn't tell."

"Were they big? Small? Thin? Fat? Anything distinguishing about them?"

"You mean like their names?"

Doc held it in. "Their names would be nice." Not even hoping they'd used their real names, but any name was a place to start.

"The one in charge was called Larry. The other was Butch."

Doc wrote in his book. "How big were they?"

Ed stared at the markings on the front doorjamb. "Larry was five-ten, five-eleven. Average build, maybe a little on the slender side. Butch was a couple inches shorter and pretty heavy. Big gut."

"How were they dressed?"

"Larry looked like he might've of been here to apply for a job. Butch was dressed like he'd been working on his car."

"So Larry had on a suit and tie?"

"Not a suit. A shirt and tie with like a blazer. Nice slacks."

"Do you remember the color?"

"Of what? The jacket?"

"Any of it."

Ed's eyes rolled up. Shook his head an inch. "Jacket was dark blue. Navy, I guess. White shirt. Striped tie. Gray slacks."

"That's good. Thank you. What about the other guy? Butch?"

"Jeans, work boots. Had on one of them dark coats with the two rows of buttons."

"A trench coat?"

"Shorter. Like sailors wear in the old movies."

"A pea coat?"

"Yeah. One of those."

"Were they armed?"

Ed glared. "Do I look like someone who'd hand over close to ten thousand dollars if they weren't armed?"

Doc's first thought would not have moved the interview along. "They got that much?"

"It's an estimate. I balanced the drawers last night before I went home. It's been slow today."

"Can you get me an accurate number? I don't mean right now. Later today will be fine."

"The insurance will ask for one, anyway. I'll call you when I have it ready."

"That'd be great. Now about the weapons. What did they have?"

"I don't know a lot about guns. All I know is Larry had some kind of handgun and Butch had something long."

"Rifle? Shotgun?"

"Yeah."

"Which?"

"You know, one of those. I didn't get a good look. All I know for sure is he slid a piece along the barrel and a shell popped out. They were both pretty pissed about that."

Doc turned toward motion at the front of the store. Teresa Shimp coming in, getting the scoop from Sisler. "So a shotgun, then. Did they threaten to shoot anyone, or did they just show the guns?"

"The fat guy—Butch—he was yelling and screaming, 'Motherfucker' and 'Up against the wall' and making a real scene. I never had the idea he was the one to worry about."

"Why not?"

"Too showy. I figured the guy to watch was Larry. He didn't try to hide his gun, but he never made a big deal about it. Least not till he took me in the back to get the money."

Doc always enjoyed statements from people who maintained such cool heads an hour after the shit went down. "What'd he do then?"

Ed shot a glance toward the two women. Shimp spoke to the one in the blue coat. Sisler had the teller. Ed turned to face Doc again. Didn't quite make eye contact. "I was taking my time. You know, looking for a chance to trip an alarm. I think he caught wise. Whatever the reason, he shoved the gun in my ribs. Told me he could break open the drawer and take what was there if I didn't open the safe and that the only way I wasn't gonna open the safe was if I was dead."

"So you opened the safe."

"Well, yeah, but not right away. I figured every second they were here was a chance for someone to look in and see Butch out there with the shotgun and call the cops. So I pretended I was real scared and had trouble with the combination."

Uh-huh. "But you did finally open the safe."

"I dragged it out long as I could until he put the gun right here," tapped behind his left ear, "and said that safe would be open in ten seconds or the next person to open it would have to clean my brains off it. Then he cocked it. The gun. Goddamn right I opened it then."

Doc wondered if he should try to break down Ed's story here or wait till later when he had all the statements. Had the impression Spicer rolled over quicker than he was willing to admit and felt the need to dress it up. Doc didn't mind that too much; everyone lied to cops. It did cast doubt on the rest of Ed's story.

About to ask what they'd done after handing over the money when his cell phone buzzed. Stan Napierkowski, chief of police. "What's up, Stush?"

"Where are you?"

"Easy Money. You know, that payday loan joint down on Sixth Street." Ed pulled a face on "joint."

"Who's with you?"

"Shimp and Sisler."

"Leave Shimp to finish up. You and Sisler get your asses out to Hilltop Plaza toot sweet. We got an active shooter in Dale's Department Store."

CHAPTER 6

Siren and lights, four minutes to Hilltop Plaza. Police cruisers formed a loose perimeter closing off the corner where Dale's discount department store served as the closest thing to an anchor Hilltop had. Wildlife Lodge and Leechburg roads already closed. Cops roamed both arms of the L-shaped shopping center to keep anyone inside from coming out.

Doc couldn't believe how fast what seemed like every cop in town got there, on duty or not. Even Lester Goodfoot—on permanent graveyard shift and dressed in sweatpants and what might be a pajama top—leaned against a cruiser with his gun drawn and pointed at the store.

Sisler pulled as close to the perimeter as he could. Grabbed the AR-15 and bulletproof vest from the trunk and took a position. Doc kept low climbing out the passenger side, which was closest to the store. Duck-walked back to Acting Deputy Chief Mike "Eye Chart" Zywiciel, standing on the roof of a cruiser scanning the scene with binoculars. "What do we have, Chart?"

"Fuck if I know. We got a call there's shots fired. Burrows was first on the scene and she radioed for help right away. Said there were people running and screaming everywhere. We're trying to get a handle on things."

"Shooter still inside?"

Zywiciel sat on the roof facing away from the activity. "Fuck if I know. We're just now getting things secured on the outside."

Jerked a thumb over his shoulder. "I got no fucking idea what's transpiring back there."

"Anyone actually see the guy?"

"Fuck if I know." Zywiciel looked at Doc and started to deflate. Caught himself before it went too far. "Fuck, Doc, I'm sorry. I honest to Christ don't know what's going on. If people are dead, if people are still at risk in there." Half turned his head toward Dale's. Let it hang for a second. "Stush and Janine are holding down the fort. I'm in command here." A chuckle that sounded like it might get away from him. "Benny, I'm too old for this shit. This is nothing like what I signed on for way back when. It's been getting worse, but—goddamn. You saw shit like this in the army. Tell me what to do."

No one called Doc "Benny" except for family and the chief. Gave him some idea how shaken up Zywiciel was. Mike had been his field training officer when Doc came back to Penns River after nine years in the army. As solid a cop—and man—as Doc had ever worked with. Handled every situation with pretty much the same casual efficiency. Till today. It killed any inclination Doc had to let slip that he'd never seen anything like this. Not in his three Iraq tours nor breaking up a riot in Leavenworth.

Doc stared at Dale's as if it were a leper colony. Spoke to himself as much as to Zywiciel. "We're gonna have to clear that building." Took as much of an inventory as he could of available resources. "Who's here?"

"Everyone except for Stush and Janine." Schoepf, the dispatcher. "Tell me who and what you want and I'll make it happen."

Doc glimpsed Tony Lutz treating a woman bleeding from the face. Gestured to Zywiciel. "What happened to her?"

"Crashed into a pole running out of Dale's."

"Anyone talk to her?"

"Burrows couldn't even get her name. I think Tony gave her a sedative. I'll have someone try again when he's done."

"We have any way to see inside?"

"I talked to the store manager and chief of security." The

way he said "chief of security" told Doc all he needed to know. "They have some cameras, but the security guy spilt soon as he heard the shots so there's no one inside to see the monitors. A company down by Camp Joann gets the feeds. Neuschwander's on the phone now to see if we can get a look inside."

"Any idea how long it'll take?"

"At least an hour, the way he was talking. They might be able to send us something over the internet we can pick up on our phones."

Phone screens too small to be much good. Doc looked toward the building. Spat. "We can't wait that long, not knowing what's going on in there." Gave a hard examination of as much as he could see. Knew he was putting off the inevitable. Exhaled until he was empty. "You got a vest for me?"

"Tac van's over there." Zywiciel pointed. "It's got everything."

"Who's around back?"

"McKillop and Speer."

Everybody really was here. Ray McKillop not even a cop, worked at the courthouse as a sheriff's deputy. "Tell them to dig in. No one comes out the back. Take no chances, but be goddamn sure they don't shoot me, Sisler," thought a moment, "Snyder, or Augustine." Another pause. "How did Burrows handle being first on the scene?"

"She did fine, far as I can tell."

"Her, too, then."

"You don't think she's a little young?"

"She's young, but she's good. And she's single."

The entry team gathered inside a diner with a view into Dale's front windows through a covered gangway. A single spider-webbed bullet hole through the front of Dale's reminded everyone this was not a drill. Two entry doors into the store with an area for shopping buggies between them on the inside. Clear line of sight from door to door. Doc and Snyder would go right, Sisler and Augustine left. Burrows would come in last and take the center.

Doc looked everyone in the eye. Liked what he saw and ordered an equipment check. One Sig Sauer in his hand. Another in a belt holster at the small of his back. A small .32 automatic on his ankle. Knife, extra magazines for the Sigs, flex cuffs, ASP baton, and a good old-fashioned sap in his pockets. Breathed a silent thank you for 5.11 Tactical Pants. Gave another eye check. Nodded and everyone moved at once. The two pairs paused at the entry points. Doc and Sisler made eye contact and opened their respective doors in unison.

Eerie inside. Lights on, some displays playing animations. Not a soul in sight. Store music so quiet Doc almost shot the popcorn machine when the heating element kicked on. He and Sisler nodded and moved apart slowly along the wall adjacent to the entry doors. Snyder and Augustine followed. Burrows came in last to hold the center. Hanging clothes and display racks provided concealment and a little cover for them. And whoever they were looking for. Five cops not enough to clear a store this size. Five cops were all Doc trusted to potentially be in each other's lines of fire if the situation turned fluid.

Doc and Sisler reached their corners at about the same time. Snyder and Augustine halfway along. Doc gestured to Burrows to ask if Sisler was in position. Got a thumbs up in return. Doc pointed forward and everyone stepped off.

He kept the outside wall on his right arm as he crept into the store. Women's clothing. Dressing rooms cut into the wall twenty feet in. Called a pause. Looked through the entryway without exposing himself. A counter piled high with clothes. More hanging from a rack. Plastic cards with numbers so whoever was on duty knew how many garments a customer took in. Violins played "Poker Face."

Doc stepped in with one quick movement, got down low. Four stalls in a single row on the left of the aisle. All open in varying degrees. The walls did not reach the floor. Doc saw no feet and caught a break: The door hinges were on the sides closest to him. Kicked open each door with enough force to make it bounce off the stall wall. No one there.

Back in the main shopping area. Moved the team forward again. Nancy Snyder's voice on the radio. "I got bodies here."

Plural? Fuck. "How many?"

"At least two. Make it three."

"Alive?"

"Not from the looks of it." Snyder's voice perfect. No sign of overexcitement or more than healthy fear. Flat but engaged.

"Leave them. Stay on the hunt."

Not two steps farther along when Burrows broke in, not as calm as Snyder. "I got one here! I think mine's breathing!"

"You need a paramedic?" Zywiciel.

"Not till we clear the building," Doc said. "There's enough people in motion in here already."

Halfway back Doc sensed movement the other side of the men's dressing rooms. Called a halt. Raised the Sig and drew a sight picture on the rack of clothes he suspected. "You! Behind the slacks. Penns River Police. Show yourself. Hands in the air facing me."

No response.

Doc keyed his radio. "Eye Chart. We get a feed from those cameras yet?"

"They're still working on it."

Kim Kardashian could flash a nipple in Malaysia and people in Kansas would see it ten seconds later. Doc couldn't get pictures of the room he was in from across town. "I need two or three bodies at the front. I got something back here and we need to tighten our perimeter. I want someone to cover our backs."

"Who do you want?"

Doc's vision locked on where he was now sure he'd seen movement. "You pick. I'm busy in here."

Commotion at the front of the store. Multiple voices on the

radio, none as calm as even Burrows. "What the fuck is going on out there?" Doc said.

"Tony Lutz just went in to find your survivor."

Should've known better. Live victim, Tony within hailing distance, he'd be in. Won a Bronze Star as a medic in Afghanistan when his reserve unit deployed. Goofy son of a bitch off duty, absolutely fearless in uniform. They should have accounted for him before going in. "Burrows! Wave him down and keep him with you. Shoot him if you have to." Eyes still locked on the clothing rack, less worried about Tony than having another piece in play.

Zywiciel gave the word three more cops were at the front. Sisler, Augustine, and Snyder had closed the loop toward Doc. Not ideal placements yet, but they had their own sectors to clear. Snyder had already proven herself. Augustine older and slower, but reliable. Sisler had saved Doc's life a year ago. No doubts there. Asked himself what he was waiting for.

"You! Behind the clothes rack! Penns River police. We have the exits covered. Hands over your head, palms facing me. Do it now."

Fingers appeared above the clothes rack. Palms. "Now stand slowly. Do not move your hands." Hair and elbows appeared. Shoulders. "Spread your arms at forty-five-degree angles, palms facing me. Keep your hands away from your body."

The man who appeared stood close to six feet tall. Thick through the torso. Down vest over an open flannel shirt over a Steelers tee. Eyes fixed on Doc's gun.

"Are you armed?" Doc said.

"Yes. I mean no. I mean—"

"Which!?"

"I had a gun but it's on the floor now."

Doc leveled his voice. "Keep your hands exactly where they are and kick the gun to your left. I want to hear it slide." The man's body moved. Hands and head steady as if nailed to a wall. Something hard slid along the floor. "Snyder. Do you have a shot?"

"I got him."

Sisler's voice, calm as paint: "I'm on him."

"I'm moving," Doc said. "Cover me." Then, "You. Behind the rack. Do not move. Do not turn. I'll come to you."

Doc took his time getting around the clothes racks. Walked heel-to-toe to minimize any upper body movement, gun sight square on the center of what chest he could see. Stepped over what looked like a .32 in the aisle as he turned the corner. Sisler and Snyder shifted as Doc moved to keep all three cops out of each other's lines of fire, Augustine alert for surprises behind them.

The man still stared at the spot Doc had left. "Can I put my arms down now?"

"I'll do it for you." Doc took a flex cuff from his pocket, slipped it over the man's left wrist. Pulled it behind him hard and grabbed the right. Didn't concern himself much with whether the cuffs were too tight.

"What? Hey, what? You're cuffing me? You think I'm the shooter! I'm the guy ran him off. You should be thanking me."

Doc jerked the man by his wrists to steer him. "What's your name?"

"Chuck Simon. Uncuff me right now. You're making a big mistake."

There were times a crook could say that and bring at least a twinkle to Doc's eye. Close to half, maybe more, of the people he'd arrested said that or something close when he cuffed them. He had made a few mistakes over the years. Never a "big" one.

Doc keyed his mike. "Eye Chart."

"Roger."

"I'm coming out. Do not let anyone shoot me."

"You got a suspect?"

"In custody. Don't let anyone shoot him, either. I got plans for him."

Doc grasped Simon's wrists and gave a nudge. "This way."

"Don't you have to read me my rights before you arrest me?"

"No."

"I have a concealed carry permit for that gun."

"I'm happy for you." Doc kept walking and steering.

"Don't be stupid. Do you think I'd just give myself up if I was the guy you're looking for? I saw what was going on and fired back. I'm pretty sure I winged him. I'm the guy that kept things under control, goddamnit!"

EMTs raced through the door with a gurney for Tony Lutz's patient as Doc pressed Simon toward the front of the store. "Since you already know your rights, use them. Open your mouth again before I tell you to and you're a dangerous suspect resisting arrest. Then I can shut you up pretty much however I want."

That did the trick. Doc gestured for Dave Wohleber standing by the door. "Your unit here? Take this asshole to the house and lock him up. Make sure no one talks to him until I get back."

CHAPTER 7

Doc took a look around the parking lot. Literally every cop in Penns River engaged. Those he couldn't see he knew were either inside Dale's or around back. Zywiciel had sent most of those in uniform to the barriers to provide a more official-looking presence. Officers who'd come in early or on their day off talked to people and tried to identify witnesses. Doc the only cop in sight with nothing going on. Found Rick Neuschwander organizing a grid search of Dale's interior and walked over. Waited for Neuschwander to set the search in motion before getting his attention. "Tell me what you need me for."

Neuschwander turned with a start. "I thought you had a suspect."

"I gave him to Wohleber for safekeeping. Give me something to do."

Neuschwander looked around considering options. "You have good eyes. There's a bullet hole in the front glass there. See if you can find the round. Don't worry about it if you can't. If it wedged into the wall of the diner we'll have to try to recreate the firing angle to have an idea where to look. If it ricocheted, well, maybe we'll get lucky. I'm hoping we'll get real lucky and it only had enough juice to bounce off and lay there." Someone called for Neuschwander from inside. "Gotta go."

"I'm on it."

Barricades at either end of the gangway kept the search field clear. Flat concrete, little or no foot traffic since the event. Doc looked at the hole in the glass. Made a mental calculation of about where Simon would have been standing when he fired, already sure whose bullet he was looking for. Let his line of sight travel along his best guess at a trajectory. Pulled on latex gloves as he walked to a spot ten yards past his estimated impact point. Took his time coming back along the side of the building. Made sure what looked like bits of gravel actually were. Wondered how disfigured the bullet would be if he did find it.

Twenty-five minutes and thirty-seven pebble false alarms later he had it. Too badly misshapen to guess at the caliber, though there was no reason to think it wasn't a .32 like the one he took off Simon. Doc had seen the head wounds of the dead and knew a substantially larger gun was also in play. Wondering what the hell Simon would have been shooting at for a round to end up here when Neuschwander approached. "You find anything?"

Doc held up his deformed prize. "Could be from Simon's gun. Good luck proving it. I'm trying to figure out how it ended up where it did."

"You mark it?"

Doc pointed to the evidence tag on the ground. Light already beginning to fail. "Beat up as it is, it must have ricocheted but I can't be sure."

"We'll figure it out tomorrow when the light's better. We have your suspect's gun. We'll see what kind of loads he was packing." Jerked his head back toward Dale's. "We found three .32 casings and three .45s inside."

"That's all? Six rounds fired?"

"We're still looking but that might be it. We only have one cluster of victims and no evidence of gunfire anywhere else in the store."

"No guns?"

"Just the one you took off the suspect."

Doc released a gentle "fuck." "So there is another shooter.

With the big gun." Neuschwander nodded. Doc pointed to Dale's. "Need any help?"

"I got fifteen people working it. We'll be there half the night. Angelo found a casing mixed in with some hair spray or conditioner or something so I'm having them take everything off the shelves. Handling every garment to be sure nothing's caught in a fold or a pocket."

"Thought of using metal detectors?"

Neuschwander shook his head. "There's metal everywhere. Hanging racks for clothes. Display supports. Spray cans. Everything has to be touched." Pulled a knit cap over his ears. "I got this. Go see what you can get from your suspect."

Doc handed over the evidence bag containing the bullet. "You need me, you know where to find me." Turning to leave when he heard shouting from around the side of Dale's. Something about another body.

CHAPTER 8

Ray McKillop pointed toward a dark blue Ford Escort coupe somewhere between fairly new and beater. "He's in the car. Christ, we been standing out here how long making sure no one comes out the back and there he is, parked in next to the Dumpster all slumped over. I just noticed him now coming around to see did you still need me."

A man who might have been in his late twenties sat slumped in the driver's seat, head resting on the side of the steering wheel. Blood and brain hung from the headliner and spread across part of the windshield and window. Doc and Neuschwander stopped ten feet short of the car. "Lights?" Doc said.

"They're in the van." Neuschwander turned toward McKillop. "Ray, do me a favor and tell Mike Zywiciel we need the tactical lights brought back here. And the generator. We're gonna need a statement from you, too."

McKillop looked disgusted. Didn't say anything. Doc asked what time he'd come on duty. "Six. I was in the locker room changing out of my uniform when the call came in."

"I'll walk over with you. We'll talk while they set up the lights. Maybe we can get you out of here before full dark. Leave it for the real cops." Winked.

McKillop's statement not much more than he'd already said behind the building. Still had to have it for the file. Doc wandered back near the car in time to hear the generator come on and flood the area with light. A couple of minutes to get everything as evenly lit as possible and Neuschwander waved him over.

The two of them stood near the driver's door. "Open it slow," Neuschwander said. "I'll look for anything that might fall out."

Doc nodded and gripped the handle. Looked back. "Locked."

"Think you can pick it?"

"Pick it? Really?"

"I'd like to avoid forcing anything inside the door. I want to disturb the insides as little as possible."

"You think if we called Shehab's with the year and model they'd have a master? Or an impact wrench?"

Neuschwander had phone in hand when Al Speer asked who he was calling. An edge in Al's voice implied his fascination with standing outdoors in twenty degree weather watching Dale's back door had worn thin.

Doc answered, Neuschwander already engaged. "Locksmith."

"What for?"

Doc opened his hands. "The door's locked. Damn, Al."

"Passenger window's open."

Doc looked at Neuschwander, who squeezed his eyes shut. "Using an open window would be quicker." Neuschwander nodded.

They walked around the front of the car, Doc kicking himself for not thinking to check the other side. Speer pointed to the door before he stepped aside. "Could that be something?"

"Where?"

Speer leaned over. Got his finger an inch from the car. "Right there. Is that blood?"

Doc and Neuschwander crouched to look. "Could be," Doc said. "Noosh?"

"I'd say yeah. We'll take a sample and test it." Gave the side of the car a good visual inspection. "Go ahead and open it. Nice and slow in case something falls out."

Doc pulled on the handle. "Shit."

"What?"

"This side's locked, too." Waited a beat, then looked at Neuschwander.

"You're an asshole."

Doc reached inside to release the lock. Eased the door open. Nothing fell out. Neuschwander leaned inside. "Looks like a contact wound on this side of the head. Do me a favor, Al? Go 'round front and get my collection kit. It's in the trunk of my unit, over by the eyeglass place. Call in and ask Janine to run this plate while you're at it. Thanks." Took a deep breath. Held it. "I don't want to crawl across the seats and possibly contaminate something. You have anything we can reach across with, unlock the other door?"

Doc three inches taller than Neuschwander. Pointed to a spot near the headrest. "How about if I lean here? Grip the top like this." Pantomimed how he'd do it without touching the seat back. "I keep most of the pressure on the forward side, the seat should stay secure."

"Grip it good. I don't want you falling into the body."

"Don't think that makes you special." Doc gripped the headrest and leaned into the car. "Whoa. Look what I found."

"What?"

"Get a bag ready."

"How big?"

Doc backed out of the car. His thumb and index finger pinched the trigger guard of a handgun. "This big."

"That an old Army Colt?"

"Looks authentic, too. My cousin has one."

Neuschwander pointed to the body in the car. "This mean he's our shooter?"

"Could be. Sure looks like it might be our gun."

Doc put the .45 in the bag and waited while Neuschwander completed the chain of custody form. Leaned in and reached across with his baton to disengage the lock.

Same slow process opening the driver's door. Nothing fell

out. Nothing noteworthy in view they hadn't seen before.

Neuschwander's breath glowed white in the floodlight. Doc said, "Well?"

"We wait."

"We wait?"

"Not much I can do until the medical examiner moves the body and she's still tied up inside last I looked. I'll work on this door and that spot Al found when my kit shows up."

Doc not in the mood to wait. Looked toward the open gangway and saw Speer lugging Neuschwander's portable evidence kit. "Here comes your stuff. I'm going inside, see if I can hustle the ME along a little."

The crowd at the front of the store had thinned. Increasing darkness made it harder to see. Increasing cold made it harder to want to. Three trucks from the Pittsburgh stations flanked the perimeter with antennae extended. Print media around somewhere, not as conspicuous.

Inside Dale's Doc saw the kinds of activity the public often associated with police, which didn't seem like much to the uninitiated. Fifteen to twenty cops who all appeared to be staring at the floor, moving things aimlessly. An undercurrent of conversation. It's what a search looked like. Everything in the store—thousands of items—had to be checked to be sure some small piece of evidence hadn't taken up residence in or around it. Shell casings were most likely to be of value, but anything that didn't belong was worth examining.

Doc walked to the location of the victims he'd already seen. Nothing there but blood on the floor and some displays. He turned to the nearest cop. "Where's the ME?"

"Just left. I'm surprised you didn't pass her on your way in."

Doc left the way he came with all reasonable haste, careful not to disturb anything. Paused at the front to shield his eyes from the television lights. Saw what might be the medical examiner packing up a vehicle. Jogged close enough not to have to yell. "You the ME from Allegheny County?"

"Yes."

"We got another customer for you." She looked confused. "Around back. We just found him." The woman's shoulders slumped for a second before she picked up her kit and walked through the gangway.

"Doc, you got a minute?" Eye Chart Zywiciel looked like he hadn't slept in a week. "Mr. Galmoff here is the store manager."

Doc wanted to talk to Galmoff about as much as he wanted another tour in Iraq. Tried not to show it. "Yes, sir, Mr. Galmoff. What can I do for you?"

Galmoff in his early forties. Average height and build with a budding paunch. Did a nice job with the comb-over, but the battle neared the tipping point. "I don't want to seem pushy, but do you have any idea when we'll be able to get in there and start cleaning up?"

"The detective who can give the best answer is busy right now, but it won't be tonight. Probably not tomorrow, either. We'll do what we can for you, but it's going to be a while."

Galmoff stared without comprehension. "I have to wait here?"

"You might as well go on home, sir."

"But I or an assistant manager has to lock up."

"Don't worry about security. We have to seal and chain the doors. We'll also keep at least one cop here all night. Probably two. Your building will be as secure as it's ever been."

"I—um—I mean, not that I don't trust you, really, I do— but...there's money in the cash drawers. It should be in the safe."

Doc fought back a comment. "Tell you what: I'll talk to the detective in charge when I get a chance. See if we can't get you in there to secure the cash and credit card receipts sometime to-morrow. That's the best I can do." Left Zywiciel to deal with any dissatisfaction.

Made ten steps before another voice called to him. "Detective Dougherty! Please? Just two quick questions."

Doc kept walking. "There'll be a presser at the station. Check there to see when."

"I know. I just have a couple of quick questions. Please? I promise not to argue with a 'no comment.' I just want to be able to say I asked."

Doc risked a look. Young woman, no more than thirty. Pretty in a wholesome, girl-next-door way. Looked exhausted and a little scared. Probably her first exposure to anything like this, getting pressure now from above. And she said, "Please." Slowed his pace, said, "Up there where the tape meets the corner of the diner. Where the light's not so good. Otherwise I'll have to talk to everyone."

She looked around as if to be sure no one else heard. Did as he asked, ignoring him along the way. Doc held up his end of the deal. Stood at the corner of the diner and the gangway, crime scene tape between them, backs to all activity. "Thanks for stopping. I'm Katy Jackson."

"Who do you write for, Ms. Jackson?"

The slightest hesitation. "I'm freelance."

Doc took a closer look. Twenty-three years old. Twenty-four, tops. "Is that the new term for 'stringer'?"

Jackson's face fell. "I can provide references. I've sold stuff to the Post-Gazette, the Tribune Review, even the AP. I—"

"It's okay. Ask your two questions." Doc extended a hand. "I'm Detective Not For Attribution."

Took her a beat to see he'd agreed. "Okay. Okay. Great. Thank you. Do you have a suspect in custody?"

"No comment."

That fleeting look again. Someone rapidly growing accustomed to disappointment, intent on soldiering on. "Do you have any suspects at all?"

Doc looked away so that wet puppy face couldn't unduly influence him. "Police sources say they have suspects and are close to providing more information after promising leads are checked out. That's the best I can do."

"Is there another body around back?"

"That's a third question."

"You answered 'no comment' to the first one."

"You said you wouldn't hold a 'no comment' against me."

"I'm not. I'm just not counting that question."

Doc looked at her from the corner of his eye. Didn't bother to fight off the smile. "Okay. One more." Held up a finger. "One."

"Is there another body around back?"

"No comment." Held out a placating hand. "I really can't tell you anymore. I probably shouldn't have told you what I did." Started to walk away, changed his mind. "How'd you know my name is Dougherty?"

"Give me some credit. There are only three detectives in this town. Shimp's a woman. You're either Dougherty or Neuschwander." Correct pronunciation of both. "The name Dougherty's been in the air since you came from around back and went inside. That or Doc. And Sergeant Zywiciel called you Doc when he asked you to handle the store manager. And I heard Dougherty was a real smart ass. It's okay. You'll always be Detective Not For Attribution to me."

Uh-oh. Smart and funny, too. "You've done your homework. I respect that. The thing is, Ms. Jackson, I really don't know a whole lot more than what I just told you. What I do know it would be unprofessional to divulge just yet. I'll make you a deal." Handed her a business card from one of his multitude of pants pockets. "Give me two days. After that, you can call and I'll do my best to either confirm or deny any concrete statements you run past me. No fishing, and only yes or no answers. You okay with that?"

Jackson took the card. "So you know, it's not just this shooting I care about. I didn't dig up all that detective information since two o'clock this afternoon."

"I didn't think you did. That's why I offered the deal." Al Speer came around the corner. Said Neuschwander needed to see Doc right now. "I have to go. Give me a couple of days and I'll see what I can do for you."

"Fair enough. Thanks."

Speer started to speak. Doc held up a hand. Gestured with his head toward the departing Katy Jackson. Mouthed, "Reporter." Took Speer by the elbow and walked him through the gangway. "What's up?"

"Rick says they're ready to move the body."

Doc turned the corner in time to see Neuschwander reach into the car to get his hands on the corpse. Thought how much easier it would be for two, the mess where the head used to be. How this was only the second time he'd worn this ninety-dollar pair of slacks. Fuck it. He was police. Neuschwander had clothing expenses, too, for a family that included four kids. "Hold up, Noosh. Let me help you."

"Not much room here for the two of us."

"Go 'round the other side. Lift his feet so he slides out easier."

"You sure you don't want the feet?"

"No, so get over there before I change my mind." Doc stripped off his coat. Pulled out his shirt to hang over his belt and provide a little protection to his pants, the shirt an old warrior nearing the end of its useful life. The ME took pity, handed him a small sheet of plastic for the head. Saved both garments from facing untimely demise.

An ambulance *whoop-whooped* to clear a path through the gangway. Doc and Neuschwander eased the mortal remains of...

"Hey," Doc said. "You get his wallet?"

"I thought you might want to do that." Neuschwander would pick through any level of blood and gore, squeamish about even a small chance of encountering excrement or urine.

"Thanks," Doc said with as little sincerity as possible. Rolled the body to one side. No wallet in that hip pocket. Made a face and rolled him back. At least the poor bastard hadn't voided. Patted the stiff's ass, then reached in and withdrew the wallet with two fingers as the ambo turned the corner.

Al Speer's radio crackled. Keyed the mike and tilted his head to listen. "Hey, Doc. Janine says the car is registered to—"

Doc held up a hand. "Let me guess. Michael Stoltz. Twenty-eight years old, five-ten, one seventy-five. Lives at—lived at—five-fifty-seven Arizona Drive."

CHAPTER 9

Stush Napierkowski didn't become beloved within the department because he was a house cat. Ten years ago he would have taken the door at Dale's with Doc. Five years ago the deputy chief would have manned the phones at the station while Stush took onsite command. Age, weight, health, and politics had cost him all those luxuries. Offered Doc some coffee and asked what the crime scene was like.

Doc waved off the coffee. What he really needed was warm milk and some Jack Daniel's. Maybe not in that order. On second thought, fuck the milk. "What do you think it's like?"

"Cluster fuck?"

"Of biblical proportions. Neuschwander's rising to the occasion, though. Giving orders, collecting evidence, making suggestions. Far and away the biggest crime scene he's ever had."

"I don't like the looks of you, Benny. You all right?" Stush the only person outside Doc's immediate family who could call him Benny and get away with it. Stush and Doc's father went back so far Doc and Drew referred to him as "Uncle Stush" well into adulthood.

Doc breathed to speak. Changed his mind and sat in a visitor's chair. Reached into the candy bowl on Stush's desk. Picked out a Hershey's Kiss. Unwrapped it. Took his time chewing and swallowing. "They're not as good since they started making them in Mexico."

"Must be the water."

Doc unwrapped a Tootsie Roll with great care. Stush took a few jelly beans. Sipped his coffee. Made a face and set the mug aside. "This guy McKillop found out back. Stoltz? You make him for the shooter?"

"Unless Neuschwander finds something says he didn't do it. I'm not ready to go public with it, though."

"No rush. I'm assuming this guy has family. Friends. We let this out and they're in for a shitty time."

Doc nodded. Swallowed another Tootsie Roll. "I'm going to the address on his license soon as I'm done with the guy we're holding. We have a unit parked a little ways up the street with eyes on the house till I get there."

"The guy you brought in. What do you know about him?"

"Full name is Charlton Peter Simon. Lives in Valley Camp. No priors. One moving violation for rolling through a stop sign. That's it."

"Any personal stuff? Job, military history?"

"All I've done so far is pull his sheet and try to get my act together."

"You think he might be a good guy with a gun?"

"Right now he's an asshole with a gun. At best. That's why I'm letting him stew. I want to find out all I can before I go in the room with him. Let him wonder what I'm doing out here all this time." Today had already been a bad week for Doc. No telling when he could take a break once he started. Eating candy with Stush the most appealing thing he could think of. "When's Neuschwander's help coming? Right now he's got every cop in town on their hands and knees picking up lint and gum wrappers at Dale's."

Stush's turn to take a Kiss from the bowl. Unwrapped it and ate. "You're right. They're not as good." Doc's stomach slipped away. "Chet Hensarling called while you were driving over. I was explicitly ordered not to request assistance from either the states or the feds." Saw Doc's expression and hurried on. "I told him this was more than we could handle. He told me that was an odd argument to make for a chief hanging onto his job by such a slender thread."

"Chet said that?"

"I think Rance Doocy was feeding him lines. You remember Rance? Hecker's piss boy?"

"Jesus Christ, Stush. What did you say?"

"I told him I strongly disagreed. Said I'd mean no disrespect if I went over his head and called in the cavalry myself. I can do it, you know."

"What'd Chet say to that?"

"Said that would be my last act as police chief."

"He can't get away with firing you."

"Maybe he can't get away with it, but he can do it. The state of grace from that Russian situation has pretty well worn off." Must have seen Doc's eyes glazing and tapped the desk. "Don't worry, Benny. It might be time for me to stop flirting with retirement and just commit to the bitch. I'll call for help on my way out."

Doc squeezed his eyes shut. Pinched the bridge of his nose with a thumb and forefinger. "I wasn't going to say anything about this, but I don't know if Mike Zywiciel's ready to be even acting chief right now. He struck me as close to overwhelmed at the scene today."

"Wouldn't be Mike."

"Who, then?" Stush dipped his head in Doc's direction. "You know I don't want the job. Hecker wouldn't let Chet give it to me even if I did."

"Acting, Benny. Not permanent."

"Then who investigates the case? No way will I have time for it."

"That's why the feds will be here."

"Chet will cancel the invitation soon as you're gone."

"The FBI's like roaches, Benny. Once they're in they're hell to get rid of." Stush using Doc's name a lot, making it personal. "What say we go talk to our asshole with a gun?"

"Give me half an hour to see what I can find out about him."

CHAPTER 10

Stush put the Miranda waiver on the table. Told Simon to follow along while he did the recitation from memory. Went back to make sure there was no misunderstanding about the right to counsel, tape rolling all the time. Simon signed. Stush added the form to the file. Then he and Doc talked about everything except the day's events for half an hour. Simon tried a few times to bring up the elephant in the room. They responded with invitations to join their wide-ranging and irrelevant conversation. The usual topics of Steelers or Penguins failed. Finally lured him in with taxes and government. Let him run his mouth and get comfortable, just three guys bullshitting. Then Stush asked, real neighborly-like, what the carry permit was for.

Simon seemed to grow in the chair. "For days like today. My wife's been on me about that. 'What do you need all them guns for?' Now she knows."

Doc asked how many guns he had.

"You mean counting the Walther you took off me in the store? Which I better get back, by the way. There's the Smith and Wesson .38 Master, the .44 mag, the Taurus 24/7," Simon looked up, counting on his fingers, "the Baby Eagle nine—which is a sweet fucking little piece—a Ruger SR-22, Ithaca Model 37, a Ruger American, the BAR," Doc and Stush exchanged looks, "Winchester Model 94—a badly underrated gun—and a Bushmaster."

"No .380 or .25?"

"Oh, shit. Yeah. Picked up a nice Glock 42 at a gun show in Butler a couple months ago. I don't like a .25. Too in-between on size. I use a .22 for target shooting, but if stopping power matters, I want something bigger."

Stush said Simon sounded like a man who wanted to be prepared for anything.

"I do what I can."

Doc asked what took Simon into Dale's that afternoon.

"I needed a couple of flannel shirts. When I got there I seen some of them reading glasses for five bucks so I figured I'd get a pair of them, too."

Stush asked what happened then.

"Like I said, I went in for some shirts." Simon moved his hands when he talked, the chains jangling against the table. "You think you could take these handcuffs off me?"

Doc looked to Stush, who said, "We could." Neither cop moved.

"Fuck yinz guys."

Stush told him he was doing fine. "Keep going and we'll see what we can do."

Simon gave them each the stink eye. "So, like I said, I went in for some shirts and I come across these cheap glasses. I'm checking out that chart they have to see how strong I need them and I hear a gun go off."

"How close?"

"I couldn't tell right away. You know how sound is in a big room like that. I look up in time to see this guy the other side of some jewelry or something just about explode some woman's head."

Stush asked what the guy looked like.

"His back was to me. Couldn't see his face."

"How big was he?"

"About average, I guess. Nothing stuck out about him. Had on a ball cap so I can't say much about his hair."

51

"What did you do? After he shot the woman."

"The first thing I did was not panic. I backed away to get out of his field of vision while I drew my gun and took my time to get a good shot."

Doc said, "What was he doing while you were angling for the tactical advantage?"

"He shot some guy in the head. That's all he did was head shots."

Doc gave Stush a look. "The one Tony Lutz worked on wasn't shot in the head."

"Maybe she moved," Simon said.

"Maybe."

Stush said to go on.

"I got some clearance between us and fired a couple rounds. I know I hit him at least once."

Doc asked how he knew.

"He yelled and grabbed his arm."

"Which arm?"

A pause. "Left, I think."

Stush said, "What did he do then? After you shot him."

"He run out the front."

"Which door?"

"I didn't see."

"So you didn't chase him," Doc said.

"I didn't figure anyone needed a gunfight in the parking lot, people all over the place."

"Good thinking. What did you do?"

"I did what I could for the people that was shot."

"Not much you could do for them if they were all shot in the head."

"One wasn't. You said it yourself."

"Yeah, but you didn't."

Stush allowed as how maybe Simon didn't see the other victim right away.

"I didn't. Which is why I didn't say anything about it."

"Man or woman?" Doc said.

"Man or woman what?"

"The one that wasn't shot in the head."

"I just told you I didn't see her. Or him. Whichever."

Everyone sat silent for close to a minute. Doc gave Simon a hard look for half that time then lost interest. Stush nodded so slightly even Doc would have missed it had he not been paying attention. Spoke as conversationally as he could. "Here's what I don't get, Mr. Simon. I found you way the hell near the back of the store, fifty feet from any of the victims. Why did you go that way instead of out the front doors with everyone else?"

"I told you. I was buying time to set up a good shot."

"I mean after. You exchange fire and the shooter runs. Why didn't you take that chance to get out?"

"I wasn't sure he left. I didn't want to run into an ambush."

The cops exchanged looks. Doc said, "You said yourself he ran out the front."

"That's the way he was headed. I didn't actually see him leave."

"He headed for the front so you ran for the rear. That about right?"

"I didn't run."

"Okay, you walked in the opposite direction. You put as much distance between yourself and him as you could."

"He'd already pulled. Wouldn't do any good for him to see me go for my gun and shoot me before got to it. I needed a little space."

Doc glared. "You were at least fifty feet—at least—from the closest victim. You're full of shit if you're telling me you shot him from where I found you. I doubt you'd even been able to see him from there. Not to mention there was no brass anywhere around you."

"You're twisting what I said. I was a lot closer when I shot. I—I had to get some space."

Doc didn't enjoy watching Simon's face and posture collapse along with his story. He also wasn't in the mood to be sympathetic after what he'd seen. Asked Simon his MOS in the Army, already knowing the answer.

"My MOS?"

Doc's lips pulled together. Wagged his head an inch. "Military occupational specialty."

"I wasn't in the Army."

"Marine Corps, then."

"No." Very small.

"Were you in the military at all?"

Simon shook his head.

"Ever fired a weapon in anger before today?"

"No."

"Ever had a weapon pointed at you? Before today?"

Simon grunted something that might have been, "uh-uh."

"What's that?" Doc said.

"I said no."

Doc left half a minute for Simon to sense how his answers had gone over. "Here's what I think happened. You were close when the shooting started. Your feet decided to get the fuck out of Dodge but your head realized the danger was between you and the exit. Once you remembered you had a gun you turned and got off a few shots. One went through the front window."

"No fucking way did I shoot out a window."

"I found the bullet myself. It might be too badly damaged to match with your gun but there's no fucking way it's a .45, either." Shit. Didn't mean to let that out in front of Simon. "One might've hit the shooter. There's a good chance the other one hit the woman who's over at Allegheny Valley Hospital right now."

Stush's voice almost inaudible. "I heard they choppered her down to UPMC."

"Trauma center. Nice shooting, Chuck."

"Somebody hadda do something." Simon's voice regained a little bravado. "Wasn't like yinz guys was gonna show up in time to do any good. Christ knows how many'd be lying there dead."

Simon looked to both Doc and Stush in turn. No sympathy in the room. Doc said, "You understand, don't you, that if we had shown up much sooner we'd a shot you, right?"

"Me? What the fuck would you shoot me for? I was the one on your side."

"All we'd see were people down and two assholes with guns. We would've shot you both and let the crime lab sort it out."

Simon's mouth hung half open in amazement at the lack of police prescience Doc described. "At least you're satisfied I ain't the one started it." Held up his shackled hands. "You gonna let me go now?"

Doc looked to Stush. The chief sat with his hands folded on his belly. "Mr. Simon, we're going to keep you with us for a night. Maybe two."

If Simon was amazed before he was stunned now. "You're keeping me? What's the charge?"

"For now let's say discharging a firearm inside the city limits." Simon stared, unbelieving. "Four people are dead and one damn near and you're the only person we can prove had a gun anywhere in the vicinity. We're hanging on to you."

CHAPTER 11

Ten o'clock Tuesday night. National media trickling in. Not too many, Penns River not the kind of place that rated the full-court press unless half the town was underwater or a tanker car full of chlorine gas derailed. A terrorist driving a truck bomb into an elementary school might do it, except no self-respecting terrorist would waste his time on a town with the media profile of Penns River. The local stations and papers milked their sources. The big cable news outlets sent their B teams while the stars covered a crisis in the federal government unlike anything anyone had seen for at least six weeks.

Rick Neuschwander and Teresa Shimp sat in Stush's visitors' chairs. Doc lounged on a window ledge. Fourteen hours into their shifts and not likely to leave anytime soon.

Stush made sure everyone had coffee and at least one doughnut, though Shimp treated hers—plain—as if it wanted to attach itself directly to her hips. Stush asked if everyone was comfortable or needed anything. They were and they didn't. "Okay, Ricky. What do you have?"

Rick Neuschwander was a good family man. What Doc's grandparents would have called "salt of the earth." Always where he was supposed to be, not much for conversation. Almost worthless in an interrogation unless the topic was his children. A tenacious investigator with an eye for crime scenes. Lacked the imagination needed to put together a full puzzle from the pieces he found. Pittsburgh came calling every time they had an opening, but that would mean shift work. Missing dinner at five o'clock with his wife and kids enough to set Rick off his feed for a week. He'd missed it tonight—as well as getting to tuck in the little ones—and it showed.

"Our suspect is the dead guy in the car behind the store, Michael Stoltz. Contact wound to the head, gun right about where it would fall if he shot himself. Ray couldn't see it from the angle he was looking at and didn't want to contaminate the scene once he saw the guy was dead."

"How many did he fire?"

Neuschwander wagged his head as if he didn't like his answer. "No more than five. Seven-round mag with three left."

Doc stopped jiggling his foot. "You're saying he only missed once? Or not at all?"

"Doesn't sound right for one of these guys," Stush said. "They're into slinging lead all over the place."

"I know," Neuschwander said. "We took that store apart. There are no discarded magazines. We found three .45-caliber casings in the store and one in the car. Three .32s in the store. That's it."

"The guy in the car," Doc said. "Stoltz. He have any other wounds on him? Left arm, maybe?"

"Not that I saw. We'll get the ME's report from Allegheny County tomorrow if we're lucky." Penns River in Neshannock County—pretty much was Neshannock County—too small for a medical examiner of its own. "Speaking of reports, no one was still working at the crime lab we use by the time I got the first batch of evidence out. I'll have more before I leave tonight. Do we have the budget for me to expedite the requests?"

"Until someone tells me different," Stush said. Everyone in the room aware Chet Hensarling wouldn't want to spend any more money than he had to if they already had the shooter dead to rights, no pun intended.

"What about ballistics?" Doc said.

"In transit like everything else. We're not going to have any lab work back until late tomorrow afternoon at best. Thursday, more likely. If we're lucky."

Stush sipped his decaf. "So as far as we can tell it looks like this Stoltz guy got a bug up his ass and killed at least three people for reasons we may never know." Looked from face to face for signs of disagreement. "We also know Simon got off a few rounds, so even if he didn't hit Stoltz he might've scared him off. Stoltz runs out to his car and—what? Overcome with remorse? Planned to shoot himself all along?"

The three subordinates looked at each other like they hoped one of the other had the answer. "That's the best scenario we have so far," Neuschwander said.

"Why'd he run away if he was planning to shoot himself, anyway? And why go back to the car to do it? Don't these guys usually raise hell then kill themselves just before the cops get to?"

Doc and Neuschwander looked at each other, then Stush. "No idea," Doc said.

Shimp cleared her throat. "Maybe he didn't expect anyone to shoot back and he panicked."

"Gets to the car and calms down enough to remember the plan was to kill himself instead of driving away?" Stush said. "I'm not picking on you, Teresa. I'm just trying to make sense of it."

"Maybe there is no sense to be made of it," Neuschwander said. "This isn't the kind of thing a lucid person does."

Everyone quiet for a minute. Cops hate motiveless violence. Stupid violence they understand. Guy at a family barbecue gets drunk and cuts up his cousin over the score of a cornhole game. Woman's had enough one day and throws something at the old man for what he considered an innocuous comment. The reasons appear weak to any outsider. Often to the perpetrator after a few minutes' thought. But they had reasons. Something like this, no rational explanation...to say it scared the four cops was too strong, drinking coffee in Stush's office, the violence past. Disconcerting as hell, though.

Stush spoke first. "Benny. You going over to talk to Stoltz's next of kin?"

"Soon as we're done here. Allegheny County's holding the body as a John Doe until I can get to them."

"Teresa, go with him. Watch and listen. You're good at the nonverbal shit." Shimp nodded. "Who did the notifications for the other three?"

"I did," Shimp said.

"All three?"

"You and I were with Simon," Doc said. "Rick was tied up at the crime scene all day. We're still a detective short."

"I'm sorry, Teresa," Stush said. "That's a shitty day. And you inherited that armed robbery downtown."

"Whatever you need, Chief." Shimp the newest Penns River detective, one of three women brought in when a consent decree encouraged the town to beef up its complement of female police. Still not with the local custom of calling the chief "Stush" to his face.

"You get anything worth mentioning from the victims' families?"

"Nothing that ties them together. Two were employees who might have been dating. The other went there to buy panty hose and some Claritin. I put everything in the reports."

"Anyone have an update on the survivor?"

"That's where I just came from." Shimp really did have a shitty day. A solo death notification hat trick followed by hospital watch. The alcoholic cop starter set. "The doctor I talked to said she won't live the night. The bullet went through both lungs and nicked an artery on the way. She said we should give the EMT on the scene a medal for keeping her alive as long as he did."

"You didn't have to call her family, too, did you?" Stush looked as close to alarmed as he ever got.

"Janine did. I did talk to the parents at the hospital. Nicole—

that's her name, Nicole Sobotka—was supposed to drop some clothes at her parents' on her way to work for her mother to mend. The parents got home and were wondering where the stuff was when Janine called. They didn't tell me anything I didn't already know. Nicole can't speak and probably won't."

Stush tapped his wedding ring against the handle of his coffee mug. One of his tells when making a decision he didn't like. Doc had a pretty good idea what was coming. A cop should be bedside at Mercy Hospital in case Nicole Sobotka woke up, or even mumbled something in her coma. The odds were against anything of value coming from it, but the base had to be covered. The problem was finding someone to do it. Penns River had no night shift of detectives. The few on staff had full plates. Costing one of them a night's sleep on a slim chance of learning something that may or may not be useful was a luxury Stush couldn't afford.

"We had all hands on deck today, right?" Nods from Doc and Neuschwander. Stush brought up the roster on the computer. "You were there all day, Ricky. Who was in the first batch to go home?"

"Whoever was supposed to have the day off. I'm not sure who all it was. Eye Chart took care of it."

Stush read the screen. "Dave Wohleber works four to twelve tomorrow. I'll send him to—where is she? Mercy?—for tonight." Picked up the phone and made the call. Doc loved to listen to Stush make assignments the recipient wouldn't like. The perfect blend of sympathy and authority.

Wohleber dispatched, Stush faced his detectives. "Where do the Stoltzes live?"

"Arizona Drive," Shimp said.

"Take your personal vehicles and go home right after and get some sleep if you want. Write up the reports in the morning."

"Can't do it," Doc said.

"Why not?"

"Rick and I are watching TV tonight. Videos from Dale's

security company." Stush opened his mouth. "Don't even think about it. You're too old for this shit. Besides, you're handling the media and you have to be fresh for that."

Stush's face didn't like either of those comments. "Teresa, you go home after the notification. No argument. I need one detective working on a decent night's sleep." Not that she'd get one after the day she'd spent. "Ricky, how close are we to buttoning up that crime scene?"

"Eye Chart detailed Al Speer to work a double and keep an eye on the place. I have a few things to prep for the lab."

Stush gave his three detectives each a long look. Doc understood better than anyone how it killed the older man to task them with things he was no longer in a position to do himself. "Tomorrow's shifts start an hour early. See you all here at seven. Oh, and tell the reporters you're sure to pass on the way out that we'll have a statement for them at nine in the morning and that they might as well go home."

CHAPTER 12

The first thing Teresa Shimp noticed was that Mark and Patricia Stoltz didn't seem all that surprised when Ben Dougherty told them their son was dead.

Patricia spoke almost as if she'd been aware of her son's death several days. "We knew something was wrong when he didn't come home for supper. He hardly ever misses and he always calls when he's late. We left messages and sent texts. He always answers them."

Mark had much the same disposition as his wife. "I called Allegheny Valley Hospital when I heard about what happened at Dale's. They said he wasn't there and they didn't know anything about him. I guess they weren't allowed to tell. I should've gone over and identified myself."

Michael Stoltz's parents and the two cops in the family living room. Mark sat in the recliner, elbows on his knees. Patricia small enough to curl up in a wing chair with a University of Pittsburgh throw hanging over the back. The cops shared the couch. Teresa felt the cushions shift as Dougherty leaned forward. Her stomach clenched. She knew what came next and wouldn't have traded places if it meant a guaranteed ticket to Heaven.

"Mr. Stoltz, do you own an M1911 A1 Army Colt Pistol?" Dougherty knew he did. They'd already checked the registration on the gun.

Teresa saw it in Mark Stoltz's eyes. Recognition the conversation was moving to a place he couldn't have imagined, not yet ready to jump to the logical conclusion. "Yes. It was my father's."

Dougherty said, "Did Michael have access to the gun?" and the color drained from Patricia Stoltz's face like water through a sieve.

Mark already had a sob in his voice and tears forming in his eyes. His answer had nothing to do with Dougherty's question. "No."

"I can't begin to tell you how sorry I am to have to say this, but your Colt was lying at Michael's feet when we found him in his car. The wound appears to be self-inflicted." Patricia drew in a sharp breath. Dougherty paused to gather himself before dropping the other shoe. "We don't have final ballistics reports back yet, but the victims in the store had wounds consistent with a large-caliber weapon, possibly a .45."

Patricia looked to Mark. He stood, holding her gaze. Said, "No" again and left the room.

No one spoke. No one looked at anyone else. Patricia fussed with the fringe on the Pitt blanket. The thermostat clicked. A few seconds later the furnace came on.

Mark Stoltz returned in less than a minute. Stood in the doorway that led down the hall. Spoke as if it pained him to breathe. "It's gone."

Teresa worked with Ben Dougherty almost every day. Sitting this close, she sensed how much this was taking out of him. Tendons stood out on the back of his hand as he squeezed the couch cushions when he spoke. His tone calm and measured. An undertaker's voice. "Did Michael have easy access to the gun?"

He might as well have asked the question in Aramaic. Both Stoltzes looked at him without comprehension. The furnace fan easing air across the room the only sound for thirty seconds. Dougherty cleared his throat as if to speak and Mark said, "Yes. He could take it whenever he wanted. He was...good with it."

"Good in what way, sir?"

Another ten seconds passed. Teresa had no sense Mark was holding back. It was taking him this long to process the questions. "Every way. He's a dead shot." Patricia released a sob. "No. No. Not like that. We go the range out there off Greensburg Road. You know, past the radiator shop? He loves that gun. Says it makes him feel like he's with his granddad when he holds it. Cleans it every time he uses it. Wraps it and puts it away in the safe. That gun's like part of his hand…"

"Had Michael given any indication he was upset about anything? Angry?"

Patricia spoke right away. "No. He's been fine. He's always a little…quiet since the accident, but nothing out of the ordinary."

"What accident?"

"Mike was in a car wreck after his senior prom. Would've been…ten years ago?" Mark looked to Patricia.

"Eleven in May."

"What happened?" Dougherty said.

"It was the damnedest thing." Mark blew air through puffed cheeks and shook his head. "Kids in a wreck after the prom. Drinking, right? Uh-uh. The kids were sober. A drunk hit them on their way to a post-prom party at one of their houses. Asshole half again over the limit T-boned them turning off the bypass onto Wildlife Lodge."

"How bad was it?"

"No one was killed. Some of the kids were hurt pretty bad, though."

"What about Michael?"

Another twenty seconds before Patricia said, "He was the worst."

No volunteers to continue. Dougherty kept things moving. "How bad was he?"

"Broken shoulder, broken collarbone, broken elbow, broken

ribs, ruptured spleen, internal bleeding." Mark recited more than spoke. "Some...brain issues."

"What kind of brain issues?"

Teresa expected a longer pause than Patricia took. "He wasn't the same after. He was...timid? Is that the word? Mark had always been so lively. Always getting his friends to do things and go places. Never anything that was trouble, but he was always the one putting together a group to play ball or go to a movie. All that changed after the accident."

"The psychologist used the word 'docile,' I think." Mark rubbed his jaw. "Makes it hard for him to hold a job. You know, he doesn't see what needs to be done and takes care of it. Someone has to tell him. He's fine then. Hell of a hard worker. He just needs a lot of supervision. Once you tell him what needs done and he says he'll do it, he's as good as his word."

"He have any anger issues?"

"Sometimes I wish he did. After the accident he seemed to accept anything that happened. Couldn't get a rise out of him."

Teresa felt Dougherty's gears working. Made a mental note to see what they'd need for a court order to talk to the psychologist. Outward docility didn't equal inner tranquility.

Dougherty sat with his elbows on his knees. Stared at the backs of his hands until the pause became uncomfortable. "Mr. and Mrs. Stoltz, I know what a difficult time this is." Looked up. "I'm sorry. I don't have any kids, so I can't imagine what this must be like. Still, I have to ask if we can take a look in Michael's room. Go through his things around the house." The search warrant in Dougherty's pocket.

"Sure," Mark said.

Patricia said, "Whatever you need."

CHAPTER 13

"Don't spend any more money here tonight than you do regular."
Jacques Lelievre picked up a twenty from the bar and put it into
Don Kwiatkowski's shirt pocket. Jacques had mixed emotions
about getting together with Don at Fat Jimmy's, their cherry-
busting robbery no more than twelve hours past. Rules Seven
("Never flash money at a bar or with women") and Eight ("Never
go back to an old bar or hangout once you have moved up")
argued against it, and Don had already spent most of his day
breaking rules like they were china figurines in an earthquake.
So far they'd got away with it.

For once Don didn't get the red ass. "Sorry. You're right.
Rule...Six? No. Seven."

"That's right. Rule Seven. People here know you so they
know you are not working. No one but you knows me, so they
might think I have money. Maybe I just got a check. I'll pay tonight."

Quiet in Fat Jimmy's. Both televisions tuned to the eleven
o'clock news, which was unheard of. Everyone wanted the latest
on the shootings at Dale's. What little discussion took place
focused on how different things would have been if any one of a
half dozen of Jimmy's regulars had been there when the balloon
went up. Another half dozen volunteered opinions about how
full of shit the first six were. All of it quieter than the usual pool
shooting or football watching. No one's heart really in it.

Jacques wanted to keep Don focused. "You paying attention to this on the television?"

"Yeah. My mother and my sister shop there. I can't believe they haven't caught the son of a bitch yet."

"Worse things can happen." That earned Don's undivided interest. "Listen to me before you get mad. This is a small town. Not much police. They are going to be busy with this shooting business for a while. It's a terrible thing, I know, but it's an opportunity, too. For us."

"What do you have in mind?"

"We have a few days—three at the most—while the local cops figure out what is going on and either catch the guy or ask for help. It will be the only thing they care about. That's when we can move."

"How do you know they didn't ask for help already?"

"Because that woman on the television just said they didn't. Maybe they already have a suspect and don't want anyone to know."

"Maybe they already called for help and don't want anyone to know."

"In case someone is planning another shooting? They would want people to know if the FBI or state police were coming. Put their minds at ease." Jacques sipped his drink. "We have time for two or three jobs if we're quick."

"Seems to me we don't want to rush into anything. What'd we make today? Seventy-six hundred dollars? That'll hold me over for a while."

"I understand that. What you have to understand is we have an opportunity that does not often come. Unless you want to be nothing but a locked-out steelworker when the bank comes for your house."

That perked Don up. "Why not take a couple of days and do it right, but take something with serious money? Like a bank?"

Didn't Americans study civics? Jacques said, "*Tabernac*" under his breath before he caught himself.

"What's that?" Don said.

"Something a friend used to say." Jacques reminded himself to only curse in English. Still looking for a word that gave the same satisfaction as *Tabernac*. "Banks are insured by your federal government. Bank robberies are investigated by the FBI, which is who we are trying to stay away from." A quick check to be sure no one was listening. "Besides, banks are ready for robbers. They have cameras, dye packs, alarms, time locks. The tellers have very little money. Two things are true about bank robbers in this country: They don't get rich and they do get caught. There are other places with cash."

"That's the only payday loan place in town that I know of."

"Doesn't have to be a loan store. Where do people pay cash for things?"

"Sheetz, I guess. When they go inside."

"What is Sheetz?"

"They're gas stations with convenience stores attached. You know, they sell snacks and drinks and lottery tickets. Hot food, too. Sheetz makes great hot dogs and those made-to-order sandwiches are really good. I used to get a couple of shmiscuits for breakfast on my way to work—"

"Okay, I understand. Sheetz are convenience stores. You ever look at a Sheetz like you were thinking to rob it?"

"No."

"Convenience stores have what they call drop safes. Anytime the register gets more than a couple hundred dollars, they drop the money into a safe no one can open until the armed security guards come for it."

"Oh." Don tipped his glass so Jacques could see it was empty. Jacques checked Don's eyes. Sober enough for one more without having to shut down the conversation. Jacques knocked back the rest of his Crown Royal and gestured for another round.

Neither spoke while the barmaid fetched their drinks. Jacques insisted on paying—"I got some expense money for my last run today"—made sure she heard. Gave a tip calculated not to draw attention to him as either a stiff or a big spender. Waited for her to leave and said, "What about money orders? People have to pay cash and the places that sell them have to have money on hand for people to redeem them."

"Post office sells money orders."

Mon dieu. "That's worse than a bank. Post offices are federal institutions. They even have their own investigators." Thought a moment. Remembered Leonard's book. *Swag.* "What about supermarkets? Do they sell money orders here?"

"Sure they do. What? Supermarkets don't sell them in Vermont?"

"I just want to be sure. Different places have different laws about what can be sold where. Like up in Vermont they can sell liquor in groceries. Here even the liquor stores are run by the state." Jacques had no idea if Vermont allowed liquor sales in supermarkets but figured Don wouldn't either.

"I guess so. I never had to buy one so I don't pay much attention where to get them." Don spoke as if buying a money order was the final act of a desperate man.

"What time do they open?"

"I don't know. Giant Eagle might be open twenty-four hours."

"I need you to do something. Tomorrow, go to all the supermarkets in town and see what time they open. I'd do it myself but I don't know where they all are. Meet me for lunch—somewhere. You can pick."

"Why do you care when they open? Won't be any money in them then. We should go when they close."

"If we know when they open, we have a good idea when the day shift of cashiers gets off work. That's when the most money will be available, when they bring their drawers in and the replacements are going out. Cash building up in the office. We'll go in then."

CHAPTER 14

Neuschwander already in the detectives' room when Doc got back. "You just missed Barb Gaydac. I would've had her stay if I knew you'd be back this soon."

"Who's Barb Gaydac?"

"Barb Smith? She got married."

Doc set a paper shopping bag on his desk. "I knew she got married. I must've forgot the name." Barb Smith Gaydac, a Penns River cop for a short time. "How is she?"

"Pregnant."

Doc paused. Replaced whatever it was he'd had halfway out of the bag. "That's as far as it goes with you, isn't it? She's pregnant, so everything must be unicorns and rainbows for her. Just because you have four kids doesn't mean the goal of all human existence is to live in a more or less continuous zone of reproductive construction."

Neuschwander let Doc finish. He'd heard this riff before. "She's fine. Says it's nice to have a job with regular hours, even though she had to work late tonight."

"Speaking of which, what was she doing here? I haven't seen her since she quit."

"Didn't you know? She's a manager at the company that handles Dale's security. She brought over the videos from this afternoon."

"Good. I was hoping we were done waiting for those. I

brought," Doc reached into the bag, "three Cokes for you, three Mello Yellos for me, and a box of that cheap microwave popcorn you like so much. We're going to stay up all night watching TV, we might as well do it right." Determined not to let a shit day turn into a shit night. Not that he had much choice considering the task at hand. At least he could make the effort.

"Nice. Thanks." Neuschwander held up six disks. "How do you want to do it? She kept each camera on its own disk in case we wanted to split up and watch them separately. Or we can both watch together and make sure we don't miss anything. You have a preference?"

"I prefer to pee. You hungry?" Neuschwander tapped a pencil against his teeth while making up his mind. "How about I put a bag in the microwave, hit the head, then we'll watch together. Two sets of eyes and that."

Five minutes later Doc was back, hands washed and popcorn ready. Neuschwander had opened one Coke and one Mello-Yello, put the extras in the mini-fridge. Doc settled into his chair. Turned to face Neuschwander's monitor. "Okay. What do we have?"

"Six cameras, which isn't great, but it's all there is. Each video starts half an hour before the 911 call and runs through till you took Simon out."

"Barb always did do nice work."

"It gets better." Neuschwander laid a rolled-up paper on the desk. "This is a map of the store showing each camera's location and field of vision."

"We owe her at least lunch. Dinner if there's anything good here." Doc put his feet on the desk. Sipped his drink. "Roll 'em."

Neuschwander inserted a disk into the drive. The camera angle covered the store's front doors. "The time stamp on the 911 call is 2:02. What say we start a quarter of?"

"You're the forensics expert. Maybe we'll see Stoltz going in."

People came and went as on any other day until 2:00:14

when a woman led the charge. Not a mass exodus, more like a steady stream of twos and threes, the store too big and not busy enough for a consolidated rush once those at the cash registers got out. A round went through the front window at 2:01:09. Burrows arrived at 2:09, gun drawn. Neuschwander let the video run until everyone who wanted to got out and Burrows had the perimeter as secure as one cop could make it. "Did you see him?"

"I thought so for a second but I changed my mind." Doc looked at his notes. "Roll it back to 1:56." Neuschwander did. "There. Coming in from the right. Blue down jacket. Steelers ball cap. Can you roll it in slow motion? I want to see his face." Neuschwander pressed a key. The video crawled ahead at about one-quarter speed until the figure in question moved out of range. "I couldn't make it out. Could you?"

"Uh-uh. Let's watch it again." Rolled back the video. Replayed it even slower. "Damn it. He never looks at the camera. Even the profiles are obscured."

"Let's follow him." Doc sat up, rolled out the map. "This is Camera Two, right?" Drew a line with his finger along the path the blue jacket had taken. "And he went here? Or an aisle over?"

"Here." Neuschwander tapped the map. "And that's where the shooter would've gone. Health and Beauty Aids." Another tap.

"Where? Here?"

"Yeah."

Doc stared at the map. "Okay. I give up. Which camera covers Health and Beauty Aids?"

Neuschwander looked at the map. Read the legend. Back to the map. "Doesn't look like any of them do. Camera Four is closest."

"Cue up Four. See if it has anything helpful."

Neuschwander swapped disks. Camera Four covered what passed for jewelry in Dale's.

"Goddamnit," Doc said. "I hoped we'd at least see motion outside the range shown on the map. The angle's wrong. Shit."

"Give it a second..." Neuschwander slowed the speed.

"There! That's him running. See the coat?"

"Barely. Back it up and freeze it." Both cops stared at the right arm and leg of what appeared to be the man they'd seen come in. "What time is it?"

"Two-oh-one and thirty-five seconds."

"Switch it back to that first camera and go to 2:01. We should see him leaving." Kicked himself for not looking there first.

Neuschwander switched the disks back again. "There's the window breaking. Yep. There he is. Running like hell."

"Still can't see his face, though."

"We knew we wouldn't. He's running away."

"I thought he might take a look over his shoulder."

"Would you?"

"I might if I thought I was being chased. Remember, Simon got off three rounds. How does this guy know he wasn't a cop and might pursue?"

"Don't get ahead of yourself. This guy in the blue jacket might just be some jagov came in for underwear and wants to get out before he gets shot."

"Back it up. Let's see our best look. There." Doc pointed. "Can you zoom in? Simon swears he winged the shooter."

"Haven't we pretty much decided Simon is full of shit?"

"Yeah, but if this guy shows any sign of a gunshot, maybe he's not as completely full of shit as I thought. Can you get any closer?"

"Yeah, but watch." The focus crawled in until the running man's back almost filled the screen. "This isn't some NSA satellite camera that can read license plates from the moon. That's all the resolution we have."

Doc pulled the map closer. "Camera One covers the outside. Let's watch him leave."

Neuschwander switched disks again. Fast forward to two o'clock. Let it run at normal speed until Burrows came in at 2:09. "Where the fuck'd he go?" Doc said.

Both cops stared at the screen. Neuschwander figured it out first. "Other door."

Doc sat back. Drew a picture in his head. Dale's had two entry doors. He and Snyder entered through one to clear the building. Sisler and Augustine the other. One opened onto the parking lot. The other onto the gangway that led to nothing but the service entrances for all the stores. "Don't tell me. There's no coverage of the other door. The one by the alley."

Neuschwander checked the map. "Nope."

"Which side did he come in from? When we saw him on Camera Two?"

Neuschwander thought. "I'm not sure. We didn't notice him right away, remember?"

"Run this back to a minute before we picked him up inside. That was..." Doc checked his notes, "1:56."

Neuschwander rolled it back to 1:53 to be safe. The blue jacket never appeared.

"Put Camera Two back in. Roll it to 1:55 and let's see where he comes in from."

Neuschwander already moving before Doc spoke. Froze the frame when they saw the blue coat. "There. From our right. He came in the alley door."

"Yeah," Doc said. "The one by the car."

CHAPTER 15

Doc cruised in on three hours' sleep at six forty-five for the seven o'clock meeting. A note in his mail cubby told him Stush had urgent business with the mayor and asked him to extend every courtesy to Staff Sergeant Gord McFetridge of the Royal Canadian Mounted Police, who waited in the lobby. Doc would have preferred to extend another hour's worth of courtesy to his pillow.

The Mountie was about Doc's size. Wore a blue suit over a white shirt and a tie with a subtle plaid. Doc wondered if it was the clan tartan. Wanted to ask where his Dudley Do-Right outfit was, remembered what a keen sense of humor most FBI agents had and wondered if Canadian feds were any different. Kept it to himself.

McFetridge accepted an offer of coffee, though to Doc it seemed more out of courtesy than any desire for a cup of police station swill. Still situating himself in his chair when McFetridge spoke. "I know this is a bad time to ask for help. I don't want to distract you from your investigation into what happened yesterday. I do have a job, though, and I need to get at it."

"Always get your man, do you?"

If McFetridge caught Doc's tone, he ignored it. "Often enough."

McFetridge seemed like a nice guy, which didn't help Doc's mood any. "Well, you're here, bad timing or not. What can I do for you?"

"I'm looking for an escaped convict named Jacques Lelievre."

"Never heard of him."

"No reason you should. You did have a robbery here yesterday. Just before your shooting? A bad credit loan store was robbed."

"And you think of all the payday loan joints in all the world he happened to walk into mine?"

"We have him traced to the Pittsburgh area. Those are the kinds of places he likes to rob. It was worth a look." McFetridge took an envelope from an inner pocket. "I don't want you to think I'm wasting your time freelancing. Here's a letter from the FBI requesting your cooperation. I want to stay out of your hair as much as possible. Point me and I can look around on my own."

Doc waved off the letter. "I don't have the kind of relationship with the FBI that I give a shit what they say. My chief says you get my cooperation and that's good enough for me. The problem is, that's not my case anymore. It was, but the shooting took me away. Teresa Shimp is lead on the Easy Money robbery. I can let you look through the file if it's here. She'll be in around eight."

"You answered the call, though. Right?"

"First uniform on the scene was Sean Sisler, but yeah, I was responding detective."

"Can I ask you a few quick questions before Detective Shimp gets here?"

Doc had the report in hand and almost tossed it across the desk and told this pain in the ass Canuck to read the fucking thing himself before he remembered his notes weren't in there. The Dale's shooting called him away and he forgot all about it in the confusion later. Took his notebook from a pocket and relaxed into his chair. "Sure. What do you want to know?"

"Well, the obvious first, I guess. Any good description?"

Doc flipped through pages. "Two guys. Called each other Larry and Butch. Larry seemed to be the leader. About five-ten, five-eleven. Average build. Butch was a little shorter and had a gut on him."

"How were they dressed?"

"Larry looked pretty sharp. Butch...says here Butch looked like he'd been working on his car."

"Let's stick with Larry. Was he armed?"

"Handgun. Butch had a shotgun."

"Anything else stick out? Impressions from the scene that aren't in the report, I mean. I can read that later."

Doc turned a page. "Manager—guy named Ed Spicer—made a big deal about how Larry was the quiet one. Butch waving a shotgun around and yelling at people. Larry keeping things under control until he took Spicer in back for the money. Spicer says he was looking for a chance to set off an alarm but Larry told him," checked the notes, "the only way he—Spicer—wouldn't open that safe was if he was dead. Then Spicer tried to play for time by bungling the combination and Larry said the safe would be open in ten seconds or the next person to open it would have to clean brains off it first."

McFetridge looked as disappointed as any cop ever shows. Doc noticed. "Don't take that too seriously. I think Mr. Spicer made the thread his life was hanging by a little thinner than it really was."

"What makes you say that?"

Doc leaned back in his chair. "You know what it's like. You talk to enough witnesses, you get a feel for who wants to make himself look good. I got the idea what Spicer told me is what he wished would've happened more than what actually happened."

"You mind if I talk to him?"

"Be my guest. Teresa will take you by when she gets here. Any information you can share with her will be a big help." Doc scanned through a few more pages of notes. Flipped the book shut, put it away. "I'm sorry. I was a pill this morning when you came in here. I'm running on about three hours' sleep after—"

"My feelings will be hurt if you apologize. I'm a cop, too. We've all had days like this, except I've never had one as bad as what yours must've been like yesterday."

"Thanks." Doc slid the case file across the desk. "I need to see a guy before the media finds out about him, so I'm going to run. Here's the file. Make yourself at home. Teresa Shimp will be here in fifteen, twenty minutes. Five-eight or so, thin, blond hair. Good cop. You'll like working with her."

McFetridge stood to shake hands. "Thanks. And thanks for the insight on this Spicer. I'll be sure to have a talk with him." Walked Doc to the door. "Hey, you don't have any relatives in Montreal, do you? Cops?"

"Not that I know of. Why?"

"I worked a couple of times with a Montreal cop named Dougherty when I was a pup. Pronounced it different but spelled it like you do, with an O. Don't see that much, the O with a G-H."

"I don't think I have any people up that way."

"It's nothing. I just thought it might be one of those small world things."

"That would be a small world. Good luck catching this Lelievre." Doc took two steps and stopped. "Oh, and if you have a thing for clean bathrooms? Teresa Shimp can hook you up. She knows them all."

CHAPTER 16

The Pucketa Gun Club sat on part of an old farm near the southern edge of Penns River. Two small signs—one facing each direction—were the only notices on Greensburg Road. Another, half hidden by a bush in summer, pointed to the driveway. A line of trees hid the buildings and range so well the place was a challenge to find even with a GPS.

Doc didn't need directions. He qualified here twice a year. Came out to practice on his own at least once a month. Pucketa—the Puck, locals called it—the only range within twenty miles that could accommodate shots up to a quarter of a mile. Sean Sisler, a Marine sniper in Afghanistan and the department's official marksmanship snob, called it an "outdoor pistol range." Tore the hearts out of paper targets at three hundred yards with the department-issue AR-15 at the semiannual qualifications.

Quiet at eight on a Wednesday morning. The door was open and the smell of coffee floated into the parking lot. Ron Blewett—"Pump Action" to his friends, unmatched at double skeet shooting anywhere in the Valley—leaned back in an old-fashioned wooden reclining office chair with a steaming Remington mug in his hands. His face sank when he saw Doc's expression. "Aw, hell. It's not one of my guys, is it?" Stood to shake Doc's hand.

"I'm afraid it might be, Pump." Doc took Michael Stoltz's driver's license photo from a folder, laid it on the counter.

Blewett's eyes closed. His shoulders sagged. "Aw, for the love of—not Mikey Stoltz. Why?"

Doc shook his head. "When's the last time he was here?"

"Yesterday. Tuesday's his regular day lately." Blewett still looking at Michael's photo. Doc had never seen anything affect him this much, Ron usually dry as sand. "Come in around...eleven? Quarter after? Christ, Doc. We shot the shit. I even talked him into bringing back lunch. I paid. I mean..."

"Did he have his dad's .45 ACP with him?"

"His granddad's, yeah. Beautiful gun. That what he used?"

"Looks like. How long was he here?"

"One o'clock? One thirty? One thirty. He was gonna leave at one and *Mail Call* came on the H2 channel, so he stayed."

Plenty of time to make it to Hilltop Plaza by two. "How well did you know him, Pump?"

Blewett threw Doc a look. "How well did I know him? You're saying he's dead, too?"

Doc nodded. "Looks like he did himself in the parking lot."

Blewett off in his own world. "I knew him as well as I know anyone here. Well as I know you. Wasn't like we socialized or anything, but he was in here once or twice a month and we always bullshitted. Nice kid. You're sure it was him?"

"Sure as we can be until we get the ballistics reports. Tell me about him."

"Shot where he looked. No one more careful about safety. Quiet, but had a pretty good sense of humor, you got him going. Smart, I think, but not the kind to show it off. His dad told me he'd been in a bad accident and it did something to him. Made him keep to himself."

Doc tried to find a non-cliché way to ask and failed. "This will sound corny, and I'm sorry, but did he seem different yesterday? Anything unusual about him?"

"You mean did I have a feeling he was going straight over to Dale's and kill a bunch of people? No."

Doc took a second, no more in the mood for this than

Blewett. "Maybe something more subtle. Did he seem down? Or a little up? Do anything you thought was out of character? More outgoing than usual? Funnier? Or not getting obvious jokes? Distracted? I don't know. Just not himself in some way."

"That's casting a pretty broad net of things to look for."

"Come on. You know what I mean. Imagine Michael Stoltz in here on any day except yesterday. Now think of him yesterday. Anything seem off? At all? Good or bad."

"The only thing different about yesterday was I talked him into going to Dairy Queen instead of McDonald's. Nothing else. He was a good kid, Doc. Nice kid. I used to look forward to when he'd come in."

Doc looked through the back door's window and across to the tree line on the next hill. Thought of firing off a few magazines himself. Something he could understand. Money, power, or sex were at least reasons to kill. Not good reasons, but they made sense on some level. Here all he had were five dead—Nicole Sobotka had passed in the night—and a shooter he half felt sorry for. Doc liked being a cop because of the closure that came with solving a case. No closure in sight here.

The two friends stood looking downrange watching the frost melt in the morning sun. Blewett spoke first. "You tell his old man?"

"Yeah."

"How'd he take it?"

Doc rubbed his neck. "As well as could be expected, I guess. He wasn't surprised when I told him Michael was dead. They heard about what happened and the kid hadn't returned their calls or texts. He took it hard when he found out Michael was the shooter, but he held it together pretty well. Going to be some shitty days for him coming up. Both of them."

Blewett took a sip. Made a face and threw the rest of his coffee out the door. "Shitty days coming up for a lot of us."

"That's another reason I came by so early. The media's in town and we're going to have to account for Michael's whereabouts yesterday. They'll be here ten minutes after the presser. Too good to pass up, him going to a gun range right before he goes off like he did."

Blewett squeezed his eyes shut. "Thanks for the heads up. When are you going to tell them?"

"Presser's at nine, be done by ten. We're closing a few loops now."

"The protesters will come, too."

"Not right away, but yeah. Maybe it won't be so bad. We're not in one of those hardcore anti-gun states like Connecticut or Massachusetts."

"They'll fly in for the opportunity to say this is what happens when you have a bunch of rednecks clinging to their God and their guns."

Doc had nothing to say to that. Never knew Ron Blewett to be particularly political, though he never forgave Barack Obama for that comment about Western Pennsylvania. If pressed, Doc didn't see the statement as an insult. People around here had lost a lot. Some damn near everything. Everyone needs something to hold onto. To Doc the problem was too many people chose the past.

CHAPTER 17

Doc and Neuschwander in Stush's office along with Shimp and McFetridge. Stush called the meeting so he spoke first. "Teresa, we're gonna need you to split your time some here. The robbery and acting as liaison to Staff Sergeant McFetridge is your primary task, but we'll call you as we need you for the Dale's business." Teresa Shimp nodded.

"Staff Sergeant, you're welcome to stay and we'd be happy for any insights you might have, but I know you have work to do. We won't take it personal if you're off on your own. Patrol units know you're in town. Just identify yourself if you have any problems, or call for a unit to go with if you sense a jurisdictional issue."

"Thanks, Chief. There is one favor everyone could do me and it won't take a minute." Stush nodded for him to go on. "Call me Gord. Or Gordie. Staff Sergeant's a mouthful and my rank doesn't really apply here, anyway. I'm here on your forbearance."

"All right, then. So ordered." Stush winked. All the PR cops chuckled. No one on the force could remember Stush ordering another cop to do anything. He asked. Requested once in a while. In dire circumstances he might say he needed someone to do something. Cops did things for Stush because they wanted to.

The moment ended. Stush tapped a finger on his desk a few times. Took a deep breath. "For those who don't know, Nicole

Sobotka died this morning in Mercy Hospital. Dave Wohleber was there when she passed. She never woke up, never said a word." Looked to Doc. "Mr. Simon is still our guest, right?" Doc nodded. "What do we have on him? Any more than yesterday?"

Doc shrugged. "Rick?"

Neuschwander needed no notes. "We know he fired three rounds from the shell casings and checking the magazine in the gun. We can't prove it was him shot the Sobotka woman, but we know it was."

"And how do we know it's him that shot her?"

"We don't have ballistics back yet, and two of the rounds are too badly damaged for comparison, but I don't see any way she was shot with the .45 we found in Stoltz's car. We also got lucky when Burrows, bless her eager little heart, found what appears to be a .32 slug with blood on it under the popcorn machine near the front door. It's intact enough we should be able to get a match. I'll bet money it came from Simon's gun."

"Write her up for that, Ricky. Especially if it turns out we can add some of that 'led to the apprehension of' shit."

"While we're on the subject..." Doc waited for the floor. "Let's say the round matches. What do we do with Simon?"

"Give the file to Sally Gwinn," Stush said. "She's the prosecutor."

"You really think Sally will charge this?" Sally famous for two things throughout Neshannock County law enforcement: She was without question the hottest woman in the courthouse, and she never met a case she wouldn't try to plead out. "What's the upside for her?"

"What would you charge him with, Benny?"

"I know, I know. Goddamn, though. It's gotta be some kind of manslaughter, doesn't it? I mean, he'll plead self-defense, but isn't there something in the law that provides some responsibility to shoot the person you're defending yourself against?" Three hours' sleep put more of an edge in Doc's voice than usual when talking to Stush.

"Sally's problem. Ricky, is she aware of any of this?"

"Just that we had a bystander that might've been shot by someone whose presumed intent was to hit the shooter. I told her we'd have more when we get the test results."

"She give you any idea which way she might be leaning?"

"Something about looking into what was covered by Good Samaritan statutes. That's all."

Doc made a disgusted sound. "Can we beat her up about requesting a high bail? I'd at least like to break this guy's balls a little."

"How much bail do you figure he'll get?" Stush said. "It's not like he's a flight risk. You heard him yesterday. He wants attention for what he did. He's proud of it."

Doc sat back. He'd killed a man in self-defense once. Shot the right guy and everything. Still woke up a few times a year hearing the man's last words. "You're right. Not our problem. Let's move on."

"Ricky." Stush left time for everyone's attention to shift. "You said the casings and rounds are at the lab. Did they say how long?"

"I tried to call in some favors."

"And?"

"They gave me a half-ration of shit when I requested expedited service."

"What for?" Stush said.

Neuschwander held back a few seconds. "Apparently we're three months behind paying them."

Doc hissed a sincere "Jesus Christ." Stush let his eyes fall shut for a beat. Said, "I'll call them soon as were done here. How long, worst-case scenario?"

"Depending on the condition of the rounds, end of the week. I should hear back on the ejector marks on the casings sometime tomorrow."

"How many bullets do we have?"

"Intact? Two, though one's beat to shit. Everything else we've found are fragments, though I think there should be a .32 we're missing somewhere. Seven casings altogether. Four from a .45 and three from a .32, which matches what's missing from the weapons recovered at the scene."

"That's all? A mass shooter walks into a department store in the middle of the day, another armed man engages him, neither one dies and there are only seven rounds fired?"

"Stoltz is dead," Neuschwander said.

"He got away from the firefight, though."

"Maybe Simon scared him off."

Doc not ready to give up completely. "The only person we know for a fact Simon shot is Nicole Sobotka."

Stush's expression said he'd heard all he cared to on that topic. "He wouldn't have to hit him to scare him off. Maybe just seeing someone willing to engage threw him." Paused as a thought presented itself. "Did the videos get delivered? From Dale's, I mean."

"Doc and I looked at them last night," Neuschwander said.

"How late were you here?"

Doc and Neuschwander exchanged looks. "Two thirty?" Doc said. "Quarter to three?"

"About that."

"How much sleep did you get?" Stush.

"Three hours or so," Doc said. "No big deal. I had to be up at six for an important meeting at seven that got canceled."

Stush gave a look to show Doc he wasn't mad yet, but could see it from here. "I wasn't asking you. Ricky?"

"About the same."

"Just so you two know, I'd much rather been here on three hours' sleep than at Chet Hensarling's house so I could brief him in intimate detail before he went to work. Not just him, either. George Grayson was already there."

Doc sat up on full alert. "The Gray Ghost was at Chet's house at seven o'clock in the morning?"

"I showed up at six-thirty and he was already there."

"I thought Rance Doocy was Hecker's commissar for Penns River."

"The Deuce doesn't draw enough water for this. Grayson came down so I could get the word as heard straight from Hecker's lips."

"And the word is?"

"Mr. Hecker is taking a personal interest in this." Doc snorted. No Penns River cop ever called Daniel Hecker anything more respectful than "Danny." Stush went on. "He's very concerned such an event could take place directly across the street from the casino and wants something done to alleviate the fears of the casino's customers."

"That a direct quote?" Doc said.

"Close as I can remember. Too many big words."

"What did you say?"

"I said Dale's is actually catty-corner from the casino but I got his point and that no one wanted to see this cleared up faster than I did."

"How'd that go over?"

"How do you think?"

Doc covered his mouth with a hand to keep the tiny smile from showing. A terrible thing had happened at Dale's, but anything that gave Daniel Hecker agita had a redeeming side. "He should be happy. Last shooting we had here was in the casino parking lot. At least things are moving away."

"I'll be sure to mention that next time I see him. Better yet, you do it."

"Anything else come out of the meeting?"

"I'd show my new asshole, but there's a woman present. Now, about those videos. Anything good on them?"

Doc and Neuschwander gave each other every opportunity to go first. As usual, Neuschwander won. Doc said, "Not really. A guy about Michael Stoltz's size and wearing what could be the same jacket and hat came into Dale's from the entrance closest to where his car's parked at the time the shooter might've come in. He left in a hurry, which is consistent with what Simon told us about shooting him. Or at least at him."

"The way you're talking, you don't think it was Stoltz?"

"We never got a look at his face."

"Can we match the garments?"

"I doubt it," Neuschwander said. "Maybe. I don't know. The color quality is pretty bad."

No one spoke until Stush got tired of the silence. "Anything else, Ricky?"

"Not until we hear back from the lab. No. Wait. There is one other thing. It's probably nothing, but I can't account for it." Stush raised an eyebrow. "There's a drop of blood on the passenger door of Stoltz's car. The shape of the drop implies whoever it came from was stationary."

"It's not Stoltz's? Could be random drops of blood all over that car the way you described it."

"That's why I didn't think much of it yesterday. I looked at it again today. It came from outside the car."

"Which raises another question," Doc said. "Why was the passenger window open? Stoltz was alone. Parking the car in back is iffy, too."

"He's going in to shoot people," Stush said. "He doesn't want to be seen,"

"Why does he care? He came heavy. Who's going to stop him? Forget why he parked around back. He does. Then he opens the passenger window, goes into Dale's, kills a bunch of people, and walks back to his car to shoot himself?"

"No reason he couldn't have opened the window after he went back to the car."

"True, but why then? He runs out of Dale's, gets in the car, decides it's stuffy and opens the opposite side window before he blows his brains out. Who does that?"

"Michael Stoltz, apparently. Be honest, Benny: It's not the weirdest thing Stoltz did yesterday. Ricky, is there enough blood for a test?"

"Already sent to the lab."

"Outstanding. Anyone have anything else?"

Doc almost didn't say it. Knew if he didn't bring it up now he might never. "Does it bother anyone that this guy walks into his own mass shooting party with only seven bullets? Guys that do this have large-capacity magazines and lots of them."

"You saying you don't think he did this?" Stush said. "I'm not trying to sound like Chet's flunky here, but we have quite a bit of evidence that Stoltz is the guy, not the least of which is a self-inflicted head wound fired from his gun, which is almost certainly the murder weapon. You have some minor variances from common practice. Where are you going with this?"

"They're just the pieces that don't fit. The bullets and the open window. I don't like them."

"There are always pieces that don't fit and I'll let you know if I find anything about this I do like. Meanwhile, I need you all to excuse me. I have to call the Stoltz family so they know we're about to tell the national media their son's a mass murderer. Unless someone else wants to do it for me."

No one volunteered.

"Mr. Stoltz? Mark Stoltz? This is Stan Napierkowski, chief of police in Penns River...Yes, sir. I know. It's a terrible thing. I wish I had something to say that would help...Yes, sir." Longer pause. "No, sir. I'm sorry I don't have any good news for you. The reason I called is that we're about to have a press conference. National media. We've held off as long as we can. We have to tell them what we know...Yes, sir. I understand. The thing is, we're going to have to tell them what we know about Michael, about him being the—No, Mr. Stoltz. I promise I won't do that. The thing is, they have a right to know, and they're going to find out one way or another. It's better for everyone if we provide enough information to maintain some level of control...No, sir. I can't do that. I only called now to give you a heads-up so it's not as much of a shock when they start calling and showing up at your house...No, sir. We're not going to give them the number or the address, but it's not going to take them long to find out on their own...Getting out of town for a few days might not be the worst idea. For sure don't answer the phone for a while. Might be best to unplug it...I'm sorry about that, but there's nothing I can do. It's a free country. What I can do—what I will do soon as I get off the phone—is send a unit to your house. Keep the street clear and enforce the trespassing laws the best we can...I wish I could do more, but my hands are tied...Yes, sir...Yes, sir...No, they won't release the body for another day or two. I can ask them to hold it longer while you and your wife get away for a bit if you like...Yes, sir...Uh-huh...Right...Thank you for understanding, Mr. Stoltz. I'll post that unit now...Yes, sir. Goodbye."

Took a minute to convince himself he wasn't as much of a bastard as he felt. Picked up the phone and dialed Mike Zywiciel's cell. "Mike? Press conference in the multipurpose room in an hour. Put the word out. And send a unit over to Arizona Drive to keep things under control when the press finds the Stoltz family."

Opened the bottom drawer of the filing cabinet behind his desk. Took out the bottle of Johnny Walker Black he preferred to save for celebrations and poured himself a double. Drank it in one swallow and let the heat move through him.

Doc had an errand of his own. Found Chuck Simon in his cell under the county side of the City-County complex. "Nicole Sobotka's dead."

"Who's that?"

"Woman you shot in Dale's the other day."

Simon deflated an inch. Said, "I did what I had to," as much to himself as to Doc. Spoke up for, "I'd do it again. Someone had to do something."

"That's exactly what I think you should tell the judge."

"The judge? You mean you're charging me? What about them 'stand your ground' laws?"

"You're probably okay as far as we're concerned. Between that and the Good Samaritan laws, I doubt the county will charge. In fact, I think your lawyer's upstairs now trying to habeas corpus your ass from under that dinky discharging a firearm rap."

Simon had almost fully recovered when Doc said, "That's not the judge I mean. I'm talking about the guy you'll see when Nicole Sobotka's husband and two kids file the wrongful death charge. I hear we dispatched a patrol unit to work traffic on their street to keep the ambulance chasers from jumping the line. I just came by to give you a heads-up so you know to get a good lawyer yourself."

Simon not nearly as cocky when Doc left.

CHAPTER 18

Lunch with Jefferson West always a treat for Doc. West a retired Army First Sergeant who saw serious shit in Vietnam. Lived alone in the Allegheny Estates, his family wanting nothing to do with him for reasons Doc didn't know and wouldn't ask. They met when two kids squatting in a vacant townhouse next door to West's witnessed a murder. Doc caught the case and West inherited the kids, their father in a Tennessee prison, the mother a hardcore fiend.

Bob's Sub used to be a Grease Monkey, sat on a rise above Tarentum Bridge Road. The roll-up doors facing the street opened in nice weather so people could eat outside. Closed today, thirty-five degrees and a light drizzle.

The sandwiches came—West a Number Four Super, Doc a Number One Bob's Delight—and small talk ceased as they unwrapped their lunches, opened bags of chips, and arrayed their food for convenient reach the way men expert in the ways of sandwich shops know to do.

Doc took his first bite. Chewed and gave West every opportunity to start the conversation, only one reason for him to call a meeting during the workday. Got tired of waiting, said, "See the boys much?"

"David more days than not. And nights. Their mama's slipping again."

"She'll never get clean. She'll just die one day. A better person

92

would feel worse for her. I only feel bad for the boys."

"I think David gets it. I hope he does. He sees what she is and I think it scares him. He still loves her, but he also knows there's not a lot left there to love."

"How's Wilver taking it? Mom's relapse, I mean." Wilver the older brother.

"The boy's got potential. Good with his hands and thinks of original ways of putting things together."

"Wilver?" Doc a little surprised. Wilver had shown no such tendencies in the past.

"David. Took my toaster apart with him last weekend and he not only picked out what was wrong, he put damn near the whole thing back together by himself."

"That's great. An ability like that's always useful. Wilver still helping him out?"

"He's a good boy. Sometimes I feel bad about keeping him from his mama, but there's nothing good over there for him unless she's clean and like you said, I don't ever see that happening."

Doc put down the sandwich. Sipped his cherry Coke. "Any reason you're avoiding talking about Wilver?"

West's turn to take time for a drink. "You seen him lately?"

"Been a few months. Why do you ask?"

Doc waited while a mouthful of sandwich required West's full attention. "He pretty much runs the drug bidness down our part of town."

Doc took a sip, nodded. "I know."

"That all right with you?"

"No, and on multiple levels. Problem is I don't have the time or the resources to do anything about it."

West raised an eyebrow. "Resources? You talking about jailing the boy?"

"Not if I can help it. If I had a little more manpower—and a little more time—I'd try to roll up the business. Get him to cop to a deal while he still can." Doc took a substantial bite, decided to talk anyway. "When I say 'time' I really mean 'energy,' I guess. There's a lot going on in town lately, Mr. West. I never seem to think of getting together with him when I have time, and when I do think of it, I don't have the energy. I have to do better."

"It's not like you spending quality time with him is up to you anymore. Boy has a reputation to protect. Hanging with a cop ain't the way to do it."

Doc remembered the last time he and Wilver spoke. Wilver coming across as an equal, glad-handing and talking shit until Doc threw him against a car and patted him down. Told Wilver if he wanted to run drugs to refer to Doc as "Detective Dougherty" when they were on the clock. Saw the glimmer of fear in the boy's eyes from the glimpse of what that life could be like. Wondered if that look was still there.

"What's he up to? I mean, I enjoy getting together with you whenever, but you asked for this lunch on kind of short notice and I'm a little pressed for time with this Dale's shooting. Is there something I need to know sooner rather than later?"

West looked as if he'd buy more time, came right out with it. "I think things are changing down my way. Now I see hoppers right on the street. What I can gather, Wilver likes to keep his action out of sight as much as he can. Now I see little crews on corners like before all them got killed last year."

"Maybe Wilver's getting cocky."

"That's the thing. These boys I don't know. When anyone looks like management comes by it ain't never Wilver. I think someone's moving in and I worry how things will go for the boy if they do."

Doc took another big bite, finished chewing. "He ran a crew off last summer. He may have a harder bark than we think. On the other hand, the last thing we need is a war over drug corners a lot of people don't think are there." Licked mayonnaise off a finger. "Okay. When I said I was short on resources, I didn't mean I don't have any. Let me poke around a little. You do what you can to keep David squared away. Call me if you need me."

"What should I do about Wilver?"

Doc rolled his trash into a ball. "Nothing. He comes to you, fine, but otherwise leave him to me. He's a law enforcement problem now."

"I'd hate to see that boy go to jail."

"Me, too. I'd also hate to see him dead. I'm willing to get him out of the life however I have to."

West wadded up his trash. Massaged it in his hands like a basketball. "What do you think will happen to a boy like Wilver in prison?"

"It doesn't have to come to that if I get him out before things go bad. First offense, I vouch for him, you vouch for him, Social Services lays out his family upbringing, maybe we can get him supervised probation." Doc didn't really believe that. Liked how it sounded, though. "Thing is, we'll have to burn that bridge when we get to it. This business with Dale's is winding down. That should free up some time for me to pay more attention to what's going on at the Estates and downtown." Doc dropped his trash in the bin. "Don't be afraid to call me if you see anything you don't like. Busy or not, I'm still police."

CHAPTER 19

Doc knew he'd fall asleep if he went home, which meant he'd be up at two in the morning. Didn't want to stop for a few beers because he knew he'd fall asleep and wouldn't be up until two in the afternoon. Farted around pretending to grocery shop until his parents' dinner time passed then drove up the hill to see them.

Tom and Ellen Dougherty ate supper at five o'clock. Every night. Ellen had the meal ready by four fifty-nine, on the table at five, and Tom's ass had better be in that seat no later than five oh-one if he knew what was good for him. Doc walked into the kitchen at quarter to six and they were just sitting down. Life didn't make sense anymore.

"You hungry, Benny?" Ellen already half out of her seat and reaching for the dish cupboard behind her.

"I ate, Mom." Doc sorry as soon as he said it, the smell of his mother's meatloaf luring him in. Took the chair that had been his since he was old enough to notice where he sat. "I figured you'd be done by now. It's almost six."

"That's my fault," Ellen said. "I forgot to take the hamburger out of the freezer and it didn't thaw in time."

"You have a microwave."

"I'm warning you," Tom said to Doc between bites.

"It doesn't taste the same if you thaw it in the microwave," Ellen said.

Doc raised an eyebrow toward Tom. "Really?" Doc sometimes thawed a ground beef patty in the microwave, then turned up the power and let it cook rather than take the time to have to clean anything else. "It's noticeable?"

Tom swirled a forkful of meatloaf in his mashed potatoes. "I warned you once."

Ellen not assertive by nature. The kitchen was her fiefdom. "Microwaves heat things from the inside out. That's okay to reheat something, but not for defrosting."

Doc looked at Tom. His father ignored him until he finished chewing. Swallowed and asked if Doc wanted a beer.

"I drink a beer now I'll be asleep in ten minutes. You have any pop?"

Tom's mouth full of food so Ellen picked up the slack. "There's Mello Yello in the ice box. Maybe some of that Fanta orange you like." Pushed back her chair and leaned on the table to stand. "Let me look in the cellar. Your dad always has Pepsi and there's probably some Faygo root beer."

Doc held up a hand traffic-cop style. "Sit down, Mom. I'll get it."

Ellen all the way up. "I'll put some ice in a glass for you."

"You can hand me a glass but the ice is in the refrigerator with the pop, which is where I'm going, anyway. Sit down and eat."

Ellen gave Doc a glass and sat, disappointed. Waited for him to seat himself, glass filled with ice and orange pop. "How come you're so tired? It's only Wednesday."

"Running on three hours' sleep."

Ellen leaned forward. "Why aren't you sleeping?"

Doc looked at his father, then back to Ellen. "You guys know what happened at Dale's yesterday, right?"

Tom gestured over his shoulder with his fork toward the television. "Can't hardly miss it. You'd think the Russians were in Vandergrift the way the news is carrying on."

"The kid that did it killed himself," Ellen said. "Why were you up all night?"

A wave of astonishment and frustration rose and ebbed. There was a time when Ellen would have grilled him for half an hour on every detail, absorbed by things other civilians never thought twice about. She started losing her eyesight several months earlier. Reading went from being her favorite pastime to a chore. Doc convinced the less she read, the less connected she was to the outside world. Not a good sign for a woman her age.

"We still have to pin everything down," he said. "Four people dead, we can't leave anything to chance. Last thing we'd want is for that kid to have an accomplice and we let him walk because we were sloppy."

"We saw you on TV last night," Ellen said.

"Me? Mike Zywiciel and Stush handled the press."

Tom put down his utensils. "You were in the background. They were showing the cops and the crime scene tape and you were talking to some woman looked like she might be a doctor."

"Ah. Probably the medical examiner from Allegheny County. That must've been right after we found Stoltz's body in his car 'round back."

"Looked like more TV there than cops," Tom said.

"You have no idea. Even worse today."

"Why today?" Ellen said. "Everything happened yesterday."

Doc sipped his drink. "Pretty much all the media yesterday were local. Quite a few of them knew us, so we came to an understanding pretty quick. Today the networks are here. I stopped by and they were taking turns slipping under the crime scene tape while Mike Zywiciel and a couple other cops played Whac-A-Mole with them."

"I saw a little of that," Tom said. "Shoulda locked their asses up, interfering with a police investigation."

"They have a job to do. I understand that. What some of them forget is that we have one, too."

"What'd you do with them? I know better than to think you walked out in the middle of a situation."

Another sip. Doc had no interest in rehashing the day he'd

come here to escape. Finish this one and go home. Should be some Sugardale hot dogs in the fridge. Buns less certain. What the hell. Wouldn't be the first time beanie-weenie came to the rescue after a long day. "I pulled them over to the side and described the local dos and don'ts while Mike got his cops to move the tape out from Dale's a little. Things settled down pretty quick after we reset the perimeter. And put two guys with shotguns on the doors."

That got Tom's attention. "Really? You had guys with shotguns?"

"Bean bag rounds. It was all for show. I told everyone there was nothing to see in Dale's, but there were people who'd talked to actual eyewitnesses working in all the other stores. Said I was sure they'd be happy to see their names in the paper or their pictures on television. Might be even more forthcoming if some money got spent."

"They go for it?"

"Most of them. One jagov from CNN kept giving me shit about the First Amendment so I reminded him we could've locked down the whole parking lot instead of just that corner."

"It wasn't that Cuomo asshole, was it? He looks for trouble."

"No, it wasn't Cuomo. Who I kind of like, by the way. I think it was a producer. Guy with a face made for the other side of the camera." Doc raised his glass. Stopped short of a drink. "He was just doing his job. Of course, so was I. Today, I won." Winked at his dad.

"What's on for tomorrow?"

"Crime lab results will be back. I hope, anyway. Nailing things down a little more. Rick Neuschwander will probably cross-reference the victims' cell phones with the shooter's. See if there are any relationships we don't know about. Maybe do a re-enactment so Dale's can have their store back. The manager's shitting bricks worrying we're going to take all the stuff out the back and sell it."

Tom rose from the kitchen chair and made his way to his

recliner. Took him a while. He told people he retired early because he'd saved enough money he didn't have to work. Truth was rheumatoid arthritis sent him home. Hands unable to grip things and feet that couldn't spend a day supporting him, even at five-ten and one sixty. Surgery helped enough for him to work an hour or so a day in his shop, but everyone knew where this road led.

Eased himself into the recliner. Said, "Dumbass." Started up again.

"What?" Doc said.

"I left my water in the kitchen."

"I'll get it."

Doc went into the kitchen for the glass. Ellen said, "You sure you don't want any meatloaf? Before I put it away."

"No, thanks, Mom. I still have some in the freezer." He didn't. Bothered him that she might think he stopped by just for the free meal, though he knew it would delight her. Walked back to the living room. Gave his father his drink.

"Thanks. Hey, why the hell are you going to all that trouble tomorrow? The kid that shot them's dead. How can the city afford this?"

Doc stifled a sigh. This happened more all the time with both parents. He couldn't decide if they were forgetting or just not paying attention. "It's the job, Dad. We do what they tell us." Finished his drink. Made a point of checking his watch. "I better go. Give Mom time to clean up before *Jeopardy* comes on." Ellen Dougherty tracked the time leading up to *Jeopardy* with the same passion Rain Man showed for Judge Wapner. "I'm beat, anyway."

The motion-sensitive light came on when Doc stepped off the expanded stoop where Tom kept the grill next to the house. Paused at the bottom of the stairs next to the garage's entry door. Saw the imperfectly repaired bullet holes in the brick, perpetual reminders of the Russians who came calling for his cousin Nick one night. Looked up the stairs at the front door and the warm glow from the kitchen and living room. Almost went back. Knew he'd fall asleep on the couch and that would just worry his mother even more.

Picked up a dozen wings with celery at the Edgecliff. Beanie-weenie wasn't going to cut it after the two days he'd had.

CHAPTER 20

"You're from Vermont? I don't think I ever met no one from Vermont before. Least not that I knew about it."

Jacques using his Bob Gainey persona in the Penns River Inn, talking to Mary Pugliese. "Way up there, though. Little town on the lake called Alburg. Aboot—not much more than an hour from Montreal."

All work and no play would make Jacques a dull boy. Mary looked like she might play. He hadn't planned to stay in Penns River but brother Sylvain couldn't just walk into a currency exchange and convert ninety-three thousand dollars Canadian into American without drawing attention. Doing it in under-the-radar-sized increments took time. Jacques looking for a temporary address to receive Sylvain's package when the opportunity presented itself to work against an overwhelmed police department that didn't strike him as too sharp even when undistracted. Tied down, he decided to kill two birds with one stone and found a source for the documents needed to pass as American.

Mary was five-three or so with dark hair and dark eyes. Light olive skin Jacques could live without was more than made up for by having a house of her own, hard earned through a divorce from a husband who sounded like a real shitheel the way Mary described him: "Jimmy was a real shitheel" her exact words. Jacques made sympathetic noises in the right places. Not too sympathetic. She'd be suspicious if he sounded like too much of a pushover. Worked the middle ground, understanding of her situation, not so much he came off as a pussy himself.

He waved for another Crown Royal and a Bud Light for Mary. "What do you do all day?" he said while they waited for the refills.

"I was working at Dale's until that guy went nuts in there."

"You were there?"

Mary sipped her fresh beer. "Not yesterday. It was my day off."

"Lucky you."

"Least them that was working got paid for the whole day. Now I might as well be laid off until the cops quits screwing around in there."

"They are still there?"

"All day today and the store won't open tomorrow, either. They said they'd call if we was opening Friday but not to count on it. Once the cops is done they're bringing in some company from down the other side of Picksburgh that cleans up crime scenes. Might not be open till Monday from what I heard. We could collect if we was laid off. Now we can't even do that."

"It's a tough break for you."

"People never think of that. How it fucks everyone up for days after."

Jacques sipped his Crown. "Does kind of free up your time, though."

Mary gave him a look that might have meant anything. "I guess I do have some time on my hands. You got something in mind?"

"I might, if you're interested."

"I might be. What did you say you did for a living?"

"I didn't say anything."

"You some kind of shady character, not saying?"

"You didn't ask. I didn't want to volunteer anything and have you think I was trying to impress you."

"What do you do that's gonna impress me so much?"

"I didn't say it was impressive. I just said I didn't want you to think I was trying to impress you."

"Go ahead. Try me."

Jacques's turn to give her a look that might mean anything. "A man could take that a couple different ways, you know."

"Impress me enough and who knows what else you could try?"

Jacques figured he had all evening to find out. "I'm self-employed. A consultant. I travel all over the area."

"What kinds of things you consult on?"

"Security. I go to gas stations, convenience stores, check cashing places and make sure their security is good."

"Any money in that?"

He smiled. "Sometimes."

CHAPTER 21

Stretch Dolewicz thanked his nephew for the fresh beer. "I wished I never heard of that shithole up the river. That was all The Hook's doing. All of it. He wanted to live there because the old time Mannarinos did. Cocksucker wasn't even from the connected side of the family."

Mike "The Hook" Mannarino not connected to any family since Stretch found out he'd been informing for the feds. Now even the thought of the two-faced prick broke Stretch's balls, all they'd been through together. Sipped his beer, said, "Okay. What's going on in Penns River now that I have to deal with?"

Ted Suskewicz even taller than his uncle. Six-seven in sneakers. A good kid. Slouched in his chair to look shorter, Stretch's sitting posture not what it used to be since a crew from New York put three shotgun pellets in his hip. "Someone's pulling robberies. Running around like their hair's on fire. Three today last I heard."

"*Three*? Today? You're shitting me."

"And one yesterday. That payday loans joint on Sixth Avenue."

"Can't be all the same guys."

Ted made an apologetic face. "I just got back from there, Uncle Stretch. The descriptions match and the cops think it's the same crew. One thin guy with a pistol and a fat guy with a shotgun."

"White guys?" Ted nodded. "You know which cop's working it? Is it that prick Dougherty, used to fuck with Mike all the time?"

"He answered the first call. Left when those people got rained on in Dale's. Now that woman's got it. Shimp, I think her name is."

Stretch had no idea how Ted got so much information from inside Penns River. Didn't really want to know. Anything that reminded him of Penns River gave him more of a pain in the ass than he already had. "I don't know her. Dougherty's an asshole, but he's smart. He think it's the same crew?"

"That I don't know."

Stretch swallowed beer. Took his time. "Understand, I wouldn't give a shit this crew stole the whole goddamn town, put it on a barge and floated it down the river." Took a second to savor the thought. "Except Fred Kaparzo pays protection to make book out of the back of that loan joint. They only got the legit money, but Fred's pissed. We don't do something, he's the kind to start getting people worked up, they ain't getting what they pay for."

"Plus, these guys ain't paying the tax."

"Yeah. The tax." Stretch exhaled, shifted in the chair. Knocking over a place that paid protection and not kicking anything up to Stretch. Two unforgiveables. Now he had a fucking task. Almost enough to make him miss Mike. Let him have the worry. With Mike and Buddy Elba both gone and the books closed, New York didn't have any made guys to run Pittsburgh full-time. Stretch more like the caretaker than the boss. Probably kicked up as much money as Mike ever did, but he wasn't Italian, so no button. Which meant he couldn't be the boss. Which was okay with him, learning every day how being the boss was more trouble than it was worth. Sometimes he wished they'd straighten out someone in the Burgh until he remembered who the prime candidates were. In moments of weakness he fantasized about walking away from Penns River and making up the lost income other ways. Then he'd figure in how much money he spun off from the casino with the loan sharking, drugs, women, and a couple of poker games.

"*Gówno.*" Stretch saw the question on Ted's face. Smiled for the first time that day. "Shit. My *dziadek* taught me that one. Worked down the old powder plant. Used to come home dark as a nigger coal miner. Curse up a blue streak. Grandma'd give him holy hell if he swore in front of the little ones so he always did it in Polish so we wouldn't understand." Stretch repositioned his hip again. Getting so he couldn't sit more than a couple minutes in any position. "Then when Grandma turned her back he'd teach us every fucking word. Proper pronunciation and all. I loved that old bastard."

Stretch swallowed beer. Fussed with the TV remote. Nothing worth watching was on, not with Pitt basketball in the shitter.

Ted must've got tired of waiting. Said, "About this crew in Penns River…"

"Put the word out. If they come to us, pay the tax, make restitution for Kaparzo's inconvenience, we can come to an arrangement. If we have to go looking for them, a little pissant two-man crew? That won't go so well."

CHAPTER 22

Rick Neuschwander tried to break it to Doc gently. "I know you're not happy with some of the things that don't add up here. I'm not, either."

"Doesn't sound like you're going to make me any happier."

Rick gave a *don't shoot the messenger* face. "I spent all day going through the cell phones and social media accounts of every victim and the shooter. The only connection I see is that Monica Albanese and Tim Cunningham both worked at Dale's and had been dating for a couple of months. The only other relationship I can find between any of them is that Nicole Sobotka and Eloise Scheftic both shopped at Dale's. Nothing associates any of them with Michael Stoltz."

Doc recognized a losing battle when he saw one. It still bothered him that they'd walked into such a crime scene and found everything as tied up as it would ever be. "Humor me a minute, Noosh. He spends the morning target shooting and hanging out with Ron Blewett. Ron knows him pretty well and sees nothing out of the ordinary. Stoltz leaves and drives directly to Dale's to kill people."

"It's not like he hot-footed it up there."

"Damn near. Ron says he left at one thirty. By—what?—two-oh-nine everything's done."

"So? It can't be more than five miles."

"Six-point-seven. I measured it myself yesterday."

"Ten minutes using the bypass. Twelve, tops."

"I also checked the logs. There was a serious accident at the intersection of Seventh Street and Stevenson. Call came in at one thirteen. Two units, a fire truck, and two ambos dispatched. Traffic was fucked up for an hour."

"That time of day, it still couldn't have held him up more than five minutes."

Doc slumped in his chair. "Still, this was a man with a mission. He wades through the traffic to go directly to Dale's to shoot people he doesn't know. He had such a hard-on to kill someone, what's special about Dale's? Why not break it off and go downtown? Shoot up the crowd at the new community center?"

"Maybe he didn't know about it. The ceremony, I mean. Wasn't it done by then, anyway?"

Doc did the math. "Yeah. It was breaking up by the time the robbery call came in." Tossed a ball of paper into the trash. "Walk me through the connections. Or lack thereof. For my peace of mind."

Neuschwander spread his notes across the desk. "First thing— the easy part—was to check all the calls in and out stored in the cell phones, along with all the phone numbers saved. Only Albanese and Cunningham had any in common, and the only numbers they had in common with anyone else is each other and some Dale's employees. Which makes sense, since we know they were dating."

"We know this how?"

"Witness statements from other employees who knew them both."

They'd done this before. Doc would sit, hands fooling with some small item, not looking at anything. He'd interrupt with the occasional question so it was clear in his mind. Sometimes they switched roles, though Neuschwander took notes and doodled when he was the audience. Their way of making sure neither took anything for granted.

Neuschwander went on. "So the phones are a dead end. We

109

opened their email accounts. The only cross-references are between Albanese and Cunningham. Then we checked Facebook.
Same thing. Lots of mutual friends between Albanese and Cunningham—mostly people they worked with—and nothing else.
Aside from those two dating, these people are as random as it
gets. The only thing I can find they have in common is they
were all in Dale's at two Tuesday afternoon."

"You ready to call it?"

"I'd like to wait for the lab results. Maybe see if the autopsy
shows a brain tumor or something that might explain it."

"A tumor would be sweet. His parents are nice people. I'm
all for anything that lets them sleep easier not thinking they
raised an evil prick for a son. Any idea when you'll hear back?"

"You know how they are." Penns River too small for a lab
of its own. Sent everything out to either the state police, the feds,
or a private company. Allegheny County handled autopsies.
Penns River's work was rarely a priority.

"Even for this? Goddamn, this is national news. You'd think
they'd want to look good."

"It was national news. You looked around lately? We're back
to just the locals. They find anything, they pass it along and do
the national stand-up themselves."

Doc thought back over his most recent contacts with the
media. "Now that you mention it, yeah. Where'd they go?"

"You didn't hear? Honest to God?"

"No. What?"

"Kimmy Schmidt."

"Who's Kimmy Schmidt?"

"You never saw the TV show? On Netflix or Amazon or one
of those streaming services?"

"I don't watch a lot of TV, Noosh. Cut to the chase."

"Some dickhead in Arkansas kept three young women in an
underground bunker for something like four years. One of them
got out yesterday and sent the cops back for the rest. No one
gives a shit about us anymore."

Neuschwander took off his glasses to rub his eyes and Doc saw how tired he was. Tucked his kids in every evening with a story intended as much to remind himself of life's beauty as it was to banish their monsters. The shootings they'd worked before were crimes and therefore explainable. What happened at Dale's was something beyond reason. Doc saw the bags under Neuschwander's eyes and thought of Mike Zywiciel in the parking lot practically begging to be told what to do.

Part of Doc wanted to shake it off. He'd seen worse in Iraq. IEDs blew pieces off of people—men, women, old, small children—equal opportunity destruction. He'd show up to establish a perimeter amidst ambulances and sirens and screaming and the fear of wondering if the explosion had been a trap to pull them together for snipers or a bigger bomb to come. What struck him most when he led his team into Dale's was how still it was.

He dry washed his face. Stared into his hands. "What time is it?" Could have looked at his watch. Didn't feel like turning his wrist over.

"Almost three."

"All we really have left on Dale's is waiting for the lab and autopsy reports to come back?"

"Pretty much."

"Fuck it. Go home. Play with the kids. I'll sign you out."

Neuschwander's feet shifted. Not a man to bend a rule lightly, no matter how much he loved his kids. "You sure?"

Doc nodded. "We're both worn out. I'll get to bed early and see if I can't help Shimp and the Mountie with the new robbery capital of the world. Don't tell anyone we're in a holding pattern on the Dale's case, though. Part of me wants to think this rash of robberies is a couple of guys that figure we're too busy with that to pay attention to property crimes. If that's true, I'd like them to keep thinking it another day or so."

Neuschwander moving before Doc could change his mind. "Anything comes up, you hear from the Allegheny County coroner or the lab before you leave, call me. I can be here in ten minutes."

Doc waved him away with the back of one hand. "Go home. Nothing's going to come in that can't wait until tomorrow."

Neuschwander had his coat half on when George Augustine stuck his head into the detectives' office. "Doc? Guy here to see you."

"Who is it, Augie?"

"Says his name's Marty Cropcho."

And so something did come in that couldn't wait.

CHAPTER 23

"How have you been, Mr. Cropcho?"

A rhetorical question. Doc wouldn't have recognized Cropcho if he hadn't stood to shake hands. Almost walked right past him. Grayer hair and less of it. Substantial weight loss on a man who hadn't been heavy in the first place. His cheeks looked as if they were about to collapse in on themselves.

Marty and Carol Cropcho had been one of those perfect matches. Best friends, lovers, inside jokes. Two years now since Tom Widmer beat Carol to death in her bedroom, Widmer the sucker in a broader scheme. The ringmaster still breathed free air right here in Penns River. Every cop in town knew who it was. Sally Gwinn didn't think there was enough physical evidence to try the case.

"I owe you an apology," Doc said. "It's been a while since I checked in."

Cropcho made brief eye contact on "apology." Looked away before speaking. "You shouldn't have to check in with me, Detective. You have a job to do. Your own life."

Doc not sure how he felt as he shook Cropcho's hand. He liked the guy. Remembered the first time they'd met, hurt oozing from Cropcho like pus from an infection. Promised to catch the person who did it. Caught him, too, though the incomplete justice hadn't provided Marty Cropcho much closure. The task now not to show he felt sorry for Cropcho. Empathy was fine.

Sympathy belittled the recipient. Doc couldn't help himself. Sympathy was all he had for Marty Cropcho.

Doc held the swinging door in the bar that separated the public area from the cop shop. Led the way to the detectives' office. Cropcho followed a step behind and to the right. Declined a cold drink or coffee with a shake of his head. Didn't say a word until Doc offered him a seat and asked what he could do for him.

"Do you know how old I am?"

"Thirty-seven." Doc knew every punctuation mark in the Cropcho file. Still read it once a month or so. Spent over a year working the case on his own time, showing photographs of the principals in lounges and restaurants. "Why do you ask?"

"How old are you?"

"Forty-one."

"Why do you call me mister?"

"It's a term of respect. You're a taxpayer."

"Do you call all taxpayers mister or missus? Even if they're younger than you? Or just the ones you feel sorry for?"

Busted. "The truth is I started because we met as part of a case. Protocol says we refer to everyone by their proper titles in an investigation. After a while I get in the habit. I don't mean anything by it. Just respect." Doc hoped he lied better than he disguised sympathy.

The only sound the occasional creaking of Doc's chair when he shifted his weight. He saw no reason to move the conversation along, if conversation was what Cropcho intended. The case was closed, the killer imprisoned. Doc still felt he owed Marty Cropcho. If repaying any part of that debt meant sitting in a room while who knew what played out in Cropcho's mind, Doc was in.

Cropcho went first. "This guy who killed himself. Are you sure he's the one? That shot those people in Dale's, I mean."

"I'm sorry. I can't discuss the details of an open investigation."

More silence. Then, "Those people that were killed. Were they married?"

"Two were. The two that didn't work there."

"Did they have kids?"

"Both of them."

"At least we didn't have kids." Cropcho said it as much to himself as to Doc. "They were shot in the head? Died right away?"

This had been on the news already. Doc saw no reason to be cute about it. "One was. The other was shot through the back. She lived until the next morning."

"Oh. That's too bad. I mean, the one shot in the head, she died right away. Probably never felt a thing. The one that lasted until morning, she must've suffered. At least getting shot in the head you don't suffer. Carol fought. I—I don't know how long it took her to die, but she fought him."

She had, too. Doc remembered the scene as if he were still standing in it. Felt the temperature of the room, the background sounds of a ticking clock and cops moving around downstairs. The unevaporated sweat on what was left of Carol's forehead. The mess in the bedroom and bathroom of an otherwise immaculate house. She'd fought like hell. "Yes, sir. She did. She never gave up."

"It's not enough, though. Is it? Not giving up. Sometimes you just lose."

"If you give up, you never find out."

That brought a few seconds of eye contact. Cropcho broke it before he spoke. "I guess not."

Another quiet spell. Doc's concentration wandered until an unusual sound brought him back. Cropcho was crying. "You're not thinking of giving up, are you Mr. Cropcho?"

Cropcho shook his head. Rested his elbows on his knees and wept. Doc started to worry when sobs shook Cropcho's entire body. Surprised himself by moving to the other side of the desk to sit next to the man and put an arm around him. Not the awkward embrace of a man unsure what else to do. Really holding him.

Cropcho buried his face in Doc's chest. "It's supposed to get better. Everyone says it gets better, but it doesn't. It's just the same as that night when I came home and found her. Why doesn't it get better?"

Doc said he didn't know. Said a lot of things. Words chosen more for their soothing sonic qualities than to convey any information or sentiment. If Cropcho heard them at all they were murmurings in Doc's chest, the shirt damp with tears.

Took Cropcho ten minutes to cry it out. Sat up and wiped his eyes and cheeks with the back of a hand. "I'm sorry. I—I didn't think I'd be like that."

Doc's voice firm and cop-like. "You don't ever have to apologize to me. We both know Tom Widmer didn't act alone. I just can't find the evidence we need for another trial."

"Are you still looking?"

"When I can."

"I'm sorry. I didn't mean to imply this should be your life-long crusade. I just wondered..."

Doc kept his thoughts to himself. What Cropcho would never understand was almost all cops who work homicide have their white whales. They keep files and work them in their spare time like deadly hobbies. Some even into retirement. Carol Cropcho's murder was Doc's. He hoped there weren't any more.

Cropcho paused at the door. Half turned to catch Doc's belt in his peripheral vision. "Today's her birthday. Did you know that?"

Sure, Doc knew. He could recite the entire murder book on demand. How many inches between Carol's head and the piece of ornamental glass that crushed it. How many cubic centimeters of vomit collected from around the toilet. The time the suspect appeared on the security tape from Arby's to dump a plastic bag full of bloody clothes into the Dumpster. To the second. Hadn't associated the date with today.

Time moved on. Cable news heavyweights moved on to the next media bacchanal. Doc moved onto the next case. Only Marty Cropcho stayed. Frozen in time by his love for a woman who would never be anything but young and pretty in anyone's memory except the cops who'd worked on her murder. Much as Doc wanted to reach Cropcho, he instinctively knew to keep his distance.

CHAPTER 24

"Take a breath and start over. Slower. You said cookies?"

Sean Sisler was way too old for this shit, his twenty-seventh birthday two months away. Opening Day of baseball season. Pirates versus Milwaukee. A buddy who knew a guy got Sisler and three other friends tickets in Section 21, six rows behind the Pirates' dugout at PNC Park. Look the players right in the eye as they came down the steps. Pittsburgh skyline in view all day.

That was still two months away and AmberLynn Feeney was here right now. She cocked her hips and parked her fists on the resulting shelves. Five-foot-five, weight between model and tweaker, shoulder-length brown hair long since grown out of any deliberate style. Two upper teeth crowded behind the one dental charts said should have been between them. She looked at Sisler is if he were acting dense just to piss her off. "He got up yesterday morning and was all in my face and my kids' faces about the cookies."

"What about the cookies?"

"We were out. He said he knew goddamn well there was cookies when he went to bed last night and he had his mouth all ready for them and now they're gone and how he's tired of people eating him out of house and home and how he pays for the place and should at least be able to get a couple of goddamn cookies when he wants them and I told him he's full of shit. His dad owns the house and lets him and us live there for nothing so he could get off his horse about what a big spender he is any time—"

Sisler held up his hands for AmberLynn to take a breath. "Why did you call for the police today, Ms. Feeney?"

"Like I's saying, I come over to get our stuff because I ain't leaving my kids around no fucking maniac who goes off about cookies thinking he'd be at work but it must be his day off or something and I'm pretty sure he's in there and I'm afraid to go in by myself."

"What has he done to make you afraid? Besides the cookie outburst?"

"He throwed a bottle of lotion and a candle at me yesterday."

"He hit you with either one?"

"Does that matter? I mean, he threw them right at me."

"No, it doesn't really matter. Throwing them's assault whether he hits you or not. You can swear out a complaint, but I have to tell you it's going to be your word against his if it goes to court. What I'm really trying to figure out is how dangerous the situation is. Does he have a gun?"

"He says he does but I ain't never seen it. He's a lot of tough talk is all he is. Raisin' hell over cookies. Shitty cookies, too, and him carrying on like they was Chips Ahoys."

"Okay. Let's get your stuff. Understand, I'm not allowed to help you carry anything. My job is to be sure he doesn't inter-fere. We clear on that?"

Sisler a little better than average size and built like a fireman even though he had a real job. AmberLynn gave him a good once-over. "You sure? Some of this is pretty heavy. I don't know I can carry it all. You look like you can handle quite a bit yourself."

She smiled and turned Sisler another two degrees gayer. "Sorry. I'm just here as security. Let's see if he's home."

No doorbell. AmberLynn knocked. No answer. Knocked again. No answer. Sisler held up a finger for her to wait and knocked with the side of his fist, cop style. "Andrew Elias!

Penns River police! Open up!"

No answer. "You have keys?" AmberLynn held up a ring, fingers already on the one she wanted. "Before we go in, show me something that proves you live here."

"Look at this shithole. Who would lie about living here?"

"You run into all kinds when you're a cop. Got a driver's license with this address on it?" Showing her driver's license appeared to be a new idea for AmberLynn. Produced the card with a flourish as though Sisler had doubted she had one. "Okay. Go ahead."

AmberLynn inserted the key in the lock and a voice called out from inside. "Who's out there?"

"Penns River police, Mr. Elias. Open up."

"Andy, open the door, you asshole."

"How do I know you're a real cop?"

Sisler looked down at himself. Dressed in full uniform, hat included. Patrol car at the curb directly in front of the house. "You could look out the window."

Five seconds' silence. Then, "You got a warrant?"

"For Christ's sake, Andy. You are such a dick."

"No, Mr. Elias. No warrant. Ms. Feeney just wants to get some of her stuff. I don't even have to come inside if you want to wait out here on the stoop with me."

"Whilst she goes through all my shit and takes what she wants? Fuck you."

"Kick it in," AmberLynn said to Sisler.

"I can't kick it in."

"Why not? My stuff's in there. I got a right to it."

"He also has a right to be secure in his home. You want us to force entry you're going to have to get a judge to sign papers."

"Then let's go."

"Go where?"

"See a judge and get my stuff back."

Sisler never much wanted to be a detective, couldn't help wondering now if Dougherty had to put up with shit like this.

"That's not a one-day thing. You need a lawyer to file a law-suit, take it to court. A bunch of stuff has to happen."

"How long's that take?"

"More than a day, that's for sure."

AmberLynn looked at Sisler like he was conspiring with Elias. "He could be in there fucking up my good stuff while we're standing out here like a couple of assholes. For all you know he could be in there jacking off on my underwear."

Sisler tried not to laugh at the image of a man rubbing out a quick one to show this bitch who's in charge before the cops broke down the door. Knew that was an image he'd be a long time un-seeing. "I'm sorry. That's the law."

"Hey, Andy! You needle-dicked piece of shit! This cop says alls I need to do is say the word and he'll kick this door in!"

Sisler stared. AmberLynn ignored him. Andrew Elias had an opinion. "Fuck you, AmberLynn. I just called my dad. He's on his way to tell you and that cop to fuck off. This ain't your fucking house."

Sisler managed to keep his voice down. It took effort. "Uh, Ms. Feeney. I just told you I wasn't kicking down any doors today."

"He don't know that." Self-satisfied grin on her face. Sisler glad someone was having fun.

A blue Ford Escort pulled to the curb. A man about sixty got out and hurried to the stoop as quickly as his gut and what appeared to be a gimpy knee allowed. "What's going on here?"

"Who are you, sir?"

AmberLynn stepped between Sisler and the newcomer. "Johnny, Andy ain't letting me in to get my stuff."

"What's a cop doing here?"

"I figured he might pull some shit like this so I brought pro-tection."

"That's enough!" Sisler usually excitable as milk. "Who are you, sir? For the record."

The idea the cop might have some authority here appeared to

dawn on Johnny. "John Elias. This is my house."

"Is Andrew Elias your son?"

"Yeah."

Sisler pointed to AmberLynn. "Do you know her?"

"Well, yeah, I do. She just called me by name."

"Identify her, please. For the record."

"Her name's AmberLynn Feeney. She lives here with Andy." To AmberLynn: "Now what the hell's going on?"

John let AmberLynn tell the story her way, occasionally asking Sisler to confirm a recent detail. "He threw stuff at you because you were out of cookies?"

"That's what I was telling this one." Meaning Sisler.

John asked Sisler if he could talk to Andrew. "Be my guest."

The older Elias knocked on the door. "Andy! It's your dad. Open the door."

"That cop still out there?"

"Andy, open the goddamn door before I tell him it's okay to kick it in." Damn cop shows. Whole family had kicking in doors on the brain.

The door opened. Andrew Elias looked past his father to Sisler and AmberLynn at the base of the stairs. "She ain't coming in."

AmberLynn halfway up when Sisler took her by the elbow. "Uh-uh. We haven't been invited yet."

"My stuff's in there."

"I know, and you called the police to get it. Now there's rules that have to be followed. Come back down here with me."

First thing Sisler heard when he had AmberLynn situated was John saying, "Honest to Christ? Cookies? You let this get out of hand over some goddamn cookies?"

"It's a lot of stuff. The cookies was just the straw that stirred the drink wrong. I had enough, you know?"

"Let her in."

"I'm not letting her go through my stuff."

"I'll go with her and make sure your precious stuff stays put."

Andy wavered. "No. I mean—shit, this is my house. Ain't a

man's home his castle?'

John's face turned a deeper shade of red. "Whose house? I'm paying for the goddamn place and still hope someone will rent it to help out instead of you living here free. I only said youns could stay so's it wouldn't sit empty and because you promised to fix it up some. Which I don't see none of it being done. Now let us in."

John put a hand on Andy's shoulder to move him. Andy pushed back. John pushed harder. Andy drove the heel of his right hand into John's chest. John half-landed a right to Andy's cheek and Andy responded with a hand on John's throat by the time Sisler got between them. "Enough! Do you two want to go to jail?"

"Mind your business," John said. "No one's pressing charges." Glared at Andy.

"Fuck alla youns!" Andy eased his way around Sisler and down the stairs. AmberLynn made plenty of room for him to get to his car parked across the street. Laid rubber leaving.

John Elias looked at Sisler. "He always was a mouthy brat." Turned to look down the stairs. "Go ahead, AmberLynn. You probably ought to let me have your keys, though. Least for the time being."

Jacques Lelievre hadn't been averse to Don Kwiatkowski's suggestion to visit a strip club that afternoon. Yesterday's three robberies a personal record and Penns River a small town. It wouldn't do to accidentally walk into someone who'd recognize them. A nice, dark room in downtown Pittsburgh where traveling centerfolds and porn stars toured might be fun. A little money to spend could make for an enjoyable afternoon.

Chubbie's right there in downtown Penns River was not what he'd had in mind. The fact that it was nicer inside than outside wasn't a major accomplishment—the outside was a storefront in a strip mall. Even worse, Don had clearly been here before. He knew where it was, knew the layout, and looked forward with anticipation when a couple of the girls' turns were announced. They might know Don didn't have much money to spend if he was anything like a regular. Spreading it around today could draw attention, unless Jacques decided to treat again as the big shot from out of town. That ruse had worn thin.

Don acting in his element. "Come on, Larry. You can pull that stick out of your ass for an hour or so, can't you?" Waved over a waitress, rested a hand on her hip as he wrapped his arm around her waist. Ordered two Bud Lights as if she had a drive-through microphone between her breasts. Jacques drinking beer because he saw no one drinking anything else and didn't want to stick out. Learned Bud didn't make the beaver-piss-tasting brand only for export to Canada.

"You have been here before," he said through clenched teeth. "You could be recognized."

"It's not like I'm a regular and everyone knows my name. Hey, there, Natasha." Natasha waved three fingers at Don and scurried away as fast as her six-inch platforms allowed.

"They're strippers. They make their living knowing who tips and who doesn't. You been in here before, don't show much money, then today you do, they will notice."

"Don't worry. It's not like I'm going to make it rain up in here." Don mimicked throwing money in the air.

"That's the plan now. What about after a few drinks?"

Don smiled like he'd known this was coming. "Just to show you I'm thinking ahead, I only brung a couple hundred in with me. So I don't get carried away."

Jacques cradled his head in his left hand. Fifty dollars probably way over Don's usual budget. "You want to look at tits, let's go to Pittsburgh where no one is going to recognize us."

Don shook his head. "Get more for your money here. Hey, what's your name?" he said to the waitress dropping off their fresh beers.

"Matilda."

"Hey, Matilda, is Summer working today?"

"Yeah. You just missed her. She's around somewhere."

"Thanks." Don slipped a bill inside Matilda's bra. Left his hand there longer than standard protocol.

"Who is Summer?" Jacques said.

Don leered. No other way to describe it. "She's the main reason we come here instead of downtown. Gives a hell of a lap dance and I think she might could be talked into more, if you know what I mean."

Jacques looked at his watch. "One hour and we leave. One hour."

Sisler cruised the old downtown area trying to decide which of the kids he saw were lookouts, hoppers, or just hanging out on a not as cold as expected day. The hoppers were easiest to spot, their heads always turned, walking away from him at an angle. The lookouts and the straight kids harder to tell apart. Close to each other in age, and half the straight kids thought it was funny to holler "Five-O" just to break his balls.

His call sign came over the radio and Janine Schoepf requested his location.

"Eleventh Street, passing the post office."

"Shots fired at 447 Fifth Avenue. Ambulance on the way."

Half a mile. Sisler turned left on Fifth. Flicked on the siren and lights. Pulled to the curb at 447 and saw John Elias in front of the house. Looked past John's shoulder and saw Andrew leaning against a brick porch pillar. A middle-aged woman in sweatpants and a Pitt hoodie fretted in the small front yard.

Andrew spoke loud enough for the neighborhood to hear. "Here you go. Get ready for jail, you old son of a bitch."

The woman asked Sisler if the ambulance was with him. "It's been dispatched, ma'am. Shouldn't be more than a minute or two. The report said there were shots fired?"

"Fucking-A right shots were fired." Andrew on the porch. "That old son of a bitch shot me. His own kid. Motherfucker."

John turned as if he might like another go at the boy. Sisler intercepted him. "That true, Mr. Elias?"

"You want to hear the whole story? Or just what he says?"

Oh boy do I want to hear this story. "The whole thing, but first things first. Where's the gun?"

"In the house. It's not like I been waving it around the neighborhood."

"Did you shoot him?"

John looked at the ground on either side of Sisler's feet as if a better answer might be there. "Yeah. Yeah, I shot him. He had it coming."

This just got better and better. "Now I need the whole story."

Andrew yelled from the porch. Something about how he had the whole story, it was his fucking life story. Sisler put up a hand to stop him. A siren sounded a few blocks away. "You all right there, Andrew? Shouldn't you be lying down? Or at least sitting?"

"I would except that old sonofabitch shot me in the fucking ass. Can you believe it? Shoots his own son in the ass."

Sisler gave his attention to John, who looked disgusted with life. "You said he had it coming."

John's expression a unique blend of pissed and sheepish. "I let AmberLynn get her stuff and helped her carry it to her car. Locked up behind her so's there'd be no question of what got took. Come back here and catch this one," jerked a thumb in Andrew's direction, "reading his mother the riot act about what a prick I am and what she ought to do about it. Today's supposed to be my day off. I don't need this shit."

The ambulance pulled in front of the house. Tony Lutz on the ground before it stopped rolling. "Who's shot?"

"Guy on the porch," Sisler said.

Tony looked at Andrew standing there like he was waiting for a ride. "Him? He looks fine."

"The wound's not in an obvious place." Tony shrugged and went up the stairs.

Sisler turned back to John. "This is your chance, while he's getting fixed up. What happened when you got home?"

"Like I said, I come home and he's all over his mother about me taking AmberLynn's side. Well, mostly about how I'm always taking everyone else's side but his. Which I don't, goddamnit. I give that kid every break I can and alls he does is screw things up."

"Let's stay on point, Mr. Elias. What happened that made you shoot Andrew?"

"I see this and I ain't in the fucking mood, if you catch my drift. Not after what happened at the other house. So I run up on the porch and give him a push. You know, get him away from his mother. He pushed me back and one thing leads to another."

"Where was the gun?"

"In the bedroom."

"So you went in and got it?"

"Not right away. We was going back and forth and Janet—that's my wife, Janet—trying to get between us. Andy goes to push me and I stumble and he pushes his mother off the porch. I see I can't handle him revved up like he is, so I hit him on the shoulder with whatever come to hand."

"Which was?"

"A wrench I set down on the swing I was fixing when I got the first call. He grabbed it off me and threw it into the yard, so I went in the house."

"For the gun?"

"Why do you keep asking did I get the gun all the time?"

"You did shoot him."

"Well...yeah. But that wasn't the plan."

Sisler took a deep breath. "What was the plan?"

"To call youns guys. You know, get the police."

Sisler confused for real now. "You're saying you called the

police, then you shot him? I was here no more than two minutes after you called."

John shook his head. "No no no. I tried to call youns but he jerked the phone cord right out of the wall. Janet tried to call on her cell but he grabbed that and threw it around the house. Mighta broke it, the way he was flinging the damn thing."

"Then you shot him?"

"Not right away. I went in the bedroom to get the gun, seeing as how he couldn't be talked to and I was afraid someone would get hurt." Proceeded with no sense of irony. "I took it out of the drawer just to show it to him, you know? Make him come up for air. He followed me in with the wrench raised up like this." Showed Sisler the classic "man about to strike someone with a wrench" pose. "He'd a hit me in the head he'd a killed me."

Sisler breathed a sigh of relief. "So that's when you shot him."

"Hell, yeah. Wouldn't you?"

Sisler paused, drawing a picture in his mind. "Sounds like self-defense. Here's what I don't get: he's coming at you with a wrench, right? How'd you shoot him in the ass?"

"He turned when he seen I meant business. I got him through both cheeks." John failed to suppress a grin.

"I'm going to have to take the gun as evidence."

"Evidence of what?"

"You did shoot him with it, Mr. Elias. It was okay to let bygones be bygones when it was just pushing and shoving, but you could've killed him. It's also illegal to discharge a firearm in the city limits."

"You're shitting me. What about them laws? You know, a man's home is his castle?"

The Eliases were big on that doctrine. "That's above my paygrade. Let's pick up that gun and get both of you over to the station. The DA can sort it out there." Yelled up to the porch. "Hey, Tony. That one gonna live?"

"Sure, if he quits bitching before I suffocate him."

"He have to go to the hospital?"

Tony looked at Andrew's rear end and pondered. "Yeah. He's got a through and through and through and through, if you know what I mean. A doctor ought to take a look at some of the whatchacall more obscured areas better than I can do it here."

"He urgent?"

"Nah. I got the bleeding stopped. The way he's running his mouth, he's sure as shit not in shock."

"Fuck you," Andrew said.

"All right. I'll call for backup and we'll get these two squared away. See what shakes out."

Jacques counted all the reasons he couldn't leave Penns River right away. More like counted all the reasons he couldn't leave Don Kwiatkowski right away, all of which included leaving Penns River, and he was stuck here for the time being. Fake documents—using his Doug Harvey alias—were pending and his brother had already mailed the package with his cash in it. How long it would take to cross the border was anyone's guess. Wondered if he should have had Sylvain mail it from Vermont. Too risky. If Customs searched the package and found the money, all they lost was the money. Sylvain going to jail for doing Jacques a favor was a different proposition altogether.

Plenty of time to do all this thinking, Don shacked up in what Chubbie's euphemistically called the VIP Room for going on an hour. Started out over-tipping dancers on the stage, which led to lap dances in a row of chairs against a wall in the back of the room, which led to going behind the curtain. Chubbie's even more low-rent than Jacques had expected if Don got this kind of treatment for the two hundred dollars he swore was all he'd brought in.

He treated himself to a few lap dances, since a man sitting

alone and unengaged for as long as he'd been there would draw attention. Natasha was better at it than he'd expected, though nothing like stopping by Chez Paree in Montreal after some *escalopines de veau polignac* at Café Bistro La Marinara down the block. What was that girl's name? Félicie. With the birthmark she swore looked like Nova Scotia on her thigh and nipples hard as pencil erasers.

Summer led Don by the hand out of the VIP room. Jacques gathered his change and swigged the last of his beer. The look on Don's face made Jacques suspect a happy ending. Decided it would be worth it if it meant they could leave now. Summer led Don to the bar and introduced him to another girl who greeted him enthusiastically. *Tabernac.* He'd been spending money.

Don spoke to the two girls a minute. They pointed toward a rear corner behind the bar. Don pointed. They nodded. Don left his fresh drink on the bar and navigated in the direction that had drawn the attention. Jacques relaxed. Men's room.

The waitress asked if he was ready for another drink. Jacques begged off. It was about time to be going, his friend was in the restroom. Thanks very much. Tipped her five bucks. The girl smiled and went on her way. Jacques turned to look for Don when a commotion at the back of the room caught his eye. Yelling followed by confusion followed by bouncers running toward the back while young women in every state of undress ran for the front. Saw Don trailing the tide of women, wave a gun—Jacques's gun, which he'd thought was in the car—and yell something. Jacques stood and walked toward the front door. No hurry. Just a guy leaving. Heard a shot and the sound of glass breaking. No one watching the door so Jacques kept walking through the parking lot. Picked up his pace once it wouldn't draw too much attention. Close enough to unlock the car with the fob when he heard the front door burst open behind him and Don's voice amidst heavy breathing: "Larry! Get the car! Get the car!" Money clutched in his hand, bills straggling away in ones and twos like leaves off a tree.

CHAPTER 25

Gord McFetridge pretty sure Jacques Lelievre was in Penns River and responsible for the rash of robberies. Unusual to see three in one day, but Lelievre's MO showed a tendency toward opportunism. Possible he'd figured the mass shooting would overwhelm Penns River's cops and wanted to make hay.

If so, Lelievre was at least half right: Penns River's cops were overwhelmed. Teresa Shimp struck McFetridge as a good cop and probably a good detective. Dougherty and the other detective up to their necks in the shooting. All Shimp and McFetridge had time to do was chase robbery calls.

A uniform named Sean Sisler greeted them at the door. "We're not going to get much. The customers were gone by the time I got here. Most of the dancers only around because their, uh, costumes had no place for car keys and they couldn't just split. No formal statements yet, but far as I can tell no one recognized anybody."

Shimp's frustration had grown through the day. "No one? Really? They strip naked and...grind up against these guys and can't recognize them?"

"They're strippers, Teresa. It's not faces and names they care about. It's wallets." McFetridge liked that one, filed it away. Sisler asked if anyone else was coming. "This is my second 'shots fired' call today. I'm going to need a week in the office just to do the paperwork."

"Neuschwander's on the way to collect evidence. A lot of people are on comp time from the Dale's shooting."

Sisler barked a laugh. "Still trying not to pay overtime."

"I can probably get us someone if I have to. All we're doing now is taking statements, right?"

Sisler nodded. "There are about twenty here to get, though."

Shimp heaved a sigh. "I guess we each take half." Looked around the room for a logical dividing point. Two male managers in sport shirts and slacks. A male bartender and three bouncers in tuxedo shirts and bow ties. Four waitresses in open-collar tux shirts showing various degrees of cleavage. A dozen dancers still apparently wearing whatever they had on when the shit hit the fan. Half a dozen nipples visible for those keeping score at home. "Can we at least get these women dressed?"

McFetridge held back a grin. Shimp wore a blazer over an open blouse that exposed as much skin as an Anabaptist funeral. Fingered a simple gold cross hanging around her neck. Cheeks redder inside a building warm enough for naked women than they'd been in the sub-freezing air.

Sisler's lips never moved but a smile showed in his eyes. Glanced around the room then pointed with both arms pulled together. Separated his hands to move everyone on each side to a respective area of the room. Eleven in each group. All the men on Shimp's side.

Some things never changed for a cop regardless which side of the border. The managers bitched about how much this was costing them, when can they open again? The employees mentioned at every opportunity they all worked for tips and this was costing them money. Some deficiency of the HVAC kept the dancers freezing in Shimp and McFetridge's group while those interviewed by Sisler—thirty years old and built like a defenceman—seemed to feel no need to cover themselves at all.

The interviews all went about the same:

Shimp: What's your name?

Dancer: Natasha.

McFetridge: Your real name.

Dancer: Sarah.

Shimp: Tell us what you saw.

Sarah: I was in the bathroom. We've got a little one of our own back there? Off the dressing room? I was powdering my nose before my next turn on stage and I hear all this yelling and some fat fuck with a gun's in there taking money off the girls.

Shimp: Did you recognize him?

Sarah: I seen him in heres before but he always gave me a creepy feeling so's I stayed away from him and that, you know?

The managers, bartenders, and bouncers knew less than Sarah. Three dancers still to question.

Shimp: What's your name?

Dancer: Jasmine.

McFetridge: Your real name.

Dancer: Fuck you. That is my real name.

So much for cooperation from Jasmine. Nine down, two to go.

Shimp: What's your name?'

Dancer: Brenda. (McFetridge cocked an eyebrow.) They call me Summer in here.

Shimp: Tell us what you saw.

Brenda (after consideration): I was standing at the bar with Tiffany when I heard a bunch of noise and saw people running. I was afraid it was a fire in back and all I got on is this. (An outfit for which McFetridge had great admiration but understood would be of little use in thirty-degree weather.) Then I saw this guy come out from behind the girls with a gun and he shoots it. Up in the ceiling, I guess, or maybe in a mirror. One or the other since I don't see anyone hurt, but still. Shooting off a gun in a place like this?

Shimp: Did you recognize the man with the gun?

Brenda (even more consideration, then a shrug): Yeah, I guess. I just came out of the VIP Room with him a couple minutes before. He had some money and I wanted to hook him up with Tiffany, but I think he might've spent his enthusiasm, if you know what I mean.

Shimp paused a second, then flushed to the roots of her hair. No way could McFetridge hold this one in, changed it to a question in time to save face. "You didn't happen to get his name, did you?"

"He said it was Butch, but I figured that was bullshit."

"How so?"

Brenda uncomfortable with this degree of specificity. "That wasn't what it sounded like he was going to say at first." McFetridge acted more confused than he was. "Like he started to say something else and changed his mind."

"What did it sound like? The name he decided against telling you?"

"All I heard was the first letter."

"Which was?"

Deep, disgusted sigh. "D."

Shimp looked ready for an acid shower with lye soap. "Anything else?"

"No. I mean, he was just a guy, you know. We get a hundred like him in here every day."

Shimp got Brenda's contact information and gave her a business card. Said, "Callmeatthisnumberifyouthinkofanythingelse-orseethisguyanywhereatall" so quickly McFetridge knew what she told Brenda and still couldn't understand it. About to question the final dancer when Sisler's voice cut through the club:

"Shimp! You're going to want to hear this. Bring the Mountie."

The waitress's name was Darla—Matilda for work purposes—and a customer came to mind when Sisler asked if anyone in there that day sounded as if "they weren't from around here." Sisler nodded toward McFetridge and Shimp. "Tell them what you told me."

"These two guys were in here a couple hours. I'm pretty sure one of them was the one robbed the place."

Shimp asked if Darla got their names. "The fat one, no. I'm pretty sure he called the other guy Larry, though."

Shimp looked to McFetridge. "Your guy's named Jacques, isn't he?"

McFetridge spoke to Darla. "You said this Larry didn't sound like he was from around here. What did he sound like?"

"It's hard to say. He had trouble with T-H words. You know, said 'dem' and 'dese' and 'dose.' Like that."

"Like he was from Brooklyn?" Shimp said.

"That's the thing. I lived in New York for a while and it wasn't like that. You know what it was like? I saw this show on Investigation Discovery a few weeks ago and a lot of the real people sounded like this guy. Not the actors doing the written stuff. You know, the people it actually happened to. I think it was filmed down south somewhere. Maybe Louisiana."

McFetridge had hoped for something like this. Used a French Canadian accent he figured sounded similar to how Jacques Lelievre would speak, especially to someone not familiar with Canadian accents. He called it, "putting on the frog." "Did it sound anything lak dis? Lak he's speaking English but it has a different inflection lak it's not his natural language. He speaks it real well but some of the pronunciations are off, and the rhythm of the sentences is awkward. Maybe uses different words from what you'd expect sometimes, lak he has to tink about dem."

"Yeah! That's exactly what he sounded like. How'd you know?"

McFetridge turned to Shimp and Sisler. "I think we found our boy, eh?"

CHAPTER 26

Stush convened a meeting after Shimp's team concluded the interviews at Chubbie's. Shimp, Sisler, McFetridge, Neuschwander all in the chief's relatively spacious office. Doc made an appearance in his role as first among equals in the detective bureau. End of January and the overtime budget damn near shot for the rest of the year unless a mild winter allowed moving funds from Public Works to Public Safety. Stush promised to sign off on comp time vouchers, but let's not abuse the privilege.

"You're sure it's your guy?" he said to McFetridge.

"As sure as I can be with no positive ID or physical evidence. The consistency in all the descriptions we have fits him, though no one at a robbery saw his face because of the mask. The waitress at Chubbie's liked his picture but wouldn't swear to it. Maybe seeing him in three dimensions will help. She definitely picked up on the accent when I tried it out on her."

"That was slick," Sisler said. "I'da have never thought of that."

Stush liked it, too, but, "Have you ever actually heard this guy speak?"

"No, but I know where he's from. Like it would be for you if someone from Boston passed through. Let's put it this way: Her recognizing the accent doesn't mean it's him, but if she hadn't recognized it, or said it was wrong, I might not be here now."

"Good enough for me." Stush sat back into his hands folded

on belly meditative pose. "So what are we gonna do about this Canuck prick?" To McFetridge: "No offense."

"None taken, assuming I'm not the Canuck prick you're talking about." Chuckles all around.

No one had any suggestions until Shimp asked McFetridge, "How well do you know this guy? Lelievre."

"Never actually laid eyes on him. Only picked up his file since he escaped. I read everything we have and talked to the cops who worked the cases. What do you want to know?"

"Would he go back to the same place? I mean, if he is staying in town because he figures we're busy, there aren't all that many likely places for him to hit. Maybe we could stake out a few and hope to get lucky."

Doc caught Stush's eye and rubbed a thumb against two fingers. Raised his eyebrows. Stush nodded.

"It's hard to guess," McFetridge said. "The robberies fit his MO. Not this last one, but I don't think Chubbie's was his idea. Like he was there with his partner and someone took a flyer." General assent. "Pulling jobs so close together in time and space isn't like him, but he's been known to seize the moment. Seeing a small town so wrapped up in something like your mass shooting might strike him as a legitimate opportunity. No offense."

"None taken," Stush said. "I think you're right."

"Do you think he'll stay in town?" Shimp said. "Will he double up?"

"Will he stay in town depends on how otherwise occupied he thinks you are. Will he double up?" McFetridge shrugged. "I have no idea. This is new territory for everyone."

Shimp cocked an eyebrow in Stush's direction. "Do we want to try some stakeouts?"

Stush spoke to Neuschwander. "Ricky, did you turn up any physical evidence we can use in Chubbie's? Fingerprints? Shell casing from the shot he fired, maybe?"

Neuschwander shook his head. "It's a public place. Thousands of prints. It wasn't worth dusting unless we knew of something one of them had touched recently and I can't lift prints from Summer's tits."

"Maybe a family man like you can't," Doc said. "Mind if I take a shot?" Chuckles from the men. Shimp cringed.

"What about the glasses at their table?" Stush said. "Did the waitress show you where they sat?"

"She showed us, but it's no help. She asked the guy we think is Lelievre if he wanted another drink and he said they were leaving as soon as his friend got out of the can. He tipped her five bucks and she cleared the table. No way to know which bottles were theirs."

"No ejected shell? I know we don't have anything to match with, but if we catch someone down the road it might be nice."

"No, and we looked. One of the bouncers knows his firearms and he said it was a revolver, so there's that, too."

"Lelievre likes revolvers," McFetridge said. "And that's why. Even though we think he wasn't the one decided to pull this job, it's a good bet he's in charge. A revolver makes sense."

Stush picked through the bowl for three jelly beans to his liking. "Teresa, I don't want you to think I've been ignoring you. Under different circumstances I'd already be working with you on places to position officers. I looked at the budget this morning, and the money for overtime isn't there. Best we can do is circulate the photo Gordie has of Lelievre and what description we have of the other guy to all likely targets. Tell them to call us if they see a couple guys who fit the description. Doesn't matter if they try to rob the place or not. These guys get together to eat or have a beer, maybe someone recognizes them. It's the best we can do right now."

"A shot was fired today," Shimp said. "Aren't we worried someone might get hurt?"

"Sure, I'm worried. I'm open to options that don't include overtime." Spoke to McFetridge: "Any chance your cooperating fed can throw any hours our way?"

McFetridge's turn to look uncomfortable. "My fed seems to

define 'cooperating' as 'I know you're in the country and won't give you any shit for doing your job.' I think if I could convince him our guy's name was Jacques Hussein al-Lelievre we could have black helicopters here in half an hour. For a run of the mill snowfrog armed robber? I don't see it."

Stush looked at his watch. "It's four twenty-eight. Meeting adjourned. Half an hour of comp time for everyone here. If we ever get a chance to use it."

McFetridge asked Doc for a minute on his way out. "I should probably bring this up with your chief, but I want to keep it informal at first. You know, not step on any toes. Do you mind?"

"No, go ahead. What's up?"

"Two things. First, you were right about Detective Shimp. She's a good cop, but I think this Chubbie's thing has her icked out."

Doc stifled a laugh. Glimpsed Shimp's retreating form. "Oh, really? Who'd have thunk it?" Smiled to let McFetridge in on the joke. "She's a good Catholic girl. Led a bit of a sheltered existence in some ways. You might do well to keep discussions of Chubbie's on a strictly factual basis with her. You said two things."

"Officer Sisler."

"What about him?"

"I'd keep an eye on him. In a good way, I mean. He's smart and he knows how to focus. When he saw Shimp had an issue with the strippers, he divvied up the interviews so she had to talk to as few as possible. I was thinking at the time it was quite a sacrifice, him choosing to interview the naked women. I kept an eye that way myself—and, okay, some of them looked pretty good—and they weren't bashful about showing themselves, nice-looking young man that he is. Had no more effect on him than a cool breeze on a rock."

This smile harder to suppress. Doc managed. "Thanks. I'm sure Stush will be happy to hear that. Sisler is nothing if not focused."

Doc about to leave when McFetridge cleared his throat. "I never worked in a small town. Never worked much with any. All the pressure you're under and everyone gets along so well. I guess I want to compliment you. It's very impressive."

"It's Stush. He's been here going on forty years. Everyone eats a lot of shit out of respect for him. I'm sure you picked up on the overtime situation."

"Hard not to. Is the budget really as tight as it seems to be?"

"OT is just about gone for the year after that Dale's business. Part of it's an artificial shortage, too. The mayor wants Stush to retire so he can put his own guy in and he has enough votes with him on the council to give us just enough money to stay afloat."

"The chief isn't ready to retire?"

Doc smiled with affection. "He's a stubborn old Polack. Wants to feel like leaving is his idea. Anyway, that's why there's so little open dissent. Everyone knows we're pushing water uphill every day and we keep doing it for him. I don't want to think about what happens here when he finally retires."

"I don't care what it takes or who you have to pay. I want at least one of those cocksuckers found and hurt, especially the one robbed Chubbie's. I own a piece of that dump." Stretch Dolewicz pointed to his chest. "That's my money he took. I have other things going on there, too. These two jagovs are fucking with me personally now. This is where it stops."

"Gotcha, Uncle Stretch." Ted Suskewicz stood. Started putting on his coat. "I'll go up there right now and shake the tree."

"See if your magical source in the police department has anything. I'll get over it if they arrest the one guy, but that asshole that robbed Chubbie's? Make an example of him."

"How much of an example?"

"A leave-his-carcass-on-the-steps-of-the-Bachelor's-Club-and-let-the-other-dumb-son-of-a-bitches-draw-their-own-fucking-conclusions example."

"And the other one?"

Stretch made a noncommittal gesture. "The cops get him first, they can have him. We get him, make sure he has a few weeks of laying up to think about his mistakes."

CHAPTER 27

Last Saturday of the month was Burger Night at the American Legion. Dollar for a third of a pound burger you dressed yourself. Lettuce, tomato, and onion lined up on a buffet table along with Heinz pickles, Heinz mustard, Heinz relish, and Heinz ketchup. Another buck bought a plate of fries with gravy available for topping. Heinz, of course.

Doc sat with his parents. Eating out didn't change their suppertime, placing their orders at five on the dot "so we'll be sure to get seats together" at one of the banquet-style tables. Drew had to work and couldn't get Paula and the girls there before six or six thirty so they were on their own. Quarter after five now, the place filling up already.

"I heard there was trouble across the river today," Tom said between bites.

This was news to Doc. "Where?"

"Didn't you hear? Over the rolling plant where they're on strike."

"They're not on strike, Dad. They're locked out."

"They're not working. Same thing." Doc had fought this out with Tom before. Didn't feel like a rematch.

"The hell it is. Hey, Doc." Steve Schlahetka eased into the seat next to Doc. Steve a Penns River slow-pitch softball legend. Three-time MVP of the local league. Pitched an honest-to-Nolan Ryan no-hitter once. Doc coached Steve's boy in Little

League one year. Helluva nice kid. Played baseball like a swan unloading a truck.

Tom didn't know Steve. Passed a dirty look over him and went on. "The company brought in some workers. There was trouble when they crossed the picket line."

"Anyone hurt?" Doc said.

"Don't know," Tom said through a mouthful of burger. "Turned off the radio when I come upstairs to clean up."

"Couple people got cuts and bruises," Steve said, mostly to Doc. "Could've been worse."

Doc still playing catch-up. "Help me out here, Steve. The company locks out their regular workers and tried to bring in others today?"

"No tried about it. Did."

Bob Onkotz sat across from Steve. "I heard they was all coloreds and Mexicans."

"That's bullshit," Steve said. "I ain't saying none of them was, but it was mostly white guys. Some of them was from that operation that laid off a few weeks ago."

"I heard coloreds and Mexicans. They do shitty work, but they come cheap."

"I just told you, Bob, it was guys as white as you and me."

Bob's always red face got redder. "Say what you want, but I know a guy was there. He says there wasn't a white face in the bunch."

"Your guy's full of shit."

"And you were there."

"My boy was. He works there." Steve took a breath. "Worked there, maybe. Word going around now is they might not get to come back. Give their jobs to the scabs."

Doc: "The union's got no say in any of this?"

Steve looked at him for the first time. "You'd think so, wouldn't you? Pay dues into it, you'd think it would do some good. Far as I can tell, the union's okay so long as it doesn't do anything the company don't like. Soon as they don't toe the line—like fighting those givebacks that got shoved down their throats last month—then fuck the union. Sorry, Mrs. Dougherty. Whatever they bargained don't count."

Tom spoke to Doc so Steve couldn't help hearing. "I used to have a union job. Never saw where it did me any good. The union, I mean."

"Maybe yours didn't. I never worked with you. Steve Schlahetka." Reached a hand across the table. Tom shook it. "Alls I know is my old man was in the union and his old man was in the union. Granddad was a miner. The stories he told us about the shit the company used to pull, even with a union, and you have to wonder what it would've been like without one."

"That could be. Like you said, I never worked with you or in a mine. What I seen, the union was only there for them that didn't want to work. Kept their lazy asses on the payroll. I can't name one time the union did dick for me."

Every so often the twentieth century American history class Doc took in community college rose up to bite him. Pitched his voice to remove some vigor from the question. "How many hours a week did you work, Dad?"

"Forty. Same as everyone else."

"You know why?"

"Do I know why? Forty hours is a regular work week."

"Do you know why forty hours is a regular work week?" Steve started to nod.

Tom stared as if Doc were jagging him deliberately. "That's what it's always been. It's a goddamn federal law, far as I know."

"That's right. It is a federal law. Do you know why?"

"Now you're going to teach me how laws get made?"

"Not how it got passed. Why it got passed."

Tom opened his mouth to speak. Had nothing to say at first. Closed his mouth. Thought. "I'll bet you're about to tell me."

"Unions."

"My ass."

"Do you know what the average guy worked in 1900?" The

figure still stuck in Doc's mind from a class ten years ago.

Tom with the red ass for real now. Sat his weight back and crossed his arms. "Tell me."

Steve Schlahetka touched Doc's wrist. Doc gave him the floor. "Average guy in 1900 or so worked ten or twelve hours a day six days a week. No vacation. No sick pay. No benefits."

"Bullshit."

"No shit," Steve said.

Doc waited for a reply. Tom's heart wasn't in it. Doc flashed to stories he'd heard when he was a kid and hadn't done his chores. How easy he had it. He needed a graceful exit line. Saw movement near the back of the room. His friend Eve waved to him. "Excuse me, gentlemen. I see someone I need to talk to."

Tom took a bite of burger. Steve clamped his fingers on Doc's wrist. Gave a little squeeze and resumed eating. The nebshit in Bob couldn't resist turning to see. "Ain't she the rug muncher?"

Doc gave his biggest shit-eating grin. "It's okay. So am I." Leaned over to his parents. "Back in a minute."

Eve Stepler had her arms open before Doc covered half the distance between them. Both wore big smiles and gathered the other for a sincere hug. Friends the way men and women rarely are, the lack of sexual tension removing a formidable obstacle to unconditional affection.

Doc spoke first. "How was...the Caribbean?"

Eve slapped his arm. "You don't even remember where I went."

"Sure I do."

"Where, then?"

Pause. "It was south of here." Arm slap. "Way south." Another. "A religious place. Saint—Something." One more. "Saint... Bart's?"

"You're such a man sometimes, Dougherty."

"Saint Thomas? Saint Croix? Saint Petersburg? Saint Kitts? Saint Vincent? Saint John? Saint...goddamnit, Eve, I know it's Saint Something. Give me some help."

"Saint Lucia."

"That was my next choice. Swear to God. Ow. That hurt, Eve."

"Good."

Doc dodged Gino Bartiramo trying to navigate the aisle with a hamburger and gravy fries on a sagging paper plate in one hand and can of Coke and a cane in the other. Steered Eve out of the flow of traffic. "So how was it?"

"Perfect. Eighty-five degrees with a breeze every day. Rained every night for half an hour or so. The food was great, the service was great. We went diving and snorkeling and got massages and seaweed wraps, saw a volcano, slept in, drinks delivered without even having to ask. It was beautiful."

Doc gave her a sidewards glance. "I know you left something out."

"Well, yeah. At night. In our room."

"Not that." Eve gave confused. "Don't tell me you flew damn near to South America and didn't go shopping. You're gay, but you're still a woman."

Another arm punch. More perfunctory. "Yeah. We went shopping, too."

"You don't sound all that enthusiastic about it."

"I bought a bunch of shit I don't want and don't know what to do with."

"That's what vacations are for. It drives the economy in those places, stuff you have no idea why you bought it half an hour after you get back. Stuff you think will look great until you get home and see it's a piece of tacky shit that doesn't go with anything you own."

"What do you know about tacky shit?"

"You've been to my house."

Eve drew a picture in her head from memory. "Yeah. Okay. The thing is, I knew this was tacky shit I had no use for when I bought it."

"Why'd you buy it, then?"

"You ever been to one of those islands?" Doc shook his head. "The resort is beautiful. Everyone on the staff kisses your ass, but in a nice way. They couldn't treat us better."

"And that provoked you to buy tacky shit because..."

"Because then you take the jitney into town and you see how these people live. Shacks one of the little pigs wouldn't rent with a cow staked out front." Eve giggled.

"What?"

"Ronnie. She's smart—you'll like her—but sometimes she's such an airhead. We're driving up over the mountain in the jitney and she's pointing to these animals staked out front of people's houses—lean-tos, practically—and she asks me what those goat-like creatures are. Just like that: goat-like creatures."

"What were they?" Doc nothing if not a willing straight man.

Eve fixed him with the same look she must have given Ronnie. "Goats." Saw Doc's reaction. "Maybe you had to be there."

"Maybe."

"Anyway, all I could think of the whole time in town was how nice everything was at the resort. How much money was spent making it perfect. How much money the owners must be taking out of it, and the people who do the most to make it a nice vacation don't have pots to piss in. It took a lot of the fun out of it for me."

"Communist."

"I bet you'd feel the same if you saw it."

"It's the way of the world, Eve." Doc hadn't escaped one funk only to trade it for another. "So, how's Veronica?"

"Don't call her that. She hates it. Call her Ronnie."

"That's twice now you've referred to her as if a meeting is imminent. What's going on?"

"I just thought, my best friend and my new lover—maybe potential partner—it would be nice if they got to know each other. You know, to keep the different parts of my life in synch."

Doc took half a step back. Gave Eve a cop look. Not the intimidating stare. More like the bullshit detector had activated. "When did synchronicity of your life become such a big deal?"

"What makes you think it's a big deal now?"

"You're not back five minutes and you're going on about how much I'd like Veron—Ronnie and how you want your life to harmonize. If you and her weren't playing on the same team this would look a lot like one of your setups." Saw the look on Eve's face. "Okay. Give it up."

Eve scanned the area. Took Doc by the elbow. Steered him to a corner, backs to the room. "One night we were in bed, all sweaty and tangled up, and she—"

"That's already more detail than I need."

"Don't be such a prude. Anyway, we're lying there letting the vibe carry us, and Ronnie looks over at me and says, right out of the blue, 'Don't you ever just want some dick?'"

Doc's torso remained still while his neck stretched back and his eyes bunched together. "She's defecting? You drove her straight?"

Eve made a fist. The quarters too close for a punch. "Didn't I tell you she's bisexual? I know I told you. You just forgot."

Doc held up a warning finger. "No. You did not tell me. A man never forgets if he hears a hot woman is bi."

"How do you know she's hot? You've never seen her." Doc eyes narrowed again. "I guess I have described her a time or two."

"In graphically flattering terms."

"So I think you two would get along."

Doc looked at Penns River's leading lesbian yenta a full five seconds before it dawned on him. "You're out of your mind."

"Don't dismiss it out of hand."

"Did you hit your head in the islands?"

"Don't be that way. It's a good idea."

"What drugs did you take?"

"Stop it! I put a lot of thought into this. Are you seeing anyone right now?"

Still the same look on his face. "No."

"Not even a fuck buddy?"

Anita Robinson had moved in with a guy six months ago. "No."

"Hear me out: Ronnie gets what she wants. You get what you want. And I get to make both of you happy." Doc increased the stare. "Okay, and I get to know she's not catting around and hooking up with someone who might move her into a different sphere of influence. You'd be like my wing man. I know you've done that before."

Doc felt his resolve start to slip. It wasn't that he was a prude, or close-minded. Eve had been his best friend one way or another since junior high. The only non-relative he'd kept in touch with the nine years he was away in the Army. He couldn't say no to Eve. That only bothered him second most.

"How about Veltri's on Monday?"

The fact that she'd known he couldn't say no before she'd even called him over. That was what bothered him most.

CHAPTER 28

Wilver Faison never planned to be a drug kingpin. Fell into the job when he was still a hopper. Someone with ambition but no foresight took out the upper echelons of the nascent Penns River drug trade and was unable to follow up. As the senior surviving member of the organization, the one the others looked up to, Wilver became de facto boss. However much he didn't know about the drug trade, he did know keeping a low profile was the way to go, especially considering how his relationship with Ben Dougherty placed extra scrutiny on him.

"What about that vacant down Fourth Avenue?" Eddie Simmonds poured himself into an upholstered chair while they brainstormed ideas for a new retail facility. Wilver ran four in town and liked to rotate at least one every week or two. "You know, the one down by the Salivation Army? Keep a higher percentage for us, we don't have to pay no rent."

"The problem with a vacant is ain't no one have bidness going in and out," Wilver said. "People see that, they start to wondering why a bunch a fiends keeps going in there."

"Ain't nobody cares what a bunch a fiends do. They just figure it's a shooting gallery."

"Think about the people live around there. And all them goes into the Sallies for shit. They don't want no fucking shooting gallery in their hood."

Wilver, Eddie, and their Number Three, Pookie Haynesworth,

all eighteen or nineteen years old. They had greatness thrust upon them without proper seasoning in a town where even the hard-core dealers would have been pit bull shit half an hour after setting foot in a place like Baltimore or Chicago. Learned what they knew about the life from movies, where they also picked up most of their dialog, trying to sound tougher than they were.

"'Sides," Wilver said, "they an old man lives up in there knows me. Watches over that little row where the vacant at. Might as well call Five-O ourself."

Pookie had drifted to the position of enforcer, such as it was. "I could explain the situation to him."

"Naw, man. This old timer been good to me. Keeps an eye on my shorty brother. He gets a pass."

Pookie looked hurt. "I ain't mean to fuck him up, yo. I'ze just talk to him. Draw boundaries and shit."

"This one don't scare, Pook. Fought in the jungle back in the day. He a hard man down under it. He might decide to set some boundaries hisself. Then you'd have to kill him and we ain't doing that."

Wilver was proud of his record of never having killed anyone, or given the order. He'd led some beat-downs, a couple of which left people in the hospital. No one dead. He knew his day was coming, but no way would he break his cherry on Jefferson West.

Eddie pointed to a map. "What about back over by those apartments on Sixth?" Drew a small circle with his finger. "We ain't done no bidness there since we run that nigger off last summer."

"We need to talk about that," Wilver said. "There's a crew working that corner again. Right out on the street."

"Then saddle up, boys." Pookie already slipping into his coat. "That corner knows how the Step Up Posse deals with shit."

"Hold on, Pook." Wilver raised a quieting hand. "There's more than just that we needs to talk about." More than a little put out to be the only member of his operation that thought situational awareness was even a thing. "There's another one down by the tracks. I think it's the same crew. I been watching them. These niggers don't play."

"I ain't playing, neither," Pookie said. "We gots to fuck up two sets of shit, ain't no time like the present."

"I seen guns. You ready to make that step up?"

"We all know it only a matter of time. Ain't like we don't got 'em."

"Ain't that easy, Pook."

"This where you give me that 'It's different shooting a man' bullshit? Ain't but one way to find out."

"That ain't it. Any a us even been in a real gunfight? How good are we? These boys I seen, they's hard niggers. They know about this shit. We go straight up against them we come back dead."

"Then we don't go straight at 'em. Pick 'em off one or two at a time. They never know what hit 'em."

"You ever done that? Set someone up? Followed them around, get to know where they be and when they be there and them not know you doing it? Eddie? You ever done anything like that?"

Eddie shook his head. "Naw, man. I ain't know about that."

Pookie still on his feet, coat draped on his shoulders. "Well, then, how you planning to go at them?"

Wilver wished his voice had more authority when he said, "That ain't what worries me right now. What I'm trying to figure is how they coming at us."

CHAPTER 29

Jacques watched Mary Pugliese rinse her last cup of coffee before leaving for work, put it on the dish drainer. She'd been at Dale's when Jacques got back from the fiasco at Chubbie's ready to throw his shit in the car and hit la route and he didn't want to leave without saying anything. Not that he cared if he hurt her feelings. The last thing he needed was for her to decide she'd been used, read the news, put two and two together, and call the police. Don Kwiatkowski's loss of sanity mandated getting out of Penns River, but the package from Quebec was still in transit. Even worse than her calling the police was the possibility of Mary on the rag opening his mail to find almost seventy thousand dollars of untraceable American currency.

"Hey, Mary. Can I talk to you a minute?"

She looked at the clock over the refrigerator. "Just a minute. I'm already running late."

"I may have to go out of town for a few days. For work."

Mary's face didn't mask the uncertainty in her voice. "You might?"

"I'm waiting for a phone call this afternoon to know for sure." Jacques's bag already packed and in the car. Leaving enough behind to soothe Mary's suspicions. Nothing he'd miss. "Just a few days."

"When are you leaving?"

"Like I said, I'm not even sure I have to go. If I do, though, it

153

will be right away."

Another look came to Mary's face. Harder. "That was quick. Ain't even been a week."

Jacques put his arms around her. "It's not like that. I told you what I do. The security work. I have a chance for a new contract. Could be a big deal for me. I'll be back once I talk to some people and take a look around. Couple three days. Hey." Cradled her chin in his hand. Tilted her head up. "I'm coming back. Go see how much of my stuff is still in the room."

"That's cause you ain't packed yet."

"That package from my brother? In Canada? That's coming here. That package means a lot to me. I'm not going to skip out on it."

"You keep going on about that package. What's in it?"

Jacques had worked on the story. "My father, he died. We weren't close or nothing, but sometimes when you're not close to someone it's harder. You wonder what might have been different, you know? My brother found some of his things from better times, and a few he thinks might help me understand better why my father was so hard to get along." Half true. Marc-Edouard Lelievre currently serving five years in the Milton Hilton, though he was a *bâtard* to get along with. "It's personal stuff. I'm not going to leave it. And I trust you with it."

Jacques watched the indecision play out on Mary's face. A look of resignation took root. "Well, it ain't like I could keep youns from going even if I wanted to. Your stuff'll be here when you get back."

Jacques waited ten minutes after she left to drive to Fayette County. He stole a car and another set of plates from a similar model before getting a room in Greensburg—Westmoreland County—where neither he, the car, nor the plates, would likely be recognized.

CHAPTER 30

"Here's something you could have used, Noosh." Doc stabbed an article in the *Post-Gazette* with his index finger. "Says here you can hire a naming consultant for your kids. Apparently some people don't feel they're up to it." The most recent addition to the Neuschwander family named Lothar, much to the joy of the other cops. "Seems to me, a couple that figures they need to pay someone to pick their kid's name should stop fucking altogether."

No reply from Neuschwander. Doc lowered the paper for eye contact. "You okay, Noosh? I'm just breaking balls here."

"I'm reading the Michael Stoltz autopsy." Neuschwander held up a sheaf of papers. "That new ME in Allegheny County—Lyle, I think her name is—she does nice work."

"Something stick out in particular?"

Neuschwander took so long to answer Doc started to worry. "It's not a contact wound."

Doc folded the paper. Set it on his desk. "No?"

Neuschwander still reading. "Entrance wound shows evidence of both fouling and stippling."

"So, what? Six inches to a foot?" Neuschwander nodded. Doc pictured someone holding a gun that distance from their own head. Didn't like what he saw.

"That's not all. She also found scars on the body and figured there was some previous trauma."

"We knew he had a serious accident ten years ago or so."

"Dr. Lyle went back and got the hospital records from the accident and follow-up treatment. Nice work since there was no standard way to save electronic records then."

"And?" Doc knew to stay patient. Neuschwander got to things in his own time.

"Probably nothing." Neuschwander set down the file.

"No. Not probably nothing." Doc's feet still on his desk. The paper put aside, his full attention on Neuschwander. "I trust your instincts. What's bothering you?"

Neuschwander looked at the closed file as if reading through the cover. "Stoltz had multiple scars on his right shoulder, some of which are obviously from surgery. Dr. Lyle appended a description of the injury and surgery from the original accident treatment."

Doc's posture stiffened. Forced himself to wait.

"I'm no doctor—I'm sure as hell no orthopedist—but what she describes here, I have to wonder if Michael Stoltz could've held that .45 in the position it was in when he was shot."

Doc's feet on the floor now. "How bad was it? That's a good-sized gun, but it's not real heavy."

Neuschwander reopened the file. "Her notes say…'injury is such as to significantly restrict motion of the rotator cuff beyond perpendicular to the torso.'"

Doc pulled his Sig P226 from its holster. Ejected the magazine and the shell in the chamber. Slid a finger in to be sure. Held the gun a foot from his temple. "He didn't have to hold it that high."

Neuschwander shook his head. "That's not the angle he was shot at." Flipped through the autopsy file. Found the page he wanted and studied. Used his right index finger to demonstrate. "More like this." Elbow well above the shoulder, wrist cocked to place the finger above the ear at an angle of about forty-five degrees. "The trajectory is downward from his right to left."

Doc held his Sig as high as he could and still maintain the proper angle. Placed his left thumb on his head and reached his fingers to touch the muzzle. Held that position and brought his left hand to eye level. Felt his stomach drop. "I can barely do it and that was no more than seven inches. We better talk to Stush."

Stan Napierkowski let his detectives talk. Sat back and laced fingers across his belly. "You're sure?"

Neuschwander said he'd have to talk to a doctor first.

Benny agreed. "But the more I think about it, the more I don't like it. Watch." Held his Sig as close as he could to the position necessary. Stush cringed when Benny pulled the trigger, even knowing the gun had been cleared. "See how my hand jerks? I know I got carried away with the video stuff before, but this is a problem we can't explain."

Stush spoke to Neuschwander. "You call the ME about this?"

Neuschwander nodded. "She says she thinks it would be difficult but wouldn't go on the record. Reminded me she's a pathologist, not an orthopedist. Suggested we talk to the surgeon who did the work."

"Did you?"

"Trying to find him now. Looks like he retired a few years ago."

Benny: "We could save some time and ask the parents. The way the ME describes this, the kid might've had a hard time combing his hair. They'd know that."

Stush lifted one hand from its resting pose long enough to wave Benny off. "No one outside this room is to know anything about this except for whatever doctors you talk to, and don't tell them any more than you absolutely have to." Saw the looks on his cops' faces. "Sounds like we already agree that if Stoltz didn't kill himself, he didn't do the others, either. Right?" Both detectives nodded. "Word gets out we're looking for another suspect? Not only does the media come down on us like a herd of locusts, the actual shooter knows we're still looking. We need to keep this as close as possible. Do not speak with the Stoltzes."

Waited for objections. Both detectives looked at their shoes. "I don't like it either, boys. Thing is, if Michael Stoltz is innocent, we have a slick son of a bitch out there who did all this and framed him. The less he knows about what we know, the better."

"Jeez, Stush," Neuschwander said. "I'm imagining what this must be like for the parents. His name all over the world and all."

"I know, Ricky." Stush rocked his chair forward to lock eyes with Neuschwander. Pitched his voice into Uncle Stush mode. "That's why we can't tell them. Imagine how they think people must be looking at them. You really believe they'll be able to resist the temptation to tell someone? Maybe Michael's brother or sister? The only way to keep the lid on this is to sit on it. Hard. We'll give them a heads up when it can't hurt us anymore. After an arrest but before an announcement."

Silent, unenthusiastic assent all around. A knock at the door, then Mike Zywiciel's head appeared through the opening. "I thought I heard your voice, Rick. Janine said you wanted this lab report right away."

Neuschwander thanked him and took the envelope. Used Stush's letter opener. Scanned more than read, obviously looking for something in particular. His face fell.

"What?" Stush said.

"The blood on the outside of the passenger door of Stoltz's car? It's A-positive."

"What's Stoltz?"

"I'm guessing it's not A-positive," Benny said.

Neuschwander shook his head. "O."

"Oh...shit." Benny's cell buzzed. He read the screen. "It's home, Stush. You mind?"

"Go ahead. I need a minute to come up with a plan, anyway."

"Hey, what's up? I can only talk for a minute...What?...Call an ambulance...No, don't do that. Call an ambulance...Jesus Christ, Mom. I know you still have your license but you can't even read the paper anymore...Call an ambulance!...All right all right. I'm on my way."

All eyes on him. "Apparently my dad cut off his thumb mak-ing picture frames in his shop. She's driving him to the hospital."

"Why are you still here?" Stush said.

CHAPTER 31

Tom Dougherty's thumb not all the way off. He'd cut into the bone, maybe through it, not much more than meat and gristle holding it onto the hand. Doc couldn't see much through the blood. What he could see didn't look good.

The Doughertys sat in the emergency waiting area of Allegheny Valley Hospital. Blood dripped from a towel wrapped around Tom's hand even though Doc had tied it into damn near a tourniquet. A girl of five or six stood between her mother's legs and stared at the drips as they splatted on the floor.

"How long you been here?" Doc said.

"We just set down when you come in." Tom held his bleeding hand up to eye level. "Thanks for this. It feels better."

"You really ought to keep it above your heart, Dad. Slows the bleeding."

No anger in Tom's voice. "At my age I'm happy the whole arm doesn't fall off my goddamn shoulder." He'd been making more such pronouncements about his physical condition of late. No rancor in them. No humor, either. "So what's going on with you? Got that mess at Dale's wrapped up yet?"

Doc stifled a sarcastic chuckle. "We're working on it."

"I'm glad that kid killed himself. I mean, not like I'm glad he's dead. Well, I guess I am, considering what he did. I—uh—I mean I'm glad you didn't have to take him in."

Doc listening to every other word. "I'd rather take him in

than find him the way we did."

"What if he decides to go out in a blaze of glory? What do they call it? Suicide by cop?"

Doc watched blood drip onto the floor. "That's what he wants, we'll oblige him. We do it right there'll twenty of us and one of him. I like those odds."

"What if he decides to take some of you with him?"

"We draw the line short of that. Anyway, that's what rookies are for." Gave his father a quick look and a smile he didn't mean.

"Rookies and the men without families, you mean."

Ellen Dougherty spoke for the first time since she'd said she was glad to see him. "It's a dangerous job, Benny. Maybe it's time you found something else."

"It's not as bad as everybody thinks it is. You know who has dangerous jobs? Loggers. Roofers. Miners. Construction workers. All of them get hurt more than cops do. A cop's job is mostly dangerous here." Tapped above his ear. "It works on your head."

Tom shifted position. "Not all that dangerous, huh?" Cinched the towel on his wrist. "Come home with us and take a look at the bullet holes in the brick from when those Russians come looking for you."

"It was Nick they came looking for. He's just a PI. I'm a real cop." Argument a breath away in any conversation with his parents lately. Especially the old man. "Hell, an average day, Drew's probably more likely to get bit by a dog than anything happen to me."

Ellen said, "I know Stan Napierkowski wants to give you a promotion. You could be deputy chief and take over when he retires. That's what he wants, you know."

Boy, did Doc know. "Stush is a good example of what I'm talking about. How long's he been a cop? Going on forty years. Not a mark on him."

Tom rubbed a drop of blood from one shoe with the other. "That's because he took a desk job after that shootout at the bank."

"No offense to Stush, but that wasn't much of a shootout. Way I heard it he was there when the guy came out. Got the drop on him, gave him the old, 'Police, drop your weapon.' Guy pulled a gun and fired too soon. Shot a hole in the sidewalk."

"You ever seen the bullet holes in the bank?"

"The one bullet hole, you mean? Sure. Stush saw the gun and fired one round. He missed and the guy surrendered."

"You have all the answers. You must've been there. Funny I don't remember that, you three years old and not getting around much on your own."

Doc kept his voice flat. "I got the story from the guy who was there."

Tom made a face. Raised his hand to eye level. A slow stream of blood trickled down his arm. "You know how Stush is. Never pumps himself up. Goddamn this hurts." Squeezed the bloody towel and recoiled. "Son of a bitch."

Doc halfway to his feet when Tom got up. He didn't look well. "I'll do it. It's my goddamn thumb." Doc let him go. Stayed handy.

Tom made his way to the desk without incident. Stood quietly while the woman worked. "Excuse me," he said when opportunity presented. "I wonder if someone could take a look at this thumb. I've been here a while and it's bleeding pretty good." Held up the sodden towel for her to see.

"Sir." She didn't look up until after she said it. "Mr. Dougherty, we'll get to you, I promise. We have to see people in the order of the severity and urgency of their conditions."

Tom held his hand over her workstation. Blood trickled out of the towel to fall on her desk. "I'm no doctor, but this feels pretty urgent and severe to me."

"Sir, I understand you're in pain, but you have to understand we have a dead man back there."

"Well, goddamn, woman," Tom said. "I gotta be ahead of him." Then he passed out. Doc eased his father to the floor, put his coat under Tom's feet to elevate them. Held the bloody hand in his own to elevate it. Drew his badge with the other hand and held it so the nurse could see. "Do you think maybe it's severe and urgent enough to get you off your ass now?"

Two hours sitting in the waiting room with his mother before the doctor came out to talk to them about as much fun as a month in Iraq . Doctor looked a little like Peter Sellers playing the president in *Dr. Strangelove.* Identified himself as Dr. Yanchus as Doc and Ellen stood to shake his hand.

Yanchus pointed to Doc's forehead. "You missed a spot." Saw the confusion. "There's a little smear of blood above your right eye. Looks like you wiped the back of your hand across it before you washed up."

Doc looked up as if he'd be able to see. "Thanks." Licked two fingers and made a half-hearted effort.

"You did well to wrap him up and get him here as quickly as you did. He'll be fine. I'm sorry it took so long but fingers and thumbs are tricky. Lots of small muscles and nerves and they all need to go in the right places."

"Can we see him?" Ellen had no trouble telling Doc the pieces of her mind she'd give to the doctor for leaving them without word for so long. Gave the woman behind the desk blue hell for making Tom pass out. Mild as a sloth on heroin when faced with an honest to God medical professional.

The doctor said they were giving Tom a unit of blood and he'd be a while and to go on back. Doc sent his mother on her way and asked if the doctor had a minute. "Since you fixed him up, can I assume you're an orthopedic surgeon?" He could. "Can I steal a few minutes of your time for some unofficial police business? It's important."

Yanchus tried to disguise his eagerness at a chance to contribute to an investigation. Doc led him to a place they wouldn't be overheard. Neuschwander answered on the first ring. "Noosh?

You still in the office?...Yeah he's fine. Doctor here got him all stitched up...Thanks, I'll tell him. Listen, you got that autopsy report handy? The one that talks about Michael Stoltz's shoulder?" Saw the doctor's posture straighten half an inch when he heard Stoltz's name. "I got a no shit orthopedic surgeon here. A good one. I'm going to put you on speaker. Read what you have to him so we can see what he thinks."

Yanchus listened with the face of a person drawing a picture in his mind. Turned to Doc when Neuschwander finished. "Show me the angle he's talking about." Doc contorted his hand and arm. "How far away was the muzzle?"

"Six to ten inches, give or take."

Yanchus pulled a device out of his white coat's pocket. Placed one end against Doc's head and positioned Doc's gun hand at the other. "That's about seven inches. How's your shoulder feel?"

"Awkward."

"Uh-huh." Yanchus put the implement back in his pocket. "How much does this gun weigh?"

Neuschwander hadn't been wasting his time. "Forty-seven and a half ounces with three rounds fired."

Yanchus tucked his lower lip behind his top teeth. Shook his head. "I don't see any way a man with the injury described held a gun of that size in that position. Especially not and have the finger strength to pull the trigger. Now he could do this." Made a gun of his own fingers, pointed it under his chin. Looked at Doc as he spoke. "Or this." Put the "gun" in his ear. "Even this." An inch above the ear, angled upward. "But not the way you're describing it."

Dead silence in the alcove where Doc and Yanchus stood. "You get that, Noosh?" Doc said.

"Enough."

"Go ahead and tell Stush. I'll be there soon as I can." Rang off and faced the doctor. "I need one more favor. You can't say anything about this to anyone. No one."

CHAPTER 32

Doc returned to the office to find a message from Stush to gather all the detectives and meet in his office. McFetridge came along.

Stush waved everyone in. Asked Doc to close the door. "Well, as the man said in the movie, 'Now what the fuck are we supposed to do?' I'm open to suggestions." A look in McFetridge's direction. "From anyone. So long as we all understand nothing we say here leaves this room except on a need to know basis. We're looking for a mean son of a bitch who thinks he's clever. We're going to show this cocksucker he's not as smart as he thinks."

The room quieter than the absence of sound. This was a Stush no one had seen. Not even Doc could remember this tone of voice or facial expression. Stanley Chester Napierkowski, Uncle Stush, had a gear he hadn't shown before.

No one wanted to go first. Finally McFetridge spoke up. "What do we know for sure?"

Doc almost smiled on "we." Cop bonding. The Mountie's case as much as theirs now. There'd be beer for him after this. "What we know for sure is that a man approximately the same size as Michael Stoltz and dressed in a very similar manner came into Dale's Discount and shot three people with the M1911A1 Army Colt Pistol we found in Michael Stoltz's car."

"Did Stoltz have residue on his hands?"

"He did, but he'd been at the range right before."

More silence. Neuschwander said, "Is it possible Stoltz did shoot the people in Dale's?"

"And someone else shot him?" Doc said. Neuschwander arched an eyebrow.

Stush decided to steer. "I think it's unlikely, but we can't dismiss it out of hand, so let's break it down. What evidence do we have that says it couldn't happen that way?"

The silence half as long as the one before when Doc said, "This won't show it couldn't happen that way, but what about the blood on the passenger side door? The Happy Vigilante swears he winged the shooter." Doc refusing to speak Chuck Simon's name since Sally Gwynn released him on his own recognizance for discharging a weapon inside the city limits. "Stoltz has no wounds except the fatal. Someone bled on that door. It's logical to assume it's the shooter."

Stush: "We know the blood on the car door isn't Stoltz's. How do we know it hasn't been there a while?"

Neuschwander already shaking his head. "The car was immaculate. I can't prove it with receipts, but I'd guess it had been washed within a day or two."

Shimp: "Didn't it rain the night before?"

Doc: "Did he park it outdoors?"

Neuschwander made a note. "I'll find out."

McFetridge asked how they knew the blood on the door wasn't Stoltz's.

Stush gave a confused expression. Looked to Doc and Neuschwander before he remembered. "That's right. You weren't here this morning. Blood work came back. Different type." McFetridge nodded.

Doc faced the Mountie. "We know now that Stoltz couldn't have held the gun at the angle and distance needed to shoot himself the way it happened. The autopsy strongly implied that and we verified with an orthopedic surgeon a little while ago."

McFetridge started slow, showing both confidence and deference. "No offense to your theory, Detective Neuschwander—"

"None taken. I thought it up the second I said it."

"The chief's right, we shouldn't discard it, but I'd like to set it aside for a minute. It requires us to believe Stoltz walked into the store, shot those people, ran out, got in the car, either gave the gun to someone else or had it taken from him, and this other person leaned in through the passenger window, shot Stoltz, and left a spot of his own blood on the door. That's a lot."

"No argument from me. I was thinking out loud."

More silence while everyone waited for someone else to go first. Stush was chief. "So. What it looks like—going with what we know to be true—is someone, as Benny said, wearing about the same clothes who's about the same size as Stoltz walks in, kills three people, and runs out when he meets resistance. Moving ahead a little, still consistent with the evidence, this mystery person goes to Stoltz's car and shoots him with his own gun. Leaves the weapon behind."

Doc nodded. "That answers most of our questions. It also explains the open car window. Guy runs out, taps on the glass or yells or something and Stoltz winds it down."

Neuschwander: "That accounts for the blood on the door if Simon did wing him."

Shimp: "If the shooter was hit in the store, where's the trail of blood to the car?"

General thought. Doc's voice gained confidence as he went. "Even Simon says he winged him, at best. So he's got a heavy coat on, grabs his arm and squeezes while he runs away. Let's go long enough to shoot Stoltz and leave a drop on the car."

"What then?" Shimp said. "There's no blood trail leaving the car, either. No blood in the parking lot at all."

Doc started to speak, came up short. Sat forward massaging his lower lip between a thumb and finger. Felt the realization creep downward through his head into his stomach. "Fuck me. Fuck us all. He sees the drop on the car and grabs the arm again. There's no other blood and we never saw him because he has another car stashed right next to Michael Stoltz's. He had the whole thing set up."

"Stoltz is an accomplice?" Stush said.

"Doesn't have to be. The clothes Stoltz wore are close enough to what we saw on the video to be the same. I can't say how he pulled it off, but what sticks out to me right now is what the parents said when Teresa and I talked to them. About how docile Michael was after the accident ten years ago. That's the word they used: docile."

Shimp leaned into the conversation. "They said he had trouble holding a job because he couldn't make up his mind to do things on his own. Once you told him to do something, he'd do it. Very conscientious, and as good as his word."

Doc tapped an index finger on Stush's desk as he spoke. "Someone he trusts asks him for a ride, he'd do it. Someone he trusts asks him to wait outside Dale's while he runs in for a few minutes, he'd do it."

"What about the gun?" Stush said.

"Ron Blewett told me Tuesday morning was Michael's regular day to come in to shoot. Our shooter knows Michael well enough, he knows that. Arranges to get together while Michael still has the gun on him."

Neuschwander wondered how the shooter got the gun in the first place. "He can't just ask for it, like, 'Hey, Mike, I gotta run into Dale's for a minute. Give me the gun.'"

Doc waved a hand in acceptance. "I haven't got that far yet. Except for how he gets the gun, everything else fits. Right?" No disagreement. "That leaves one other piece: the cameras. Luckiest sumbitch in the world, walking through a store with security cameras and never once showing his face, right? Fuck that. No one's that lucky. Someone who went to this level of effort would know there were cameras there."

"What was his plan, then?" Stush said.

"He knew where they were, and what they could see."

CHAPTER 33

"Detective Dougherty!"

Doc halfway across the parking lot when he heard. Turned and saw Katy Jackson trotting toward him. Said, "I'm kind of pressed for time, Ms. Jackson. Can this wait?"

"This will just take a minute. Can we get together later to go over the Dale's case? I don't want to be a nag but you promised me an exclusive if I held off."

"I can't comment on an ongoing investigation."

That brought her up short. "Am I missing something? It's been announced, all the outlets ran their stories. Your chief even said there wouldn't be any more pressers because there was nothing left to tell. Sounds like it's closed to me."

"It is and it isn't. We still have threads to tie off before the report can be filed. Nothing the media would care about but could matter in case of a lawsuit or new information coming to light."

"What kinds of threads? I mean, your chief announced the investigation was closed."

Doc shoved his hands in his pockets. Looked straight over Katy's head. "And it is, for all practical purposes. I don't want to be a jerk about this, but you're inexperienced. There are a lot of procedural requirements of a case like this. We're crossing Ts and dotting Is. Nothing you'd care about."

"Maybe I should be the judge of what I care about."

"Let's not make a First Amendment issue out of this, all right?"

"I'm not. All I want to do is ask a few questions about the case. Which you promised me you'd do."

"When it's closed."

"According to your boss, it's closed now."

Goddamnit. She wasn't going to let this go. "It is as far as the public is concerned. We're just making sure all the boxes are checked, is all."

"What you're saying, then, is that nothing is going to change. Based on what you're continuing to look at. This filling in of boxes."

Doc almost said she was right. Shut her up and get rid of her for the time being. Knew lying was a bad idea. Not that he never lied. He'd lie to a suspect in a heartbeat if the situation called for it. He also knew better than to lie when the truth might turn up, and this truth would turn up. He also remembered a line about how it never paid to make enemies of people who bought ink by the barrel. Katy Jackson was a glorified stringer, but these guys talked to each other and reputations stuck. There was also no telling who she'd turn out to be. Megyn Kelly hadn't always been Megyn Kelly.

"Off the record. Not on background. Not on deep background. Not for attribution. This conversation never happened. You okay with that?" She nodded. "I can't say for a certainty that nothing will change. That's already more than I should tell you, but I don't want to lie to you. You burn me and I'll ruin you with cops all over Western Pennsylvania. Understood?"

"Understood. Thanks." She made no move to leave.

"What?"

"Nothing. Well...I guess I never thought much about what it must be like. To have to deal with something like this from your side. You saw all the bodies, didn't you? I mean in the place."

"Not the first bodies I've seen."

"Did you do the death notifications?"

"Just Michael Stoltz. Another detective drew the rest of them. You're looking for a human interest story, talk to her. She had a genuinely shitty day. Anything else?"

Katy folded shut her notebook. "No. I guess not. Thanks for your time." Hesitated. "Detective Dougherty?"

Jesus Christ. Doc wanted to get moving. "Yes?"

"I appreciate your patience. With me, I mean. I really do."

"We all have jobs. I have to go now."

CHAPTER 34

First time Doc saw Barb Smith—Gaydac now—since she left the force. They almost sorta kinda dated when they worked together until a disagreement made them both realize dating another cop on the same small force didn't bode well for continued harmony, either on- or off-duty. They remained friendly but fell into the great expanse of acquaintances everyone has: people I used to know.

Barb worked as a supervisor for Commercial Security, Inc. Now people in uniform answered to her. She offered Doc coffee and they took the obligatory couple of minutes creaming and sugaring and stirring and making banal conversation until each could give full attention to the other, as though diluting coffee required the concentration of a high iron construction worker. Doc hated small talk. Appreciated the social lubricant provided by Barb's pregnancy.

She took the first sip and opened the door for business. "Did those videos we sent over help any?"

Doc half smiled. "You have no idea. Listen, what I have to tell you today can't leave this room. Even if you have to get some help on your end, I need you to say it's police business. Nothing about why we want it."

"As much as I can. We may need to check with Legal, depending on what it is."

"Fair enough." Doc tasted his coffee. Better than the cop shop, not as good as Cabrileo's on Tarentum Bridge Road. "Michael Stoltz didn't do it."

Barb's jaw dropped, not enough to open her mouth. "How'd you clear him?"

"We're keeping that very close. The last thing I want is for the guy who really did shoot those people to find out he's not in the clear anymore."

"I'll bet. What do you need from us?"

"I need the names of everyone who worked on the cameras at Dale's since they were put in."

Took Barb a few seconds to decipher the implications. "You think one of our guys did this?"

"Let's just say it's something we need to look into."

Barb showed obvious discomfort. Doc doubted it was baby-related. "I don't have any serious objections. I am going to have to get someone above me to sign off."

"We're not looking for anything personal. Right now all we need to know is who worked on those cameras, and what those people's work schedules were last Tuesday."

"The cameras went in before I started here, so I'd have to check to see when they were installed. I know for a fact not everyone who's worked on them is still here."

"I never thought they would be. We'll clear whoever we can with what you have. The rest we'll run down ourselves."

Barb aimed unfocused eyes at her blotter. "I still need someone to sign off. I don't have the authority to say that's okay." Reached for the phone. "It shouldn't take more than a day. They'll probably want something in writing, though."

Doc breathed. Took a folded document from an inside pocket. "This warrant gives me access to maintenance records that show anyone who's touched those cameras or viewed the videos, and what their work schedules were last week. I know your lawyers can make a stink about the personal stuff. I don't care about that now. Just who was working."

Barb still had the phone in her hand. "Why didn't you tell

me you had a warrant when you came in?"

"I wanted to give you a chance to consent."

"I still have to pass the word."

"Go right ahead. As soon as you set me up with the records."

She took him to an administrative assistant with a cube right outside the office. Kid was about nineteen years old, her first job out of school most likely. Doc kept one eye on Barb retreating to her office even as he explained that Claudia could tell no one what they were doing. "Opening yourself up to a possible obstruction of justice charge" was overkill. He used it anyway. Not only would it keep her from arguing today, it would give her cover should her conscience bother her later.

The phone call Barb started before she even sat down didn't appear to be going well. She kept her back to Doc, with occasional furtive glances over her shoulder. Body language implied a lack of understanding and compassion on the other end. She picked up the warrant and read from it. Waited, fingernails tapping on the phone. Hung up one degree short of slamming it down. Lowered her head an inch and shook it slowly. Took a breath and recovered her posture. Sat down and looked through the glass wall to the cube where Doc sat. He turned away, not quick enough to prevent one of the daggers she stared at him from pricking him on the cheek.

It took Claudia a few minutes to figure out how best to get what Doc needed. Once she did things went better than he'd expected. CSI was sensitive to the possibility of employees leveraging their positions to act as inside men. Claudia pulled up the records of who'd worked at Dale's, when they worked there, the purpose and work done on each visit, and who had access to the videos. Felt pretty good about herself until Doc said this was all well and good, what he really needed to know was who still worked here and what they did last week. Didn't narrow it down to the shooting's time frame in the faint hope Claudia might think he was there about something else.

Barb's door ajar a foot when he knocked on it two hours later.

He asked if she had a minute and she offered him a seat. "I hope I didn't get you in Dutch with your bosses. I'd've given you more time if I thought I had it."

"He'll get over it. You owe me a favor, though."

"Fair enough. The way you were standing during that call I'm half surprised a lawyer hasn't shown up already. Claudia's pretty sharp, by the way."

"She's a nice kid, too. I hope we can keep her, but she's working on an associate's at Penn State." Motioned for Doc to shut the door. "About the lawyers. I told my boss it was related to the Dale's shooting and we probably didn't want to do anything that looked uncooperative." Doc shot her a look. "I had to. I didn't say it was about a new suspect. I gave him some BS about procedure and reports. That got him worried you were looking for something the victims' families can use in wrongful death lawsuits."

"He hadn't thought of that already? Not that they'll win, but the families are going to sue everyone who ever drove past Dale's."

"I reminded him of that. I said that made it even more important for us to appear cooperative. I told him the warrant was carefully worded and there was nothing you asked for we wouldn't have to provide in discovery for a private lawsuit. He started to pull rank and I reminded him I used to be a cop and I know how search warrants work a little, too. Like I said, you owe me."

"I'm good for it. Mind if I ask a few more questions?"

"Go ahead. I now have detailed instructions of what I can and can't tell you."

Doc held up a sheaf of printed pages. "Four of the people who worked on Dale's system aren't here anymore. We'll set them aside. That leaves two who worked on Dale's setup at least once and were working Tuesday. Can you account for their whereabouts? I mean, can we prove they were where they were supposed to be?"

"No problem. Their vans all have GPS locators. We can pull up their ten-twenties going back since the system was put in. So long as they're in the van, of course."

"I doubt we'll need that level of detail. No one said anything about one of your vans being there that day so the GPS data should be enough to clear them. Now, there's one guy who was on vacation all week."

"Chris Hudak. He went skiing."

"Do you know where?"

"Uh-uh. Someone here probably does. I felt bad for him. He fell and hurt his shoulder. Had to cut the trip short."

"How bad's he hurt?"

"I asked if he wanted me to put him on light duty and he said no. You know, he might still be out there. He had some paperwork to do before he left for his calls today."

Barb stood to look. Doc put up a hand. "Leave him be. Just point him out if he's here."

She shook her head. "Doesn't matter. He's gone. You probably walked right past him. You want me to find out where he went last week?"

Doc didn't answer right away. Lost in thought about a man who knew the layout at Dale's and had a convenient arm injury. "Nah. Keep everything on the down low for now. You don't happen to remember which arm he hurt, do you?"

CHAPTER 35

Chris Hudak knew the guy was a cop the second he walked in the door. Half surprised they weren't here sooner. Had his story ready if any questions came up, though he'd prefer a few more days for his arm to heal.

Still couldn't quite believe his bad luck. Everything going to plan. Mike the Retard waiting for him in the car like Uber for hit men. Dumb fuck would've waited there all day and all night. Chris should have known something would go wrong when he walked to where Monica usually worked and found her and Cunningham together, making moony faces at each other like they were still in school, both of them on the clock. Those stupid looks nothing like the one on Cunningham's face when Chris blew the back of his head off with that old Army Colt. Monica stood there with her mouth hanging open so Chris could have uncapped a beer on her overbite, no idea what was going on. That woman to his left at least had the common sense to scream. Would have run if she had any brains. Might have saved her life. As it was she stood not five feet from Chris after he put a round through Monica's eye and he needed some collateral damage. Five or six had been the plan. Give the cops a hell of a mess to clean up and a convenient patsy waiting in the car for his own .45 caliber, 185-grain ticket punch.

But some asshole had to be a hero. Graduate of the Helen Keller School of Marksmanship, killing a woman he wasn't shooting at who stood farther away than the target. Pure dumb luck he hit Chris. Burned like a bastard going through the fleshy part of his upper arm. He knew it didn't hit bone or anything vital, but the heat. Like a fireplace poker shoved through the muscle. Must have nicked an artery, too, all the blood.

Chris should have taken care of him when he had the chance. Pissed now that he'd let the moment pass. Kill the Good Samaritan, then pick off a few more on his way out as they ran for the doors. Give the cops even more to look at, a confirmed shooter down. It was surprise that threw Chris off. Not fear. Asshole couldn't have hit him again with an AK-47 and a full banana mag. It was the surprise that did it. And the bleeding. What else could he do? He'd been shot. No, it wasn't fear that pushed him away. It was common sense.

Chris smiled a little to himself about how quick he'd recovered. Thinking to put the gun in his coat pocket while ice cream turned to shit all around him. Got out in a hurry, like he might be a victim himself, just in case he'd misjudged an angle and one of the cameras picked up his face. Squeezed his arm to put as much pressure as he could on it like they'd taught him in the Army. Hoped he didn't leave a trail out to the car. Glad now he'd worn the warmer coat, most of the blood soaking into the material and lining. Put it on as a compromise to Mikey Stoltz, who wanted them to be dressed alike when they went to the Penguins game only Chris knew they had no tickets for.

It wasn't fair, calling Mikey a retard. He was a stupid fuck, which was worse. The look on his face when Chris knocked on the window? Priceless. Rolled it down and leaned forward like he wanted to give the best angle to blow his brains all over the headliner.

Chris's arm throbbed as he turned the steering wheel for a left. The wound was healing. Not as fast as he wanted, and he had a bad feeling something wasn't knitting together the way it should. Still felt better than on the drive back to Pocono Springs. Arm hanging limp as a hot dog, blood dripping down the sleeve and onto the floor. That was what scared him more than anything, that someone would recognize him from the Walmart where he'd stopped for supplies to dress the wound. So far no one had. As far as he knew.

He'd check in with Barb Gaydac when he got back. Maybe even wait till morning, not to look too eager. Not too worried. CSI had a lot of local accounts. Cop might have been there about any of them. Still, might not be the worst idea to get a go bag ready. Just in case.

CHAPTER 36

Rick Neuschwander really was as neat as Doc wished he was after half an hour spent looking for a document he'd had in his hand ten minutes earlier. Rick's desk always showed order, no matter how much paper he stacked on it. Today he had printouts everywhere. Some clipped together, some carefully placed, some in piles. Post-Its of all sizes and colors. He leaned over the sprawl, sleeves rolled halfway up his forearm, tie hanging loose.

Doc waited to see how long it would take before Neuschwander noticed him. Got bored and said, "Doing your taxes already? And on the clock? Jeez, Rick."

"The victims' cell phone records are here."

Doc tossed his coat onto its hook from eight feet away. "You see anything good?"

Neuschwander kept his eyes on the paperwork. "If you mean nothing we didn't already know, then, yeah, it's pretty good. None of them ever called or texted any of the others except for Monica Albanese and Tim Cunningham, which we already knew because they were dating and their phones had the calls."

"You said just 'pretty' good."

"These records go back a year. I haven't looked at anything like all of them yet, but I have found one thing I didn't expect." Paused as if deciding how to phrase what came next.

Doc didn't want to wait. "And?"

"There's a number that Monica Albanese and Michael Stoltz both called and received calls from. Albanese and Stoltz never call each other, but they have this number in common. Then all of a sudden, no more calls from Monica. Then the number drops off Stoltz's list altogether about a month ago."

Doc forced himself not to be too excited. "You have a name that goes with that number yet?"

"Still looking for other connections."

Doc sat at his desk. Woke his computer. "What's the number?"

"724-814-3379."

Doc tapped keys. Clicked the mouse. "It's unassigned." Clicked and tapped some more. Felt the smile grow on its own. "I got you, you son of a bitch."

"Got who?"

"Christopher Hudak. 1126 Woodmont Avenue. He's our boy."

Neuschwander gave a skeptical look. "I'd say he's worth talking to, but this is nowhere near enough to do anything with."

Doc rotated his chair. "Hudak works at Commercial Security, the company that does Dale's cameras. He worked on Dale's setup. Went skiing last week, they're not sure where."

Neuschwander looked like he was afraid to get too hopeful. "There's more, isn't there?"

"He came back with an injured left arm. Said he hurt it skiing."

"So he was away. How's that help us?"

"It might not. It might just be a hell of a coincidence. What we need to know is where he went and to prove he went there."

"I don't follow you."

"If he went to Whistler or Vail or Bennington and we can prove it, he's clear." Doc took a second for effect. "What if he went to Seven Springs or Blue Knob? Hell, even Snowshoe. Checks into the hotel, makes a day trip back here to kill a few people, drives back to sleep in his paid for room. Weirder things have been done."

"Sure they have, but why would he do that? He has no motive to kill anyone."

Doc held up a finger to let the thought fully form. "How often were he and Monica Albanese talking before the calls stopped, what? Three months ago?"

Neuschwander looked at a printout. "Pretty regular. Almost every day there for a while."

"What about him and Michael Stoltz?"

More study. "Regular but not as frequent."

"When's the last call with Stoltz?"

"December twenty-ninth."

Doc looked at his computer screen. "Service disconnected December thirty-first. He switched up on the phone. Probably went to a burner. See if any numbers show up beginning of the year that weren't there before on Stoltz's record."

Neuschwander searched a stack. Took a page from it. Worked a ruler top to bottom line by line. Doc watched his eyes scan each entry and flick to a spreadsheet on the computer monitor. "412-314-2246."

"Any others?"

"Yeah, but that's the one. Frequency of the calls is about the same as before."

"It's him."

Neuschwander sat. "Okay. Let's say we found a connection. So what?"

"You don't see it?"

"I think I might. I want to hear it from you first."

"Hudak was dating Monica Albanese. Or at least wanted to. How far back do the calls between them go?"

"At least a year. That's all the records I have right now."

"Okay, so let's assume they were dating, or at least friendly. Then the calls stop three months ago."

Neuschwander shuffled pages. "A few came in to her phone from that number after that. None outgoing."

"So she broke it off." Neuschwander nodded. "Or something

like that. Now the calls between Stoltz and Hudak. They go right up until the contract ends, and start on the new phone right away. They're buddies. They spend time together." Doc leaned back in his chair. Tapped a pencil against his front teeth. "Hudak gets Stoltz to give him a ride to the shopping center. Or he meets him there. Either way. Meeting him there is easier."

"Why?"

"Because Hudak already has his car stashed for later." Gave time for disagreement. "However he does it, he gets Stoltz's gun."

"Whoa. No 'however.' How's he get Stoltz to give him the gun?"

"Doesn't matter. He does." Doc saw Neuschwander's expression. "It doesn't matter yet. We're still working up a scenario. Hudak gets the gun, shoots up Dale's, runs out—"

"Why's he shoot up Dale's?"

That brought Doc up short. "You don't see it?"

"See what?"

"This is all about Monica Albanese. People at work said she was dating the Cunningham victim. She dumped Chris for that loser Tim Cunningham. Chris couldn't just let that pass."

"Jesus, Doc. That's a hell of a leap."

"Is it consistent with the facts?"

"Yeah, but, still. Sally's going to need a motive."

"I hate to say it, but Willie Grabek's attitude might be just what we need here." Grabek a former Penns River detective who Stush once described as "sometimes wrong but never in doubt." Knew his stuff and broke a lot of cases, had little patience for detectives he considered not his equal, which was all of them. "Willie used to say motive wasn't his problem. He went where the facts led him. If it could still be more than one person, then he worried about motive. If only one person fit," Doc opened his hands, "Willie had his man. Fuck the motive.

"Right now we're going down a road that sure looks like it leads to Christopher Hudak's door. I know, I know. We have things to check, like where'd he go skiing? Credit card records should tell us that."

"What card's he use?" No note of challenge in Neuschwander's question. Why Doc enjoyed working with him. They had their rhythm down. Either slipped into Devil's advocate mode in a heartbeat.

"Three ways we can find out." Doc held up one finger. "Get a subpoena for his bank records. See who he pays, then subpoena them for the recent charges."

"Which bank?"

Brief pause. "CSI probably direct deposits his pay. Let's see where it goes. Barb Smith said I used up my favor but we also know they don't want us to let it out they dragged their feet on something like this, an employee using inside information to kill a bunch of innocent people."

"But if that's what happened they'll want to bury it altogether."

Doc deflated an inch. "Good point. Option two is a trash run. Let's find out what day his gets picked up and make an intercept."

Neuschwander sounded less than convinced. "I'll check on that, but...it's been a little while. What if we already missed it? Or what if there's no bank or credit card statements there? Say we do get the bank info and they take their time? What if the credit card company drags its feet? This could take weeks."

"Anyone ever tell you you're a real buzzkill?"

"Only you." Doc threw him the finger. "What's the third option?" Neuschwander said. "For finding out where he went."

Doc sat back. Tapped a thumb against the keyboard tray under his desk.

"We could just ask him."

"I thought we didn't want to spook him."

"We don't, but think about it. If we're right about this guy, look at all he's done to pull this off. If he's willing to kill all these other people just to get this chick he thinks did him dirt, he's not just a psycho. He's an arrogant prick. He thinks he's the smartest guy in the room and he knows he's smarter than a couple of jerkwater cops. He might jump at the chance to tell us. Especially if we appeal to his ego."

"What if he is smarter than we are?"

The smile climbed halfway up Doc's left cheek. "He's not. They never are. Watching a lot of Investigation Discovery doesn't make you a cop. There's something he hasn't thought of."

"What's that?"

"Don't know. I haven't thought of it, either. Yet."

CHAPTER 37

"Please sit down, Mr. Hudak. Can we get you anything? Coffee? Pop? Bottle of water?"

Chris Hudak not all that surprised the cops asked him in. Everyone who'd worked on the Dale's cameras received an invitation. Chris just happened to be first.

The cops didn't impress him much. The big one—Dougherty—projected an air of competence but not much authority. Deferred to Chris at every opportunity. Sorry to have to bring him down here, hoped it wasn't too much of an inconvenience. The other guy—New something—might as well have been a deaf mute for all the more he said.

Dougherty wasn't done kissing ass. "Let me start by thanking you for coming in."

Chris shrugged. Mister Humble. "I'm on the clock."

Dougherty chuckled. "That was nice of CSI. They've been more than cooperative. Anyhow, you understand this is informal. More procedural than anything else. Crossing Ts and dotting Is. That kind of stuff. You're not under arrest and you don't have to talk to us. Do you understand?"

"Don't you have to read me my rights?"

"No, sir. You're free to get up and leave whenever you want. If you were under arrest—what they call a custodial interrogation—then yes. Absolutely. This is what's called questioning. You can refuse to answer anything we ask and we have to stop any time you say so. Of course, nothing says I can't read them to you if you want me to."

"No. That's okay. You see it all the time on TV is all." Playing dumb, like he didn't know how this worked.

Dougherty leaned back in his chair. Looked like he might want to put his feet on the desk. Mister Cool. "That's because all the cops on TV are badasses. Breaking down hardened suspects. Leaning on them. Getting up in their faces trying to trick them into saying something they shouldn't. This isn't Chicago. This is Penns River. We'll even keep the door open if you want so there's no misunderstanding about you being able to leave." Neuschwander pretended to take notes but Chris saw he was only doodling.

"It's cool. It's just I've never been in a police station before."

"Kind of a disappointment, isn't it?"

Chris stifled a laugh. "Actually, it is a little."

"Think how we feel. We have to come in here every day. How long you been working at CSI?"

"About seven years."

"You like it?"

"It's okay. Gets boring after a while. This new equipment hardly ever breaks. The problem is, when it does break, it's usually a pain in the ass to fix."

"How so?"

"Some of the cameras are hard to get to. Last month a connector went bad and I had to trace the cabling through a crawl space that was a no shit crawl space, if you know what I mean. Fifty feet of it until I found the problem."

"I see how that would suck. You planning to make a career out of it?"

"I never really thought about it. I guess I better make up my mind before I get too old to learn to do anything else."

Dougherty made a dismissive gesture. "What are you? Thirty? You got plenty of time."

"How old are you?"

"Forty-one." Forty-one years old and this is where he was. Quite a career this cop had going. "Not to waste any more of your time, we have a few questions about the Dale's setup. You mind?"

"What do you want to know?"

"The camera deployment. You worked on that, right?"

"Just setting it up and maintenance. They have guys who design the layout. You know, how many cameras, where they go, where they're aimed." Guys who'd never secured anything more than their dick in their pants. Chris met some of them in training once. Not impressed at all.

The cop made a face. "Come on. You've done how many of these installations. Worked on lots more you didn't install. What do you think of Dale's setup?"

Chris tried to make it look like he was deciding whether to talk out of school. "This is just between us, right? I mean, I say something critical, it's not going to get back to my boss, is it?"

Dougherty tossed his pen on the desk. "I won't even take notes."

Chris took a deep breath. Not as nervous as he'd expected and having more fun. "There aren't enough cameras and what they have isn't top quality. They cover most of the places you should cover if that's all the more you're going to have, but there's too many holes. Their on-site guy—what's his name, Genovy—probably has less in-store apprehensions than any-place I cover. You ask me, a lot of that is he can't be bothered to get off his fat ass and work, but he pretty much has to catch them red-handed. He sees someone lift something and he has no way to be sure they didn't dump it when he lost sight."

"You mentioned the quality of the cameras."

"You can make up a little of what they're missing with some of these newer cameras. Broader fields of vision, better range, higher resolution. I'm guessing you looked at the video from the other day, right?" Both cops nodded. "You know what I mean, then. Can't see shit in tight, can you?"

"Not as much as we'd like, no."

They went back and forth another fifteen or twenty minutes. New something left the room. Came back. Dougherty asked a lot of bullshit questions. Fishing. Had no good idea what to ask, where to go with it. Chris a little disappointed in a way. Relieved, too. Careful as his planning had been, there was no way for him to know how much the cops had. Turned out they had Mikey Stoltz and paperwork and nothing else.

Dougherty looked at his watch. "Whoa. I'm sorry. I didn't mean to have you in here this long. You understand all we're doing is filling out reports. It's the cop's burden. This one's a slam dunk. A tragedy, but damn...I mean, the killer's in the car with the gun. The file's still gonna be this thick." Held a thumb and index finger as far apart as he could get them. "Procedure." The cop moved papers around the desk. "Yeah. One last thing and we're done here. We have to account for the whereabouts of everyone with access to the security system. The prosecutor insists. Why she insists...who knows. It's not like there's gonna be a trial. Anyway, everyone who worked that day can be accounted for. You were on vacation. Skiing, right?"

Chris was having a ball with this asshole. "Yeah."

"Where'd you go?"

"Pocono Springs. Off of eighty about forty-five minutes or an hour from Wilkes-Barre."

Dougherty made a note. "How'd you like it? I got some time off coming and thought I might do some skiing myself."

"It's nice. Seven Springs is closer but I run up there on weekends when I get a chance. It's been going downhill since that douchebag owns the Pirates bought it, anyway. Thought I'd try someplace different. I liked it."

"How's your arm?"

That got Chris's attention. "My arm?"

"I heard you fell and jacked up your shoulder."

"Oh, that. Still sore. I tend to sleep on that side so every morning it's stiff as a bitch."

* * *

"Where'd you put the GPS?" Doc asked Neuschwander.

"Passenger side rear wheel well. He keeps the extra key in the driver's side front. I thought about using the key and putting it inside but didn't know if the warrant covered access."

"That'll be fine." Doc read from his computer screen. "Looks like four, four and a half hours to Pocono Springs from here. I hope the weather's good tomorrow. Right now I gotta run."

CHAPTER 38

"You're a hard man to get ahold of," Delonte Bickerstaff said.

He didn't seem too put out. Didn't seem all that happy either, that it took Doc six messages to get back to him. Doc reminded him he had returned two of the calls. "You weren't here."

"Here" was the Penns River Youth and Community Center. Doc and Bickerstaff sat in a multipurpose room. Twenty school-style chair-desks spread randomly across the floor. Old-style blackboard on one wall. A dry-erase board with multihued remnants of drawings and lists on the other.

"This is the closest thing I have to a permanent residence right now. I volunteered like you suggested and they took me up on it. I can shower and use the phone within reason. Said I can sleep in one of the empty offices for the time being if I need to."

"So they trust you already."

Bickerstaff gestured around the room. "You see much here worth stealing?"

Doc didn't have time to engage in one of Bickerstaff's ball-breaking sessions. "Now that I'm here, what can I do for you?"

"Just like a cop, thinking anyone who calls must want something. Did it ever occur to you I might want to do something for you?"

"Not really. I mean, you never have before." Doc winked.

"This how you treat all your confidential informants?"

"Is that what you are now? A confidential informant?"

"It sounds a lot better than snitch." Doc nodded. Left time for Bickerstaff to continue on his own. "You know I'm still clean, right? That don't mean I don't remember what drug-related activity looks like. That Faison boy been the closest thing we have to a real player here since them others got shot up in the religious mall last year. Player's a good word for him, too. That's all he really does is play at it. I'll give him credit, though. He does keep his shit off the streets."

"How's he do it? I'm not looking to put together a raid. At least not yet. I'm just curious. Most people think those murders took care of the drug situation here."

"You don't, do you?"

"Give me some credit. Putting the suppliers down doesn't mean demand disappears. Someone would step up. We caught everyone involved in the shooting, which is good. Wouldn't want people thinking all they had to do to take over was wipe out the competition."

"Caught or killed, you mean."

"Okay. Caught or killed. It should be pointed out we did kill the right guy, and barely before he would've shot me."

"I'm not saying he didn't need to go. Not everyone involved went to jail, is all."

Doc considered that too fine a distinction to argue. "So how does Wilver Faison run a drug business and keep it off the streets?"

"Nothing new or clever. He has some indoor locations he uses. Moves them around so no one gets too suspicious."

"How do his customers know where to go?"

Bickerstaff looked disappointed. "How much ground we talking about here? Square mile? Mile and a half? Any junkie worthy of the name should be able to smell his drug of choice at that distance."

Doc waited for more. Didn't get it. Said, "You didn't just figure this out, which must mean you're okay with it. Frankly—off the record—I am, too. I have no delusions we can get rid of drugs. So long as citizens are safe in their possessions and person and bodies don't start showing up on corners, I prefer to spend my time catching actual criminals. If they happen to be junkies... that's the best chance some of them have to get into a program."

"What if you had reason to believe that was about to change?"

"Then I'd want to know about it."

"That's why I been calling you. There's a new crew in town. Selling in the open and acting like they don't give a shit who knows it."

"You're the second person to mention that. You're sure they're not Faison's boys?"

"Drive out of here up Third or Fourth avenue to the old glass house and east as far as the tracks. You'll see them. Hard boys. Tell to look at them. Faison's crew, you see them doing something they shouldn't be, you tell them to move along. They may give you a little sass, but they do it while they're moving. Take one look at these newcomers and you know not to tell them shit."

Doc stared at the desk surface of his seat. TK had been there. K-Wash was a baggy-ass bitch. "You think it's going to break bad?"

"Unless Faison and his crew melt away into the woodwork like little mice. And I don't see that happening now that they got a taste of money. It's not like they have a plethora of financial opportunities available to them down here."

Doc smiled internally at the thought of having the only semi-homeless snitch within hundreds of miles who knew how and when to use "plethora" in a sentence. Sat back in the chair as much as six-plus feet and two-hundred-plus pounds allowed. Laced his fingers on top of his head to assume a posture of thought and hoped one came to him. "I'll talk to Patrol. See can we send some cars down that way to at least give the street crews something to think about besides bumping ugly with Wilver Faison. I'd look into it more directly myself, but I'm tied up with another case." Saw the look on Bickerstaff's face. "I know.

It's what I can do right now. You'll keep an eye open for me?"

"You know I will. What if something happens that requires more immediate attention than you can give it?"

Doc hadn't thought this much since he shit the bed taking the college boards. "Call 911. Tell whoever answers you're working for Detective Dougherty and the code word is 'snowflake.' Give them a location and they'll scramble every available unit."

"They'll take my word for it? Some anonymous source calls it in?"

"They will once I tell them this is my CI's code word and I trust you. Just don't fuck me on this."

"Don't worry. I hate standing in line for shit."

CHAPTER 39

Veronica—Ronnie—Cavanaugh was every bit as hot as Eve said. Five-eight or nine by Doc's estimation. Chestnut hair, blue eyes, and built the way models were back in the days before popular taste decided hips were passé. Green turtleneck sweater as tight as it needed to be and long enough to flair over gray slacks. Low heels. A brush of freckles showed as she moved closer and into better light. A fine, fine Irish lass. Grandma Dougherty would have been proud of her Benny if she were still around. Maybe not so much about the whole bisexual angle. If Grandma knew what bisexual meant, rest her soul.

Eve handled the introductions. Ronnie had a comfortable confidence about her. More than Doc could say about himself. The hostess at Veltri's—who clearly knew Eve—took them to a center table at the glass wall overlooking the Allegheny. Best table in the house. Doc pointed to one still at the wall, but in the corner. Ronnie gave Eve a look. Eve mouthed, "Cop." The hostess moved them to the corner.

"Do you always sit with your back to the wall?" Ronnie said.

"When I can."

"Do you think we're in that much danger?"

"Not now." A wink.

Doc liked that she didn't ask if he was armed. Didn't seem to care about him being a cop at all. She was smart and funny and had a throaty laugh and a voice phone sex operators would have surgery to get. Doc understood right away why Eve thought she was a keeper.

Drinks served, food ordered, conversation moving to how Ronnie came to Western Pennsylvania from her native Massachusetts. Carnegie-Mellon or Pitt was Doc's guess. He was right both times. Bachelor's from CMU and an MD from Pitt. Gastroenterology.

The waitress stepped away after dropping off their salads and Doc saw something that made him put down his fork and dip his head in disgust. Eve asked what was wrong. "The table they were going to give us? Look who just sat there."

Eve and Ronnie turned in unison. "Who is it?" Ronnie said.

"Marian Widmer."

"That's Marian Widmer?" Eve said.

"Who's Marian Widmer?" Ronnie said.

"You tell her," Doc said to Eve. "If I get rolling we'll be here till closing and I'll ruin the evening."

Eve gave the CliffNotes version of Doc's relationship with Marian Widmer. Certain she was complicit in two murders and an attempt at a third. Beat one charge and the DA wouldn't prosecute the second without more evidence than Doc had. Ended by asking Doc, "Do you still carry her picture and the one victim's when you go out? In case someone recognizes them together?"

"Not since Stush asked me to stop."

Ronnie took another look. "She swings both ways, huh? You want me to get to know her a little? See if she tells me something she shouldn't?"

"NO!" Doc and Eve in unison, louder than either meant to.

Ronnie pretended to hide a smile. "You don't mind she's getting away with murder?"

"The two guys who actually did the work are off the board permanently," Doc said. "Both cases were cleared. That's more justice than we get a lot of the time."

Ronnie gave him a long look. "Still breaks your balls, though. Doesn't it?"

"Yeah. It does. What's worse is this is a small town. We bump into each other once in a while. Couple times a year, maybe. Let's see...bank, post office, gas station. Now here. It's like Moby Dick following Ahab around to taunt him."

"You think she does it on purpose?" Eve said.

Doc waved that away. "No. These are random. I stopped by the bank with another cop last time. I didn't even know I'd be there until five minutes before we went. Or tonight. The reservation's in Eve's name. No one but the three of us knew I'd be here."

Eve changed the subject. Salad eating resumed with talk about her current job. Ronnie had a funny colonoscopy story. Salads finished, she pushed back from the table and stood. Dropped her napkin on her chair. "I need to go to the ladies' room before dinner comes. I'll be right back."

Eve leaned across the table. Spoke in a whispered hiss. "Well? What do you think?"

"Did you tell her to go to the bathroom just so you could get a progress report?"

Eve kicked him under the table. Hard. "No. And tell me. She won't be long."

Doc looked over Eve's shoulder so she'd be sure to see him admiring Ronnie walking away, which was as impressive as he'd expected. About to reply when Ronnie stopped at Marian Widmer's table and leaned down to speak. "Oh, shit." Doc dropped his head and shielded his eyes with a hand.

"What?"

Doc pointed over Eve's shoulder with his free hand. Couldn't resist peeking through his fingers.

Neither Doc nor Eve could hear, but it was obvious Ronnie was reading Marian the Riot Act. Leaning in from the waist to a point only someone paying attention would consider confrontational while invading Marian's space. Marian looked up at her with a vacant expression. Ronnie said her piece and continued on to the rest room.

Marian stared straight ahead, stunned. Her eyes came to rest on Doc and Eve. Eve smiled and wiggled the fingers of one hand in a wave. Doc covered the lower part of his face to hide his amusement.

Ronnie had a parting shot for Marian on her way back to the table. Sat down as the food arrived. "This smells great. I'm starving."

Doc almost busted a gut waiting for the server to leave. "What did you say to her?"

"Who?" Ronnie took a bite of her chicken. Made a savoring face.

"The White Whale."

"Oh, her. She was with some guy who looked kind of—I don't know, what's the word?—small-handed?"

"That's Rance Doocy. He's Danny Hecker's man in Penns River. They're an item."

"Really? Well he looks like one of those guys who can only satisfy a woman with his wallet. Anyway, I said I noticed her looking over at our table and told her in no uncertain terms that I saw you first and that if she planned on going home with you after she got tired of being her date's beard she should think again. You and I have plans."

Eve choked. Spit a bit of pork chop into her napkin. Doc danced around a laugh. Figured he might as well hear it all. "What did you say on the way back?"

Ronnie cut off a piece of chicken. Displayed it on her fork. "This is really good. On the way back? You mean after I went to the bathroom? It occurred to me I might have been a little hard on her and maybe I should do something to make up. So I pointed out a spot her surgeon missed up by her eye. That's all."

* * *

198

They lay in bed together at Ronnie's place three-quarters of a mile from the Oakmont Country Club. Doc on his back. Ronnie rolled over to squish a still-hard nipple between them. "It happens. Trust me. I'm a doctor."

Doc stared at the ceiling. "I don't think that's it."

Ronnie nuzzled his ear. "You don't think I'm attractive?"

"It's definitely not that. It's just…when I went down on you. I couldn't help but think of you with Eve. It killed it for me."

Ronnie rose up partway. Breast still pressed between them, her face in position to give him a hard look. The seduction left her voice. "I thought you'd be a little more open-minded than that. You knew why we got together for dinner."

"It's not that, either. Eve's been my friend since we were in elementary school. Third grade, I think. My only sibling's a brother so she's the closest thing to a sister I ever had. I get busy with you, think of her naked…it's weird."

Ronnie rolled to put an arm around him. Laid her head on his chest. He felt her smile. "Honest to God? That's it?"

"Who would make that up?"

She kissed his sternum. "Well now I'm really disappointed. I like you, Dougherty. You're smart, you're funny, and you got some size on you. I can see why you and Eve are so close. You're a sweet man."

They lay like that for a while. Doc not sure how he felt, how he should feel, or how he wanted to feel. All he was sure about was that Ronnie felt good there against him. Still no appropriate physical reaction.

"Is it hard for you? Being a cop?"

Her question caught him by surprise. "How do you mean?"

"It wouldn't have taken me three guesses to get to cop when I saw you, even if I didn't already know. I bet you're good at it. What I'm wondering about is that sweet man in here." Tapped his chest. "How does he handle the people you have to deal with?"

"It was tougher when I worked patrol." No problem talking

to her now, knowing they'd never be naked together again. "Then I used to roll up as things were happening or right after. Hear the kids crying. See the looks on the victims' faces. Now things have calmed down by the time I get there. I can put whatever energy I get from the victims into finding who did it. Those are the people I spend most of my time with, either researching or interviewing."

"You must get the wrong guy once in a while."

Doc flashed to Michael Stoltz. "Sure we do. Not as often as some people think, though. We're much more likely to get no one than the wrong one."

Ronnie rose to rest on an elbow. Supported her head with one hand to look at Doc. "You worry about it, though. Don't you? That you have the wrong guy."

"Sometimes. I have a rule for myself. Never ignore evidence just because it disagrees with the current theory. Something new comes in, consider it."

"Ever change your mind?"

"Once in a while. Understand, it's not like on cop shows. We're rarely desperate for clues. More often than not we're drowning in them. The hard part is to figure out which ones matter."

"Don't they all?"

Doc shifted to look more directly at her. "Say we lift a convicted felon's fingerprints off a windowsill. There's no easy way to know those prints aren't three weeks old and the guy left them working his new, straight job as a handyman. Weed through a metric shit ton of clues and follow the logical connections, there aren't usually a lot of suspects left. It really is like Sherlock Holmes said: After eliminating the impossible, whatever remains must be the truth. Doesn't matter how improbable or weird it seems."

Ronnie's eyes smiled. "You love being a cop, don't you?"

"The Army made me an MP and I realized I didn't want to do anything else. And that sooner or later I'd want to do it here."

"In my bedroom?"

Doc tickled under her breast. "Penns River, smartass."

Ronnie nestled her head against his shoulder. "You're soooo warm. Can you stay the night? I'm just so comfortable right now. I promise we won't do anything." Slid a hand down his belly. "Unless you want to."

"I have to get up early, is all," Doc said. "Long drive tomorrow."

CHAPTER 40

Sean Sisler on duty half an hour when the call came to see the woman on Paige Street. She looked to be mid-fifties with short steel-gray hair. A little extra weight, not unhealthily so. She met Sisler halfway up the walk, worrying a paper towel to bits. "It's my mother. My car wouldn't start and my brother had to leave for work and we figured she'd only be alone for a few minutes. Couldn't be more than twenty minutes after he left till I got here and now she's gone."

Sisler took out his pad. "Slow down for me. What's your name?"

"Me?" The woman on the brink of tears. "We need to find my mother."

"We will. First I need your name."

"Maureen Donnelly."

"What's your mother's name?"

"Rose. Rose Burke."

"Is this your mother's house?"

"No, it's—can we please look for her? She's been gone half an hour now, far as I know."

"This'll just take a minute. Whose house is it?"

"My brother, Pat. Patrick Burke."

"And your mother lives here?"

"He has an extra room. His kids are grown so she sleeps in one of their old rooms."

"Your brother. Is he married?"

"His wife passed a few years ago. She had the cancer."

"Your mother lives here with your brother and, what? You watch her during the day?"

"We take turns. I do a couple days, my sister Maggie does a couple, and our brother Mickey's wife Sharon does one while Pat works. Sometimes one of us comes over an evening so Pat can go out for a beer and some chicken wings if he wants to."

"Sounds like your mother's never alone."

Maureen tore the paper towel a few more times, wadding the pieces in her hands. "It's the Alzheimer's. She can't take care of herself no more."

"So this morning you were on your way over and had car trouble. Your brother had to leave, so your mother had a few minutes to herself. When you got here she was gone. Is that right?" Maureen nodded. "Where did you look?"

"He locked her in. We have a rule about not leaving the doors unlocked so she can't get out."

"Were the doors locked when you got here?"

Maureen nodded again. "I checked them all while I was looking for her."

"And you're sure she's not in the house."

"I looked in the yard and knocked on the neighbor's doors on both sides. They all know her and would've held onto her if they saw her out in this weather." Which was twenty-eight degrees when Sisler left the station forty minutes earlier. "Her boots and coat's still here. She can't have any more on than her housecoat and slippers."

"Any idea where she might've gone?"

"She barely knows where she is half the time, let alone where she's going." A look passed over Maureen's face. "I know. That's a terrible thing to say. It's true, though. Half the time when I come to see her, she don't know who I am. Fights me once in a while. Can you and me please look for her now?"

"We'll do better than that, Mrs. Donnelly." Sisler keyed the microphone on his shoulder.

Within five minutes every available unit was on Paige Street, including Neuschwander and Shimp. Even McFetridge pitched in. Said it was the least he could do, off-duty cops coming in on their own time to look for Rose Burke.

Should have been an easy job. How far could a ninety-three-year-old woman dressed in a housecoat and bedroom slippers get in wind chill of twenty degrees? "Just because she's old and demented don't mean she's not sneaky," Stush said to Sisler two hours later, standing on Pat Burke's porch while Sisler got some hot coffee in him. "She decided she wanted out and got around all those locked doors."

"Goddamn it. They know she's that bad. Why the fuck isn't she in a home or someplace?" Stush recognized the frustration and fear in Sisler's eyes as he scanned the yard in case they'd missed Rose Burke behind a trash can or a clump of dirt. "Cassidy House isn't a quarter mile from here."

Stush looked at the younger man. "Your grandparents still alive, Sean?"

"One set is."

"How they doing?"

"They're old, but they get around okay. Still living in the house."

"No mental issues?"

"They forget things. All old people do that."

"Do they forget where they are? Who you are?"

"If they did we'd get them some help."

"Look at this house."

Sisler looked, didn't see. "What about it?"

"It's neat, it's picked up. Needs some work, though. One gutter's hanging and I can see a couple loose shingles from here. Shutters need some paint and the garage door don't close all the way."

"I don't see your point."

"These people can't afford Cassidy. The whole family's mortgage payments don't add up to what that would cost in a month, especially with the Alzheimer's. They're doing the best they can, and it sounds like she's a handful."

"She's ninety-three years old, Stush. How much trouble can she be?"

"She got all us out here, didn't she?" Stush not sure Sisler saw the humor in his answer. "My grandmother was like this near the end. Spent the last five or six years not knowing where she was or who most of her family were. She knew my Aunt Ethel because Ethel stayed with her all day every day while the rest of us pitched in for household expenses. Wasn't much of a life for Et, but she did it."

Stush sipped coffee. Sisler was a good boy and Stush knew he had his attention now. "I remember one Thanksgiving. Mom and Dad had Grandma and Ethel down the house for dinner. Snowed off and on that week and the driveway was packed down and a little slick. Grandma was afraid and wouldn't get out of the car so my dad asked me to get her. I leaned in and unhooked her seatbelt. Talking to her, you know, set her at ease. Must've helped a little, because she quit fussing and looked right at me—right in my eyes, closer than we are now—and said, 'Wow. You're a big one.' Me, probably her favorite grandson. Knitted an Afghan extra-large special for me. Had no idea who I was and I'd seen her the weekend before."

"Honest to God? I mean, I've heard stories, but...she really didn't know you?"

Stush sipped again. Remembering. Deciding how much to tell. "You'd go to visit her and she wouldn't know where she was, sitting in the house she'd lived in over fifty years. Didn't know her own children. Swore she'd talked to Pap that day, him dead four years, pissed he wouldn't come out of the bathroom to say hello, here we are with company." The wind burned Stush's eyes so he wiped them. "One day I went up with my mom and for a few seconds—no more than that—she remembered

Mom. Not her name, though. Grandma looked at her and you could see the wheels turning and she smiled. Said, 'I know you. You're the one that lives with my Janusz.'"

Sisler stared across empty yards to the other side of Chester Drive. "Did anyone check that church?"

"Neuschwander's over there now with one of the deacons looking in every room." Stush drank from an empty cup. Thought of all the things he'd done, and hadn't. "That didn't mean Grandma didn't hop out of bed once or twice a year on a Monday morning ready to bake bread. She baked on Mondays since before any of her kids were born until she couldn't do it no more. Couple times there wasn't enough flour or yeast or whatever. Ethel'd call me at work and I'd run by Giant Eagle and bring what they needed. Usually by then Grandma'd forgot all about it. Or she'd get halfway in and not remember what came next. You could see her trying to think of it and she'd get so frustrated, knowing this was something she used to do all the time. She'd cry like a little girl, big fucking sobs. Get me going and I'd cry with her. Grown man, decorated police officer, standing there in uniform, bawling." Not all that far from it now.

"This family does what it can, Sean. What it can afford without ruining everyone's retirement. They're entitled to that, 'cause it ain't much of a life they have now. Let's go find their mother for them."

Sisler was a smart kid. He'd turned down a job with the State Police because they would have moved him to Scranton or Allentown, as far away from people he'd known as they could get him. His parents lived in Saxonburg, half an hour up the road past the racetrack at Lernerville, his mother losing her eyesight. Sisler took the Penns River job to guarantee he'd be close as she aged. "Jesus Christ, Stush. We're out there slipping and sliding and freezing and there's damn near twenty of us. Where the hell is she?"

Stush smiled. Police work showed him every day the complaints his friends at the VFW had about the "younger generation" were bullshit. "She could be in a woodpile back of the house if they had one. Thing is, they get out because they think they have someplace to be. She walks a ways, gets cold, forgets where she was going, and she gets scared. Now everything's a threat. She's too cold to stay out and can't find her way home. Afraid to ask for help. She'll hide. I doubt very much we'll find her walking down the street."

They didn't. Sisler discovered her forty-five minutes past the end of his shift, looking on his own time. Walking Paige Street with the sun low on the horizon, his unit needed for the next shift. Three doors up from where Rose Burke left her son Pat's house, she'd found a neighbor's car parked in a canvas garage, aluminum poles with material stretched over them. Car wasn't locked, which wasn't all that uncommon in this part of town this time of year. She must have crawled in to get out of the wind and cold and laid down on the back seat, which had to feel warm compared to outside. She looked asleep curled up with one hand under her head and her housecoat pulled tight. Sisler made himself think of her that way as he opened the door and reached in to shake her. Called her name but felt the cold through her pajamas and knew she couldn't hear him. Leaned in farther to feel for a pulse. Skin not as cold as the surrounding air, but closer to that than to Sisler's skin. He almost picked her up to carry her home—couldn't have weighed ninety pounds and her house was only three doors away, he could see it from here—then remembered this was officially a crime scene. Radio turned in with his unit, pulled his cell from his pocket. "This is Sisler. I'm requesting an ambulance at...I think it's 2584 Paige Street. Tell them they'll see me."

"Ten-four, Sean." A pause. "Is it..."

"Yeah," Sisler said before the name went out over the air. Blew air through his nose. Watched the silvery white cloud evaporate. "Yeah. Patch me through to Stush when you're done. He said to let him know right away."

CHAPTER 41

Long day for Doc, Penns River to Pocono Springs and back. Drive up was okay, PA-28 to I-80 which went damn near right past the place. The number of staff was impressive, how many people it took to make things seem to happen by themselves. Manager couldn't have been more helpful until Doc asked to see the key audit logs for Chris Hudak's room. Doc stepped past any privacy concerns by mentioning the solution was for him to drive back to Penns River, get a court order, then drive it right back up here, by which time he wouldn't be nearly as cheery or patient as he was now. Armed with Hudak's comings and goings, talking to Housekeeping and the wait staff told Doc more than he'd expected. Felt jazzed on the way home until it started to snow in Brookville, coming down like a bastard by the time he got to New Bethlehem then all the way to Penns River. At least six inches in his parking space at home and he cleaned another three off the car to come to work that morning. Pulling into the parking lot at the station when he remembered it was his day to bring doughnuts. Woe betide anyone who forgot his turn to "honor this venerable police tradition," as Stush put it. Started for Arnold's Bakery and saw the slippery mess on the hill leading into town and decided fuck it, went to Giant Eagle for two dozen Entenmann's.

Stush pretended to be disappointed when Doc brought him two chocolate iced. Everyone knew Arnold's had the best doughnuts this side of Oakmont. Stush had a weakness for store-bought Entenmann's. Preferred them even to Krispy Kreme, which no one but Doc understood.

"I see you couldn't bring yourself to drive a mile and a half for real doughnuts." Stush grabbed the two Doc offered before he could change his mind. "That's okay. I guess you drove enough yesterday. Worth the trip?"

"I think so. Let me get Rick and we'll start."

"I'll get him." Stush picked up his handset. Pushed two buttons. A phone rang down the hall. "Ricky? Benny's here. Grab yourself a couple doughnuts and some coffee and come on in. Hey, and Ricky? Bring one for me, would you?"

Stush had eaten both his doughnuts by the time Neuschwander got there and saw the chief with none and Doc with one and a half. "You good, Stush? I can get you another one."

Stush nodded toward Doc. Gave Neuschwander an exaggerated "good help is hard to get" expression, hands open, eyes upward. Doc shook his head. "No no no no no. Don't even do that. Sit down, Rick. I brought him two. He ate them already." Rick looked back to Stush, who raised his eyebrows and cocked his head. Worth a try.

A quorum gathered, everyone situated, Stush got the ball rolling. "What did you find out?"

"Christopher Hudak did, in fact, go skiing at Pocono Springs. Checked in the Saturday before the Dale's shooting. Checked out the Friday after." Doc paused. He could milk a story as well as the next guy. "How much time he actually spent there can be debated."

"How so?"

"I talked the hotel at the resort into letting me see the key audit logs, so I know every time anyone's keys accessed his room's door from the time he got there to the time he checked out. Doesn't tell us when he left the room, but it does tell us when he got back."

"And?"

Doc looked at his notes. "He checked in at 11:17 Saturday morning. The room wasn't ready yet so he went skiing. At least he picked up his lift ticket at 11:58. The next activity we can account for is entering the room at 5:24."

"So he did some skiing and packed it in for the day."

"Most likely. The next time the key opened the door was 11:48, though he did use his credit card in the restaurant at 7:01 and 11:42."

"Goes to dinner and has a few drinks. Anyone there able to identify him? In case he tries to claim someone else used his key and credit card."

"I showed his DMV photo to the wait staff and a bartender. It was him."

"They'll swear to it?"

"Yep."

Stush sat back, waved for Doc to continue. "Sunday and Monday he came into the room between 5:00 and 5:30, then again between 11:15 and 11:50. Same patterns with credit card receipts."

Neuschwander asked if Hudak ate lunch.

"If he did, he didn't charge it. They have like a pub down by the slopes. He could've eaten there and paid cash. It's what I would've done. In fact, I had lunch there myself. It's convenient and the food's good."

Stush noted Doc had lumped Sunday and Monday together. "What about Tuesday?"

"Ah. Tuesday." Doc flipped over a page in his notebook. "He used it twice on Tuesday. Once at 9:51 p.m., and again at 10:11." Left it to sink in.

"So..." Stush looked at Neuschwander. Asked Doc, "They have night skiing?"

"Lifts close an hour before sunset."

"So he doesn't clean up this time. Skis, goes straight to the restaurant, has a few drinks, and goes to his room. Steps out for ice. Maybe he got lucky."

"He didn't use his credit card in either the restaurant or the bar."

"She paid. Best kind of sex to have."

Doc happy to have Stush try to break down his case for him, keep him from missing anything. "Okay, though I should mention no one saw him with anybody in the restaurant or the bar."

Neuschwander suggested Hudak ate somewhere else that day.

"He could have. Now that we know what credit card he used we can get a court order to see did he spend money someplace else on Tuesday."

"I'll get on it as soon as we're done here."

Doc waited fifteen seconds to see if Stush had a contribution. The window closed and Doc said, "Now it's Wednesday. He returns to the room at 9:07 a.m., 1:43, and 6:52."

Stush's eyes got that look all the kids liked so much when he played Santa at the Vets. "Did he eat?"

"Only credit card receipt is at 6:40."

Neuschwander: "Could've paid cash for breakfast and lunch like he did before, so he could stay close to the slopes."

Stush: "But he went back to the room."

"Doc said the food's good in the snack area. Maybe he preferred it."

"When you boys had him in here," Stush said, "when did he say he fell and hurt his arm?"

"I didn't ask," Doc said. "Didn't want to spook him."

Stush's nod more acknowledgement than agreement. "What about Thursday?"

"Pretty much the same as Wednesday."

"He use his lift ticket?"

Doc shook his head. "They don't track when the tickets are used. Just when they're purchased."

"Friday," Stush said.

"Checked out at 9:25 a.m."

Neuschwander said, "We knew he hurt his arm and left early."

Stush: "And it looks like he hurt it on Tuesday. The missing time could've been him getting it looked at."

Doc: "Could be, though no one I talked to remembered him asking for medical assistance, and they log that stuff for liability reasons."

Neuschwander: "So the big question is, how'd he hurt it?"

"Any ideas on that, Benny?" Stush said.

"I might." Doc flipped pages. "I found the maid who did up his room on Wednesday and Thursday. Or would have if the Do Not Disturb sign hadn't been up." Neuschwander a little skeptical she remembered that room specifically. "Key audit verified her story. Only Hudak's key opened the door those two days."

Stush said, "Maybe he was in pain from the fall and wanted to be left alone." He didn't really mean it.

"I don't doubt he was in pain," Doc said. "She got into the room on Friday." Stopped so they'd have to ask.

Stush played along. "And she found…"

"He must've had things on his mind. The trash can in the bathroom had no plastic liner but he left behind a plastic Walmart bag. She looked inside before she threw it away in case it was something he'd want to have returned. The contents stuck in her mind."

"Are you going to make us pull every goddamn piece of this out of you?" Stush said.

"Bag had gauze, adhesive tape, purified water, and salt."

"No receipt?" Neuschwander said.

"Nope. Could have come from any Walmart. He could even have brought the bag up with him when he checked in."

Stush spoke as much to himself as to the room at large. "Gauze, adhesive tape, purified water, and salt."

"Yeah." Doc's smile started. He knew what was coming.

"This guy. Hudak. He ever in the military?"

"Regular Army."

"What MOS?"

"Eleven Bravo."

Stush and Doc locked eyes. Two cats who'd eaten the juiciest canaries in the pet store.

Neuschwander the one with no military experience. "What's an Eleven Bravo?"

"Infantry," Doc said.

"So?"

Stush took pity on Neuschwander. "All that stuff the maid found in his room? He was field dressing a wound. He took the trash can liner so no one would see the bloody gauze. Must've forgot the Walmart bag." To Doc: "Start typing the affidavit. I want a warrant by the end of the day so you can organize your team to pick him up first thing in the morning."

CHAPTER 42

The affidavit typed and sitting on his desk waiting for the judge to come back from lunch, Doc met Drew at Crouse's. Drew had a turkey club, Doc a bacon cheeseburger. Drew slid a folded-over letter-sized envelope across the table.

Doc stopped eating. Glared. "Could you make it look any more like a payoff? Maybe I should get up to go to the bathroom and you put it under my plate and leave when you see me coming."

"Blow me. You break my balls on a daily basis. I get to have some fun, too."

Doc opened the envelope. Two tickets for that night's Penguins-Maple Leafs game. Gave them a long look. Conjured a seating chart in his head. "These are right behind the net three rows back."

"A little to one side, but yeah. Nice seats."

"And you can't go?"

"Bobby got them from a guy he did some work for." Bobby D'Alessio a well-regarded contractor. Even Eve raved about his work, and they were direct competitors. "He's sick as a dog and just wants to spend the night in bed. I was gonna see if you wanted to go with me but I still got the extra bathroom half tore up. I remembered you mentioned about that Canadian cop and figured some hockey might make him less homesick."

Doc reached for his wallet. "What do I owe you?"

Drew waved him off. "Bobby says he got them for free."

"You sure Bobby got them for free? It's not like he might not pay for them and tell you he got them free so you wouldn't think it was a gift." Face value of the tickets was two hundred nineteen dollars. Each.

"I can see him doing that, but he has connections, too. Here's the thing: I went to his house to pick them up and asked him specifically if he was sure these were free, since I wasn't going, either. I didn't say I was giving them to you, just that I had someone who'd probably take them. He said fine, so long as they went to a good home. So, if he did pay for them, well, I'm not gonna kiss his ass to take money he doesn't want."

Doc shrugged. Replaced his wallet and tucked the envelope into a coat pocket. "I'll call and thank him. After the game."

Drew laughed, one exhalation. "Yeah, I'd wait. He's still pissing and moaning about those motherfucker fines you kept track of at the party."

Doc's turn to laugh. "I never met a guy willing to double down on a mistake as much as Bobby."

"It's a gift." Drew drank some water. "It's funny. The reason I thought of you is that Mountie."

"Me being your only brother—your only sibling—wasn't enough?"

Drew made a point of extending his middle finger to push a stray bit of lettuce into his mouth. Chewed to one side. "Not five minutes after Bobby called, I delivered a parcel from Canada. Don't the Pens have someone from Sorel, Quebec?"

"Not anymore. That's Fleury's hometown."

"I hope they didn't make a mistake letting him go. Anyway, the return address was Sorel." Drew looked at his watch. "Gotta go. I only get half an hour for lunch. Big Brother is watching."

"I'm not going to say anything if you're late."

"Not my big brother, dumbass. The Big Brother. Have fun tonight."

CHAPTER 43

PPG Paints Arena open six or seven years now, still had the new arena smell. Doc old enough to remember its predecessor from before Mellon Bank bought the naming rights. Missed the distinctive atmosphere of the old Igloo, in its day the largest retractable dome in the world. Cramped concourses and jammed-up entry gates, and the food and rest facilities weren't quick to get into or out of, but the space overhead in the seating area made it obvious where you were. No place in the world had the internal ambiance of the Civic Arena.

He and McFetridge sat in Section 108, Row 3, third and fourth seats in from the aisle. Less than ten feet from being directly behind the net the Pens would shoot at twice. Good looks in the corner and as the lanes formed on breakouts. Bobby D'Alessio didn't just know somebody. He knew somebody with juice.

"Good seats. Nice building." McFetridge gave the arena a lookover. "You ever been to the Air Canada Centre?" Doc hadn't. "The Hangar's nice, but it's hard to tell them apart if you can't see the marking on the ice or the banners. My dad used to take me to games at Maple Leaf Gardens. That was a place to watch hockey. Had the problems I guess all the old buildings had, but, man, it was Maple Leaf Gardens. He took me to a game at the Forum in Montreal once, too. Amazing. All the championships and the history. The announcements in French.

I still have the program. Borje Salming and Mike Palmateer signed it after the game. Two grown men waiting for them in twenty below weather. Celsius, yeah, but minus twenty is fucking cold."

They talked about hockey and being cops in the States versus Canada. Cops were pretty much cops and crooks were crooks. Biggest difference was in Canada the language conflict was English to French and in the States it was English to Spanish. Toronto the hardest place to work now, crooks and witnesses might speak anything from Thai to Ukrainian to Punjabi. McFetridge liked it. Kept him on his toes.

Five minutes before puck drop a man and a woman took the seats between Doc and the aisle. Good-looking woman. Very good-looking woman. Even better looking than Ronnie Cavanaugh, though a little thin for Doc's taste. Vaguely familiar, but she also had the air a lot of celebrities had and attractive women cultivated, so he didn't say anything.

The game started and the two cops left work at the station. Talked about their lives and hockey. Entertaining game held their attention. Both teams liked to skate and kept the pace up. Evenly played, both goalies sharp. Pittsburgh up 3-2 midway through the second period when Doc noticed a cameraman coming down the aisle. Figured he was there for a different angle close to the net until he recognized Penguins' announcer Dave Prentice with him. Prentice knelt next to the woman seated on the aisle. They chatted until a commercial break with 5:28 left in the period and the camera light went on.

"Thanks, guys. I'm here behind the Maple Leafs' goal with actress Ainsley Riordan, best known for her role in *Life and Death in Little Italy*. She's here in Pittsburgh shooting a movie with Ryan Gosling and Will Arnett and it turns out she knows quite a bit about hockey."

Doc turned to McFetridge. "Well, of course she looked familiar. The two greatest detectives in the world sit five feet from one of the ten most recognizable actresses in that same world and had no idea who she was."

"I knew she was hot," McFetridge said. "Does that count?"

Doc looked at Ainsley chatting with Prentice. The guy with her didn't look like muscle, but he wasn't obviously an actor, either. Certainly not Gosling or Arnett. Turned to McFetridge and cupped a hand so no one else could hear. "How many times you figure your boys jacked off to her?"

McFetridge stifled a laugh. "Probably none. They're in high school. She's old enough to be their mother. Almost." Chanced a quick peek in Ainsley's direction. "She is on my list, though."

"Your list?"

"You single guys don't need lists. My wife and I each have one. Five people we can sleep with and it's not considered cheating. We can't know them personally and they have to be famous. If I give you twenty bucks, will you take that guy out for a beer? I might never get another chance."

Later in the parking lot—Pens won 5-3—Doc smacked his forehead. "I'm an idiot. I'm so wrapped up in what's going on with the Dale's case I forgot to tell you how I got these tickets." Gave the quick and dirty story of Bobby's illness and Drew's bathroom. "My brother delivered a package from Canada and it reminded him I was working with a Mountie. Your boy Lelievre doesn't know anyone in Sorel, Quebec, does he?"

McFetridge did a miniscule double-take. Smiled. "Just his brother."

Don Kwiatkowski walked out of Fat Jimmy's with a nice buzz. Not drunk—not by his standards—feeling no pain and happy with the state of the world. Saw two guys leaning on his car and started that way.

"That's my car," he said.

The guys stood. Both tall, one the tallest white man Don had even seen in person. The older guy walked with some stiffness as they moved a few feet apart.

"You say this is your car?" the older one said.

"Yeah. You two jagovs looking to boost it or what?"

"We don't want nothing to do with this piece of shit. It's you we're looking for. We hear you don't like paying for things."

"I paid for everything I own. Retail, usually. Who says different?"

"You like to pay with other people's money, though, don't you?"

That set Don back a little. Reaching for a comeback, remembered something Larry told him. "Money belongs to whoever's pocket it's in."

"Or whoever's pocket you took it from." That was when Don noticed the younger guy had a gun.

CHAPTER 44

Jacques Lelievre watched the local news while he nursed a motel bathroom cup of Crown Royal. A revenue shortfall predicted for Allegheny County. The Turnpike Commission scheduled hearings to consider raising tolls. Pens beat Toronto 5-3. It was the breaking news that caught his attention.

"This just in from Neshannock County. An unidentified white male has been shot to death in the parking lot of Fat Jimmy's Lounge in the 1400 block of Greensburg Road in Penns River. Police have yet to release the victim's identity pending notification of next of kin. A Penns River spokesperson tells Channel 11 that the victim was shot twice, once in the chest and once in the head, execution style, and that police have no suspects at this time. Anyone with any information or who might have seen something at that location between nine thirty and eleven tonight is urged to contact Penns River Police, or call Crimesolvers at 888-555-5428. Stay tuned to the Eye Team for updates as we learn more."

Tabernac. Jacques didn't need a positive ID to know it was Don Kwiatkowski in that parking lot, and that robbing Chubbie's was what put him there. Strip clubs, porn shops, anything that involved the sex trade, almost always had some organized crime tie-in, whether it was from off-site prostitution or keeping the girls in drugs. Heroin or oxy for whores. Cocaine for strippers; meth skanked them out too fast.

Could be worse. At least the mob got to him before the police. No doubt Don would've turned on him faster than a windmill in a hurricane. True, he hadn't known where Jacques lived, only had the number for a burner phone, and didn't even know his real name. There were things he could've told them that might have kept Jacques moving faster and farther than he wanted.

Sylvain mailed the package last week. No telling how long to cross the border and Jacques must have missed a digit in the tracking number because the package he looked up was going to Connecticut. He drove past Mary Pugliese's house after she left for work. No parcel on the porch, which could mean she'd taken it inside or that her daily mail hadn't arrived yet. Don's shooting added to the urgency. Once the police identified Don—which they had already and just not made public—they'd come looking for the partner. Penns River was officially too hot to stay in.

He couldn't walk away from $70,000 American, either. Tomorrow Jacques would drive to Mary's again. She worked second shift, so she'd be gone around the time most people were coming home from work. Jacques would let himself in—she hadn't trusted him with a key but made no secret where she hid the extra, stupid salope—check the mail, check the house, and hope it was there. Couldn't remember her day off, had a plan for if she was home. "Baby, I'm back! I got the deal. Let's go out and celebrate. Get dressed and we'll go wherever you want." Wait for her to go in to change, take his parcel and not look back.

And if that happened and for some reason the money wasn't there yet? *Tabernac.*

CHAPTER 45

Busy day for Doc. Went to work early to get ready. Called Drew first, his brother always up by five thirty.

"I need a favor. If walking your route jogs your memory about which house got that parcel from Quebec yesterday, can you give me a call right away? Leave a message if you have to."

"Mary Pugliese, 2027 Leishman Avenue. She's usually home in the morning. I think she works evenings at Dale's or K-Mart or Altmeyer's or someplace."

"You know this off the top of your head? You two got something going on?"

"I've delivered her mail two hundred thirty days a year for the last six years. I sort it, bundle it, and personally walk it up to the house. You figure some things out."

Doc not yet over his amazement. "What does she look like?"

This at least made Drew think. No more than three seconds. "Short. I don't know, five feet or five-two maybe. Dark hair and eyes. Late thirties. Dark complexion."

"You ever think of going into burglary as a sideline? You know everything you need to and no thinks twice of mailmen coming and going from houses."

"Haven't you heard? We're so overpaid we don't need to steal. We should be leaving cash at people's houses, what they pay for postage now. Did you know stamps used to only be like three cents? Don't you ever wonder what happens to all that money?" Paused his rant to reset the tone. "How was the game last night? I caught most of the third period after I finished with the bathroom."

"You see Crosby score on that mid-air deflection?"

"About five minutes after I turned it on."

"Right in front of me. Best view in the building. Before I forget, the Mountie—McFetridge—wants to buy you a beer before he leaves town. Shit. That reminds me. That package you remembered might be the break he's been looking for in his case. Since you have such an encyclopedic memory, you wouldn't happen to know the name on the package, do you? Assuming it was sent care of Mary."

Drew made a sucking sound with his teeth. Doc imagined his brother's head lolling back, eyes rolling up. Then a part chuckle, part grunt that always accompanied a little smile. "Yeah. I do, actually. I wondered why this name stuck in my head, but I couldn't place it. Bob Gainey."

"Who's Bob Gainey?"

"You never heard of Bob Gainey? Forward for the Canadiens. Won like five cups and at least four Selke Awards. Helluva a hockey player."

"When? Before we were born?"

Short pause. "Nah...we were born. Still little shits, though."

"And you know so much about this guy, why?"

"He's one of the hundred greatest players. I looked him up. You know, on the internet. You should try it sometime. Imagine what you could learn."

"Imagine me giving you the finger. There's a steak in this for you if it pans out, you know."

"At a restaurant, okay? You can't grill for shit."

"Hyde Park good enough for you?"

"Wow, this guy must be a big deal."

* * *

Shimp wanted to go to Leishman Avenue right away. Doc had to piss on her oatmeal.

"First of all, you can't just go kick in the door. There are thousands of people in this town in Quebec. Could be from any of them. Second, you don't have anyone to go with you. Stush wants us to take down the Dale shooter first thing. Barb Gaydac's finding some bullshit task to keep him busy till we get there. We're leaving in the next five minutes."

"Who are you taking?"

"Me, Neuschwander, Sisler, Snyder, Burrows, and Augustine. You want to take a door with who's left, be my guest. It can't be McFetridge, though. All he's allowed to do is observe."

"If this is our guy and it is his package, how do we know this isn't what he's been sticking around for? What if he's gone already?"

"Then he's gone. Drew dropped it off yesterday morning. If Lelievre was waiting for it he's already twenty-four hours ahead of us. If not, then he's still there. Stake out the house and see who comes and goes. You and McFetridge know what he looks like. He comes out, pick him up. He goes in, sit on the house until some bodies free up."

Shimp looked ready to say something. Doc beat her to it. "I already talked to Stush. Four bodies trumps five robberies any day."

Doc collected his team in the rollcall room. "I don't really expect any trouble, not with us showing up with numbers in a space we can control. Still, everyone wears vests and checks weapons. Enter the building with your holster straps open."

"How're we doing it?" Sisler said.

"I'll go in with Rick—he's earned it—and you and...Burrows. Nancy, you and Augie watch the back. Any questions?" None. "Saddle up. We leave in five minutes."

Doc took Nancy Snyder by the elbow as they left the room.

"You okay with taking the back? I thought about sending Burrows out there with Augustine, but...well Augie's solid, but not the most authoritative presence. Kathy's good, but young. I want an experienced hand I trust back there."

"I don't mind watching the back. Really."

"You prefer Augie or Kathy? Sorry. I should've talked to you about this before."

"I'm fine with Augie. He's fun to pass the time with. Probably be good for Kathy to see how something like this goes down. Keep us in the loop, is all."

"Chris? You have a minute?"

Barb Gaydac gestured with her fingers for Chris Hudak to come to her office. Turned her back to pretend to look at something on the credenza behind her so he couldn't see her take a deep breath. Kept her hands solidly on the desk when she turned around to speak so Hudak wouldn't see them shake.

"I know it's not your favorite thing, but I need a second set of eyes on the Turnkey/Patrol/Surveillance reports. Can you take a look before I send them in?"

"Doesn't Libengood usually do that?"

"He has a doctor's appointment this morning." True, which was why she used this as her excuse. "I should've had him take a look yesterday but I forgot. Pick the call you least want to drive to today and I'll square it with them."

"Sure. I'll do them. I slept on that arm funny again, anyway. Be nice to stay inside where it's warm and let it loosen up."

Teresa Shimp shifted her butt to try to get comfortable. Allegedly heated, any warmth in this seat came more from Shimp's rear end than internal wiring. Ran the engine only enough to keep the windows from frosting. Street parking plentiful on Leishman Avenue, but it would attract notice if a car sat idling in the same spot all day. No place from which they could see the front and back doors of Mary Pugliese's house, so McFetridge had gone around to Vine Alley. Shimp felt bad about him being in the cold. And unarmed. Resolved to switch in an hour if nothing happened.

The car in front of the house already identified as Mary Pugliese's. Shimp's impulse was to knock on the door and see who else was there. Problem was all the other cars on the block belonged to known residents. No reason to believe Lelievre was inside. No desire to tip Mary and let her tip him. Even if Lelievre was in there, Shimp and McFetridge were not anyone's idea of the overwhelming force prescribed for taking down an armed robbery suspect.

"Base, this is PR-21. Any ETA on Dougherty's team?"

"PR-21, Base. Nothing yet. We'll let you know when we have news."

Fifteen minutes later: "Base, this is PR-21. Any ETA on Dougherty's team?"

"PR-21, Base. Nothing yet. We'll let you know when we have news."

Looked like a long day shaping up for Teresa Shimp. Maybe even longer for Janine Schoepf on the other side of the radio.

TPS reports were a pain in the ass. Usually Chris would have pitched a bitch but his arm was sore. The wound was closing but something didn't feel right inside and it wasn't getting any righter. Worse, maybe, like something was moving in there even when resting. A little hungover, too. Ibuprofen wasn't cutting it for the pain and he'd done more self-medicating than usual last night. Of all the days to pretend to proofread TPS reports, this was a good one.

Poured himself a second cup of coffee and bought a bag of Famous Amos from the machine. Positioned his cup and cookies, brought up the report on his monitor and settled in to look busy for an hour and a half or so. About shit when the main door opened and that big cop from the other day walked in with his deaf-mute partner and two uniforms. The detectives didn't look nearly as deferential as the first time Chris saw them.

Doc and his team hit the door as soon as Snyder radioed to tell him she and Augustine were in position. Crossed the room like a formation of geese, Doc walking point. Sisler two steps behind and to his left, Burrows the same relative to Sisler; Neuschwander behind Doc and to the right. He'd tried to think of all contingencies:

1. Hudak runs. Snyder and Augustine had the back and Snyder tolerated no bullshit.

2. Hudak throws down. All four cops in vests. Sisler and Burrows had their holster straps undone, hands on the butts of their weapons. Doc had his sports jacket pulled back behind his holster, Wyatt Earp style. He was good, Sisler was better, and Burrows had shown sand in the past. Neuschwander probably the weakest of the four, but no way could Doc ask him to miss this.

Doc badged the receptionist. She stood and walked out like four cops armed and loaded for bear came through the door and told her to blow two or three times a week. The main room an open bullpen with offices and storage areas along the walls. Barb Gaydac saw them enter and sat behind her desk, hands on the surface. Only Hudak in the room now that the receptionist was gone.

Doc used the voice the Army taught him. More resonant than loud, supported from the diaphragm, it left no room for dissent. "Christopher Hudak, you're under arrest. Raise your hands above your head, palms facing me. Slowly. Make sure I see they're empty."

* * *

Sean Sisler drew his weapon the instant Hudak's hands moved. Kept it pointed forty-five degrees toward the floor. No way for Hudak to do anything dangerous before Sisler could raise the Sig and blow him out of the chair.

Hudak had his right hand up, left less than half way. "Both hands," Doc said.

"My left one's hurt. I told you before."

Doc gestured with his head. Sisler and Neuschwander spread out to get sight lines on Hudak while keeping Doc and each other clear. Burrows filled Sisler's previous spot. Everyone except Doc had weapons aimed now.

"Are you armed?" Doc said.

"No, I'm not armed. Look at me."

"Do not move. Keep your palms facing me." Doc took his time approaching. Drew handcuffs from the case on his belt. Put one cuff over Hudak's left wrist and pulled it down and behind his back.

"Ahhh! Goddamn it. I told you I hurt that arm skiing."

Doc pulled back the right arm and cuffed it to the left. Raised Hudak from his seat by jerking up on the chain. Patted him down. Ran his arms along Hudak's left sleeve and stopped. Kept his hand on a spot three-quarters of the way between the elbow and shoulder. "What's this?"

Sisler saw Hudak sweat from fifteen feet away. "That's the bandage for the fucking ski injury and it hurts like a bastard right now."

"I'll bet it does." Doc drew a knife from his slacks. Cut the sleeve at the shoulder and pulled it down to expose a gauze wrap. A little blood had worked its way to the surface. Doc leaned to speak in Hudak's ear. "Skiing injury, eh?" Pushed Hudak in Sisler's direction. "Lock him up."

CHAPTER 46

"It's not enough."

Knowing Sally Gwinn was right didn't make it any easier for Doc to accept. Willie Grabek, retired a year now, would escalate this into a full-scale pissing contest. He'd lose—cops can't win arguments with prosecutors—though winning or losing such discussions never entered into Willie's calculations. Doc wanted to tell her to just try the case for once, don't look for reasons not to. Settled for, "We have a lot, Sally. That's his blood on Stoltz's car door."

"His blood type."

"Do you really think the DNA test won't confirm it's his?"

"When was it put there?" Doc didn't answer right away. "That's the first thing his lawyer will ask. We all know it." Gestured to include Stush and Neuschwander, also seated in Sally's office.

"It rained the night before. The car was not garaged. The color and consistency were not degraded like they would be if the car was left out overnight in the rain."

"That's too technical a distinction for a jury to draw."

"A few months ago you wouldn't try a case because you said there wasn't enough of a CSI effect to take to a jury. Now they're too stupid to understand something as simple as rain washes blood off cars. Make up your mind."

"What about the weapon?" Sally said. "It was found at the

scene with no traces of Hudak on it. We have nothing that ties him to the weapon."

"Hudak and Michael Stoltz were known to go to the range together. Ron Blewett picked his picture out of an array in no time flat."

"Did Hudak go with Stoltz that day?"

"No."

"So I don't give a shit when else he might have gone with him. It doesn't put the gun in Hudak's hand."

"True, but it shows he had access."

"Everything we know about Stoltz says he would've locked the gun in its case in the trunk. How did Hudak get it? I doubt he asked him to borrow it while he went into Dale's, because... why? Just in case? Just in case of what?"

Doc was tired of not having an answer to that. "I don't know. The only person who could tell us is dead."

"And I'm sorry about that. I really am, and not just because it fucks up our case. It does, though. Fuck up our case. We can't put the gun in Hudak's hand, and we can't prove for a certainty he was there."

"We don't have to prove it for a certainty. Beyond reasonable doubt is all we need."

"We have enough lacks of certainty for a jury to decide they add up to one reasonable doubt. I can't guarantee what we have right now is enough to keep the judge from throwing the case out."

Neuschwander spoke up. "Come on, Sally. It's better than that."

"Maybe. We all know Hudak's lawyer will move to dismiss as soon as we rest. We catch the judge on the wrong day and he dismisses with prejudice—which he will, if he does dismiss—we can't retry the case."

The room hung quiet with post buzzkill depression. Sally went first. "For what it's worth, I think he did it. That makes him as detestable a piece of shit as I've ever had to deal with.

Way past Marian Widmer." Threw Doc a look. "We only get one shot. We have to get him then."

Stush finally had something to say. "What if we didn't try him on all the murders at once?"

"I don't follow you."

"Charge him with one or two, hold off on a couple. If we crap out on the first try and new evidence comes to light, we can come back later. Double jeopardy won't apply."

Sally blew air from her cheeks. Played with a loose strand of hair. The pulse in her neck that gave all male law enforcement pause late in quiet nights ticked its siren song. "We could. It's tricky, though. It's possible his counsel will see what we're doing and ask the judge to join them, which he might. Same scene, same event and all."

"Not if we make Stoltz the separate case. He's special, out there in the car."

Sally gave a noncommittal nod. "Maybe. And maybe the defense convinces the judge we know we have a weak case and are using this as a test trial to refine our arguments. We're fucked for sure then." A breath, followed by a softer tone. "It's also going to be harder to come up with evidence as time passes. You saw how well things worked on the Widmer case even after Dougherty made it his mission in life." Doc scratched his nose with the nail of his middle finger. "We need to give it our best shot now."

Neuschwander: "Can we at least hold him for something? What about failing to report a gunshot wound?"

"It's a misdemeanor. Judge won't even set bail. Look, I'm not saying it can't be done. Don't you have a witness? The guy who shot the bystander?"

Doc out of patience. "You mean the other guy you won't charge who killed someone that day?"

"I charge what the law allows. I'd rather not charge him than establish a precedent for some other asshole if we're overturned on appeal."

"What difference does it make if you're going to use that logic to never charge anyone?"

Stush slapped the flat of his hand on Sally's desk. "Enough. Mr. Simon appears to be out of town and isn't returning our calls. Soon as we find him, we'll get him in here. Meantime we need to see what we can get from Hudak before our window to hold him runs out."

CHAPTER 47

Mike Zywiciel intercepted the detectives on their way to the interview room. "Doc, Janine asked me to tell you there's a couple people here who insist on seeing you. She says they're pissed."

"She say who they are?"

"Michael Stoltz's parents."

Doc closed his eyes. His "Fuck" soft and emphatic. "They found out we cleared him, didn't they?"

"All she said was they want to talk to you and they're pissed."

Stush stepped between Doc and Zywiciel. "This is my fault, Benny. You and Ricky wanted to tell them. I said no. I'll talk to them."

"I'm the one that interviewed them. Shimp and me. I'm the one made promises. If I don't talk to them it'll look like we're giving them the runaround."

Stush took a second. Nodded. "We'll both see them. Ricky, go get the recording equipment set up for Hudak. Go on in and bullshit if you want. Put him at ease."

Stush went first into the waiting area. Patricia Stoltz gave Doc one withering look, then stared at the floor. Mark had no trouble maintaining eye contact. Stush waded right in. "Mr. and Mrs. Stoltz? I'm Stan Napierkowski, chief of police. Why don't you come back to my office?"

Mark Stoltz stood, faced Stush directly. "We don't need your office. This one," pointed to Doc, "asked us questions and we told him everything we knew because we trusted him. Now we find out our Michael hasn't been a suspect for going on a week and no one thought we might like to know. We have things to say and we can do it right here. I don't give a shit who hears me."

"Yessir. I know you do. We have a few things to say, too, and this isn't the place for it. Let's go back to my office."

The Stoltzes declined coffee, pop, and water, in that order. Probably would have passed on air had it been offered. Everyone seated, Stush twitched in the direction of his bowl of jelly beans, thought better of it. "I'd like to get one thing on the record right away: This is my fault. Detective Dougherty followed my explicit orders. That's why you weren't told sooner. I had my reasons for making him wait."

"I'll bet," Mark Stoltz said. Then, when Stush didn't answer right away: "I'm waiting."

"You get to tell me what you think of me first. I have kids myself but I'm not going to lie to you and tell you I understand how you feel. I can't imagine it. So go ahead. Tell me what you came here to say."

Doc had seen Stush do this before. His way of sorting legitimate grievances from those used as cover. People who had already stepped in the dog shit would invariably respond with the reasons their outrage was justified, every word weakening their argument. More than a few received years at state expense to reconsider their error after Stush turned the gambit against them. This didn't apply to the Stoltzes, so Doc had a good idea how they'd respond. It still frustrated him that he wasn't better at it after all the times he'd seen Stush do it.

The anger remained in Mark Stoltz's voice. "No, go ahead. We're listening."

"It came to our attention a few days ago that your son couldn't have killed himself the way it was done. Without going into too much detail, we took some of the autopsy findings to an orthopedic surgeon. He said a man with Michael's shoulder injury couldn't have held the gun at the angle and distance he was shot from."

Both Mark and Patricia deflated noticeably. "His arm," Patricia whispered. "I never thought of it. We took it for granted after all this time. It was just how he was."

"No reason for you to think of it. Benny, show the angle the gun would've had to be held."

Doc demonstrated the best he could. "No," Mark said. "He couldn't even comb his hair with that hand."

Stush continued while the Stoltzes were still absorbing. "That didn't mean he couldn't've shot the people in the store, but it made him a far less likely suspect. I mean, what are the odds Michael would shoot three people in Dale's, get in his car, and someone else shoots him with his own gun? That pretty much cleared him in our eyes."

Mark looked like he might speak. Stush didn't give him time. "Detective Dougherty and his partner wanted to talk to you then. I wouldn't allow it. The real killer was out there, resting easy in the belief we had our shooter and no reason to continue the investigation. I wanted him to keep thinking that."

Mark's anger had lost its edge, hadn't disappeared. "And you thought we'd tell him?"

"I thought there was a good chance you'd tell somebody. Someone you trusted. And they'd let it slip to someone they trusted and on and on until pretty soon it gets to the wrong person, or the media gets ahold of it." Patricia's posture sagged as Stush went on. "People have to talk about these things. It's human nature. You have no idea how many criminals we catch because they couldn't help talking to someone and we found out. It was too great a risk."

Mark Stoltz looked far from placated. Patricia broke the silence with a sob. "I would've told Glo. My sister. Michael's godmother. She would've told her friend Kathy at work."

"And once you tell Kathy you might as well take out an ad

on television," Mark said.

Stush let it sink in. "For what it's worth, we have the guy we're sure did it. Picked him up this morning. It's been a busy day—another big case might go down—but I swear to God I would've come by the house before we released anything publicly. You have my word on that."

Patricia showed something that looked like hope. "So Michael's innocent? You can prove it?"

"Yes, ma'am. You rest easy on that. Your boy didn't do this." Stush, always the cop, wasn't finished. "While you're here, can I ask a relevant question?" No objections. "Did Michael share the combination for the lock box in his car with anyone?"

Mark gave it a little thought. "Not that I know of. He wasn't secretive about it, though. It's not like he shielded the touchpad when he opened it."

Stush exchanged a look with Doc. "Okay. Thank you. Again, please accept my apologies."

Doc spoke as the Stoltzes reached the door. "If you don't mind me asking, how'd you find out Mark was no longer a suspect?"

"A young woman reporter came by the house last night," Patricia said. "Her name was Jackson. Or Johnson. Pretty girl. Thin. Mark, do you remember her name?"

"Katy Jackson. We have her card at home."

Stush said, "Did she happen to say how she came by this information?"

"That's okay," Doc said. "I know how to find out."

CHAPTER 48

Wilver Faison had a dilemma. Too early to pack it in. Much as he liked to keep a low profile, the people working the drug houses still needed to see him at least once or twice a day or they'd get wrong-headed ideas about accounting. Didn't want to go home, either. Last thing he needed was for whoever was in the car that followed him all day to find out where he lived. If they didn't know already.

"Yo, Eddie. Pookie with you?" Wilver on his phone in the kitchen of the apartment on Eighteenth Street, around the corner from the Chinese place. Watching a crew a block down by the old glass house. "Where you at?"

"Arby's. Finally eating lunch, yo. Leander a complete fool, you know that?" Leander Watts ran the drug house on Sixth Avenue.

"Forget about Leander. Where Pookie?"

"Pookie said he had a pointment. We both know what that mean."

Wilver knew. It meant Pookie was fucking that shorty he met last week in Homewood when he picked up the new package. "Whose crib he at? His or hers?"

"Don't know. Prolly hers. I don't think she got a car."

"Find his ass and get him over here. You, too. Tell him park over by the flower store on Fifth Avenue and come in the back. Make sure no one sees you."

"Which one?"

"Which one what?"

"Which flower store? They's two a them over there."

"I don't give a fuck which one. Just get your asses over here in the next hour. And don't go near Eighteenth Street. Cross over the alley and come up on the Fourth Avenue side all the way."

"What's wrong, Wil?"

"Someone been following me all day. Waiting outside on Eighteenth now."

"You sure?"

"I'm looking right at him, nigger. Been on my ass all day. They either scoping out where we do business or looking to take me out. Get you and Pookie over here right now and come heavy." Broke off the call.

Wilver glanced into the empty living room. Business done out of the master bedroom, which had its own bathroom in case evidence needed flushing. Wouldn't do for anyone but Eddie to hear him in this state. Not the best thing in the world for Eddie to hear it. He had no one else.

That wasn't exactly true. There was one other. The last person in the world Wilver wanted to call. Found the number in his contacts. Looked out the window. Swallowed hard and made the call.

Voice mail. "Yo, Doc—I mean Officer Doc—sorry, Detective Dougherty. It's Wilver Faison. I...uh...I was just thinking it's been a while since we talked. Wondered if you wanted to get together some time. Hit me when you get a chance. Out."

Disconnected the call. Looked out the window for the twentieth time in the past fifteen minutes. Car still there. Hoppers still down by the glass house. Walked into the bedroom. Wilver's employees joked with someone Wilver didn't know. Older guy, thirty maybe, looked like he lived kind of rough. "Who you?"

"Dominique Washington. People calls me Tink."

"Lemme me see your phone."

"My phone? What you gonna do with it? I mean I needs my phone."

"You think I steal a phone off some raggedy-ass nigger like you? I need one that bad? Gimme your goddamn phone. Two minutes is all I need. Jamal, give him a free sample."

The free sample made all things possible. Wilver took the phone into the kitchen. Closed the door. Pressed four buttons and waited.

"Nine-one-one operator. What is your emergency?"

"They's some boys selling drugs off of Fourth Avenue and Drey Street. Right out in the open. Why the police let that go on? There's a car 'round the corner from them, looks like he with 'em, dropping off drugs or picking up money or something. Two guys in it, been sitting there on Eighteenth Street between Fourth Avenue and Ivy Alley at least half a hour."

"What is your name, sir?"

"I gots to go. Oh, shit. I think they seen me." Hung up. Walked into the bedroom. Tossed Tink Washington's phone back to him. "Sorry about before. 'Bout being rude and shit. Been a bad day."

Tink put away his phone. "We cool. You get what you needed?"

Wilver nodded. "It's all good. Thanks for the phone." Returned to the kitchen. Waited until he heard the sirens before he looked out the window. Saw the car on Eighteenth Street peel out. The hoppers scattered. Waited thirty seconds. Told Jamal and LeAndre he'd be back later. Left his car and walked home a roundabout way. Didn't face the street unless he had to. Waited until he was halfway there and felt safe before he called Eddie and Pookie with the new plan.

CHAPTER 49

Stush and Doc in the interview room with Christopher Hudak. Neuschwander behind the two-way mirror, video running. Stush drank coffee from a Tervis, Doc Coke from a twenty-ounce bottle. Hudak fussed with an empty Mountain Dew can.

Stush twisted in his chair to face the mirror. "You ready, Ricky?" Neuschwander tapped twice on the glass. Stush turned back to face Hudak.

Q (Chief Napierkowski): You okay there, Mr. Hudak? Get you anything?

A (Mr. Hudak): I'm good.

Q: I see Detective Neuschwander advised you of your rights and you signed a waiver. Do you have any questions before we start?

A: No.

Q: You understand you can ask for a lawyer whenever you want and we'll stop, right?

A: Yeah. I understand.

Q: Do you know why you're here today?

A: You think I shot those people in Dale's last week.

Q: We don't just think you shot them. We know. Now, do you know how we know you killed those people?

A: You can think you know whatever you want. I didn't kill them.

Q: Where were you last Tuesday?

A: I was skiing up Pocono Springs.

Q: Checked in the Saturday before, checked out the Friday after. That right?

A: You know it is.

Q: Yessir. You see, we're going to ask you a lot of questions. Some of them we already know the answers to. You won't know which ones. How you answer is going to tell us how much to believe the rest of what you say. You see how it works?

A: Yeah, I see. Let's go.

Q: You know Michael Stoltz?

A: I knew him. He's dead.

Q: How did you know him?

A: What do you mean, how? We were friends.

Q: How'd you meet?

A: I don't remember. Long time ago.

Q: Did you know him before his accident?

A: No. He was kind of fucked up when I met him.

Q: Fucked up how?

A: Not too smart? Kind of dopey? Never came up with an original idea.

Q: But you were friends.

Q (Detective Dougherty): That's why they were friends.

A: What do you mean?

Q: He'd do whatever you wanted. You wanted company, he'd come along.

A: Yeah, but that wasn't why we were friends.

Q: No? You practically called him a retard a minute ago. What other qualities did he have that made you so close?

A: I didn't say we were close.

Q: Your cell records say different. Last time I talked to anyone as often as you talked to him, I was fucking her.

A: It wasn't anything like that.

Q: Like what? Like you were fucking him? That's not what I meant. We checked. Michael was straight.

Q (Chief Napierkowski): What kind of stuff did you do together?

A: You know. The usual stuff guys do.

Q: Different guys do different things. What did you and Michael do?

A: You know. Go out for beer. Ball games in the summer. Coupla Pens games a year. Once in a while we'd bowl when Mike didn't have a league game.

Q: How often would you say you two saw each other? On average.

Q (Detective Dougherty): Remember, Chris. We know the answers to some of these questions.

A: I don't know. It wasn't like we had a regular date. Once a week, maybe. Sometimes more. Sometimes less.

Q (Chief Napierkowski): You ever go shooting with him?

A: Sure. He liked to shoot.

Q: Ever use his .45 Colt?

A: That M1911 was his grandfather's. Beautiful gun.

Q: You ever shoot it?

A: Yeah. Lots of times.

Q (Detective Dougherty): So it wouldn't mean anything if your prints were on it.

A: Wouldn't surprise me if they were. Unless he just cleaned it.

It went on like that for an hour. Stush exploring the relationship Hudak had with Michael Stoltz. Doc interjecting reminders of how serious the situation was. No voices raised. One cop or another would drop in the occasional relevant detail.

Stush shifted gears after a bathroom break.

Q (Chief Napierkowski): Your reservation at Pocono Springs was supposed to run till Sunday. Why'd you check out on Friday?

A (Mr. Hudak): You know why.

Q: Say it for the record.

A: I hurt my arm skiing.

Q: How'd you hurt it?

A: Like I said. Skiing.

Q (Detective Dougherty): Skiing how? Not very well apparently. I mean I never skied straight down a mountain and hurt myself so bad I had to leave a trip early. What'd you do? Ski into the wall of the lodge?

A: I fell, all right?

Q: Looks like he doesn't ski any better than he lies.

Q: (Chief Napierkowski): He says he fell, he fell. Skiers fall. That's why I never did it. (Eleven-second pause.) How'd you spend your time at Pocono Springs? After you fell, I mean.

A: In my room, mostly. Hurt like a bastard.

Q: You go out to eat?

A: Pretty much all I did. Got breakfast, lunch, and supper. Rest of the time I laid around the room and watched television.

Q: You see a doctor?

A: No.

Q: Pocono Springs offer to set you up with one?

Q (Detective Dougherty): I had a buddy tore up his knee skiing once. Resort had a doctor on site. Glorified EMT's what he was. Stabilized it for him. The resort offered a ride to the hospital but my buddy preferred to come home and see his regular guy. Funny they didn't offer at Pocono Springs, bad as you were hurt.

A: I didn't tell them.

Q (Chief Napierkowski): Why not?

A: I didn't think it was that bad.

Q (Detective Dougherty): You spent two full days and parts of a third in bed from the pain and you didn't think it was that bad?

Q (Chief Napierkowski): What time did you fall on Tuesday?

A: I didn't check my watch.

Q: Approximately. Near the end of the day? Before lunch?

A: It was after lunch. Maybe two or two thirty.

Q: What did the doctor say was wrong with your arm?

A: I just told you I didn't go to a doctor.

Q: Not even when you got home?

A: No.

Q: It hurt so bad you cut your stay short and you still didn't go to the doctor when you got home?

A: It was late Friday. By Monday it felt a lot better.

Q: Ah. (Seven-second pause.) How'd you hurt it this time?

A: What do you mean, this time?

Q: I've never seen a skiing injury that bled. For sure not over a week later.

Q (Detective Dougherty): Me, neither, but that's because this is a gunshot wound. How'd you get it?

A: It was an accident.

Q: I'll bet.

Q (Chief Napierkowski): How'd you do it?

A: It was stupid. You know, like they always say, I was cleaning it and didn't know it was loaded. I'm lucky I didn't blow my head off.

Q (Detective Dougherty): That what the doctor said?

A: I—uh—I didn't go to the doctor.

Q (Chief Napierkowski): How'd you stop the bleeding?

Q (Detective Dougherty): What kind of gun?

A: I was in the army. I know how to dress a wound.

Q: Whose gun was it?

Q (Chief Napierkowski): You had all the stuff handy? Gauze, adhesive tape, distilled water.

A: Yeah. It's common stuff.

Q (Detective Dougherty): Not in a hotel room it's not.

Q (Chief Napierkowski): Why not go to the hospital?

Q (Detective Dougherty): Where's the gun now?

A: I guess I was embarrassed to tell how I did it. I knew how to take care of it. It was a clean wound.

Q: You're a good enough medic you could tell it was a nice clean wound when you couldn't see the point of exit? Funny, your military record doesn't say anything about you being a 68 Whiskey.

Q (Chief Napierkowski): How many guns you own, Chris?

A: A couple.

Q: So, two?

Q (Detective Dougherty): Where were you in the house? We're going to go right over there and look for bullet holes.

A: A—a shotgun and a rifle. Thirty-aught-six.

Q (Chief Napierkowski): You didn't do that with either a shotgun or a rifle.

A: The bullet went through a window.

Q (Detective Dougherty): So we'll find a broken pane of glass.

Q (Chief Napierkowski): Do you own a handgun?

A: I replaced the window. It was just a square.

Q: What about the handgun? Where is it?

Q (Detective Dougherty): We still need to know which window. We can tell if the repair work is recent.

A: What difference does it make? I didn't do anything wrong. I don't have to prove where I was.

Q (Chief Napierkowski): I'm afraid you do, son. We can place you at Dale's that day. We have your blood on Michael Stoltz's car. We have the man who shot you. You have an obvious handgun wound you can't account for and I'll bet money a doctor will say it's about a week and a half old. You can't otherwise account for your whereabouts on the day of the shooting.

Q (Detective Dougherty): You produce the gun you say you shot yourself with, show us the pane of glass you replaced, then we may have to reconsider. With what we have here, you're going away forever.

A: I told you, I fixed the pane of glass and threw the broken pieces away.

Q (Chief Napierkowski): What about the gun you were cleaning? Help us help you. Show us evidence in your favor and we're back to Michael Stoltz as the shooter.

A: It's not mine. I borrowed it to go to the range and was cleaning it before I gave it back.

Q: Whose gun is it?

Q (Detective Dougherty): Which range? Did anyone see you?
A: I want a lawyer.

Stush, Doc, and Neuschwander convened in the hallway. Stush asked Neuschwander if there was any word from Simon. Neuschwander shook his head.

"All right," Stush said. "Enough's enough. I'll get Mike Zywiciel to put a unit on Simon's house twenty-four seven. Bring him in as a material witness." Jerked a thumb toward the interview room where Chris Hudak awaited a phone to call a lawyer. "He's going to identify this piece of shit or else."

Doc sounded almost apologetic. "Stush, I don't think the budget's there to sit on Simon's house like that. I'll do it off the books if you want."

"Fuck the budget and fuck Chet Hensarling if he doesn't like it. This shithead killed four people and might as well've killed the other. He's eating a charge. I'll take the money out of my retirement if I have to."

CHAPTER 50

Jacques Lelievre turned onto Leishman Avenue from Drey Street at 6:02 p.m. No car in front of Mary Pugliese's house. No light except for the front porch. Turned left on Ewing, left again on Vine Alley. Saw nothing but the light over the back stoop and a faint glow from the kitchen.

A second pass to see if anyone was watching. Jacques knew no one had followed him. Couldn't be one hundred percent sure no one knew about Mary. Had no interest in walking into the kind of situation Don Kwiatkowski had. The documents were ready, as was a clean car. All Jacques needed was the money from Sylvain, which delivery tracking showed should be in the house by now. Hate to have his last thought be about how he shouldn't have rushed anything.

Nothing looked suspicious on the second circuit. Pulled to the curb and let the car idle on the corner of Moore and Leishman while he made up his mind. One more pass up Leishman to be sure, then park the car in Vine Alley and go in the back. The extra key usually under a fake rock near the stairs. If it wasn't there, the back door into the kitchen had four small glass panes. Getting in was not the problem.

Jacques pulled onto Leishman. Crept down the street hoping to give the impression of someone looking for a house number. Left on Ewing. Left again. Pulled to the curb between two houses, one of which sat on Vine Alley directly behind Mary Pugliese's.

* * *

Ample parking on Leishman Avenue, so when Teresa Shimp saw the dark Chevy in her side mirror the second time, she copied the plate number as it went by. Called it in more for something to do than out of suspicion. She'd been sitting on Mary Pugliese's house for going on ten hours with two pee breaks. McFetridge hadn't had even that. Said he found a spot where he could relieve himself and that the front could be uncovered for a few minutes at a time if she had to go.

Teresa snuggled down even more in her seat, which had become surprisingly cozy from body heat and judicious use of the heater. A Suburban that parked behind her at four fifteen disguised much of the exhaust when she ran the engine. All of her that appeared above the driver's door was a navy blue ski cap.

The radio crackled. "PR-21, that license plate was reported stolen in Connellsville a few days ago. It should belong to a 2011 Chevy Cruze, light blue."

"Roger. This is a darker, larger car. Request backup at 2027 Leishman Avenue. We may need to make entry. No sirens, no lights. Assemble on the corner of Moore and Leishman. Call me when they're ready."

"Roger PR-21. Good luck, Teresa."

Had her cell in hand when headlights made the turn onto Leishman from Moore. Turned down the phone's screen as the dark Chevy rolled past a third time at no more than ten miles per hour. Waited until she saw the brake lights and left turn signal at the corner of Ewing before she called McFetridge.

Ben Dougherty didn't go straight home. Too wound up from the day with Chris Hudak to let himself brood alone. Not in the mood to deal with a lot of people, either. Stopped at the Edgecliff because it wouldn't be busy at four thirty and Denny Sluciak knew when to leave Doc alone. A baconburger on Syrian bread—lettuce, tomato, slice of sweet onion—and fries with gravy. Two Cokes with the meal, not ready for beer yet lest it go down too smooth and want company.

Went home and watched the last half of *Pardon the Interruption* because ESPN was the channel that popped up when he turned on the television. Used to like the show until Kornheiser and Wilbon became too full of themselves, acting like they actually knew what they were talking about. Let his distaste distract him until *SportsCenter* came on at the top of the hour and he went into the bathroom. Shower running and stripped down to his shorts when Stush called.

Not bitterly cold in Penns River. Nothing like the time Gord McFetridge and Scott Albert went to the First Nation Reserve at Norway House to arrest a Cree who'd raped a woman in Saskatoon and gone home to hide amid the bosom of his family. Thirty below at noon—minus-twenty-two Fahrenheit, doing the conversion in his head to pass the time—evil bastard of a wind whipping across Little Playgreen Lake at forty kilometers an hour. Wind chill so bad he'd have sworn an affidavit the vitreous in his eyes was freezing, that and his lips the only exposed parts of him.

Thirty degrees Fahrenheit and a breeze coming off the river four hundred meters away with lots of houses between to break it up was a mere inconvenience. McFetridge could stand here all night—and would if he had to—to arrest this fucking Queeb and go home to make love to his wife and watch his kids play hockey, not simultaneously. Got the call from Shimp and shrank a little more behind the tool shed he used for concealment.

A black or dark blue Chevy—or Buick—came toward him on Vine Alley. Glided to a stop between the house directly behind Mary Pugliese's and the one next to it. Lights went out and the exhaust stopped. McFetridge made himself even smaller behind the shed. A direct path to Mary's door would take whoever was in the car within a few feet.

The driver's head already turned so McFetridge caught no light on the suspect's face when the door opened. A man of the same approximate height and body type as Jacques Lelievre walked a not quite straight line to Mary's back stoop. Fussed around with something on the ground. Stood and unlocked the door. Went in.

McFetridge called Shimp. "Send someone to cover the back so I can come around and talk with you."

Teresa Shimp was grateful it had only been an hour since her last bathroom break. No telling what mayhem might have ensued when Ben Dougherty opened her passenger door and slid in un-announced.

He saw the look on her face and gave an apologetic shrug. "Sorry. I should have told you I was coming up. What do we have?"

"Looks like Lelievre just let himself in. I sent Speer and Rinella around back to relieve McFetridge. He'll be up as soon as they're in position."

"Where's Snyder?" Doc said.

"She's sitting on Chuck Simon's house. Is there a problem?"

"No. Al and Dewey can handle this. I guess I've gotten used to seeing Nancy in the shit. What's the plan?"

"That's what I want to talk to you and McFetridge about. We have options."

McFetridge slid in on the passenger side back seat. Rubbed his hands together. "I didn't notice how cold I was till I came in here."

Teresa choked back a guilty comment. "You want some coffee? I filled a Thermos last time I went to the bathroom."

"If you wouldn't mind." Doc handed McFetridge the jug. "Thanks. How do you want to do this?"

"We don't have a compelling reason to go in right away."

Teresa left opportunity for dissent. "We could wait and grab him when he leaves. Any arguments?"

McFetridge sipped coffee. "It's dark. Clouds and no moon. Your patrol officers have good positions but I can't guarantee they'll see him leaving, especially if he turns out the porch light."

"They're not right up against the back door?" Shimp said.

"I told them to lay back a little so he can't catch a random look at them and go barricade. If they're off a little he might not see them. They can get him in the open if it comes to that."

Doc: "They have his car blocked off, right?"

McFetridge nodded. "Yeah, except it's a patrol unit. Where they have it would be hard to notice from the house, but if he gets in the yard and catches wind he'll walk away."

"There's another problem," Doc said. "The woman owns the house will be home sooner or later. Then we have a potential hostage situation. Dale's closes at nine thirty. She could be home anytime from nine forty-five on."

"I agree with both of you," Teresa said. "I'd prefer to go in, but we don't have a warrant. We can't just start kicking in doors that aren't his even if we did know for a fact he's in there."

McFetridge leaned over the seat. "I have a warrant. It's Canadian, but I also have the paperwork from your FBI that authorizes its execution."

Doc wanted to know if McFetridge was absolutely sure Lelievre was inside.

McFetridge took a brief glance at the house. "He's in there."

Doc zipped his jacket. "Then let's go."

Teresa felt her position slipping away. "Hold on a minute. How are we going to do it?"

"Well, Snyder's out. Is Sisler here?" Doc's security blanket.

"Not yet. He lives up near Saxonburg. I haven't heard he's coming for sure."

"Who else do we have?"

"Us and Speer and Rinella around back," Shimp said.

"I'd like to have another weapon for the entry." McFetridge

arched an eyebrow and opened his hands. Doc said, "I'd love to, but the absolute last thing we need is for a foreign national police to shoot someone, or be shot. Cause an international fucking incident the way things are now. No offense, Gord."

"None taken."

Teresa held her phone to an ear. "How far out are you?... We're on the even-numbered side of Leishman between Moore and Ewing. Park around the corner and walk up...Okay. See you then."

She turned to Doc and McFetridge. "Sisler will be here in ten minutes. He says he's in plain clothes so don't shoot him."

Shimp, Sisler, and Doc on the front porch. McFetridge at the foot of the stairs on the paved walkway that led to the street. Doc raised his hand to knock. Shimp stopped him.

"No offense, but you get to have all the fun. This is my case, mine and Sisler's. I'll take the door."

Doc almost reminded her they were only here because of the lead he'd got from his brother. Decided this was no time to argue. And she had a point. Took a step back and gestured with his hands. Be my guest.

Shimp pounded three times with the side of her fist cop style. "Penns River police! Open the door and raise your hands!"

No answer. Ten seconds went by. Shimp tried again. Same result. "Do we have a ram?"

Doc opened his hands. Looked at them as if maybe he'd get lucky. Sisler patted his pockets and showed his palms. "Sorry," Doc said. Positioned himself to kick it in.

"Wait. My case, my door. Right?"

Doc gave her a once-over. Five-seven or so. Hundred and ten pounds, tops. Flat-soled, sensible plainclothes policewoman shoes. Doc moved away this time with considerably less flourish.

Shimp stepped into the door. Perfect form, heel strike a few inches above the knob. The door shook, but held. Leaned over and wrapped both hands around her knee. "Son of a bitch!"

"You okay?" Doc had done that himself, caught the door with his foot and shin a micron off the angle he'd wanted and felt the vibration go damn near to his hip. Like hitting a baseball off the end of the bat in cold weather.

Shimp nodded. Lined up the door again. Doc cleared his throat. Pointed to her feet, then his, shod in tactical boots. "Size twelve."

Shimp looked at his feet. Nodded and stepped aside. It occurred to Doc as he raised his leg he had better kick this fucker in on the first try. Shattered the frame and sent the door rebounding so hard off the wall it tried to slam shut again. Shimp went first and broke right. Sisler broke left. Doc took the center. He loved those shoes.

No telling how long it would have taken Jacques to find the parcel if the cops hadn't knocked. Walked right past it in the dining room the first time, eyes not yet accustomed to the indoor darkness. Turned to look for options when he heard the pounding and noticed Sylvain's package on the table. Mary hadn't opened it, left it right where he'd see it.

He didn't know the house well enough yet to have instincts about it. Cops would be front and back. No panic rooms or secret panels like they'd have in a movie to give him a fighting chance. His one saving grace was the front door had no line of sight to where he was now and the cops would have to assume he had a gun and take care clearing each room. Jacques did have a gun, no intention of using it. Prison was bad enough but he could do the armed robbery and walkaway bits. Maybe even walk away again if he got the chance. Killing an American cop was a death sentence. If they even gave him the opportunity. He'd heard a local cop died in the line of duty last summer and had to assume the ones fucking around at the front door would take no chances.

His opinion of the local constabulary not enhanced by their efforts to gain entry. Gave Jacques plenty of time to look for alternate ways out. The dining room had a window on the side of the house. Jacques gave a tug. Locked. Reached for the usual place and felt the typical window lock. Turned it and pulled up again. The window slid open. He kicked away the plastic storm window and slipped out into the small side yard.

A little more light out here. Police in back for sure. In front, maybe everyone came in. Jacques took a second to orient himself then ran like hell for Leishman Avenue, a shoebox with seventy thousand American under his left arm like a football. He was almost to the street when something hit him from the side and knocked him flying. Held onto the shoebox, though.

Gord McFetridge didn't mind waiting outside. Not that he didn't want to go in, but he understood why he couldn't, this not his first international stampede. Hesitated, not believing his good luck, when he saw Jacques Lelievre run from around the side of the house big as life. Didn't see a gun and Jacques didn't seem to be paying too much attention, so Gord lowered a shoulder and used the form he'd been taught in rugby. Drove through Lelievre's torso and wrapped arms around legs. Form so good the contact was harder than expected, knocked Lelievre sliding across the slippery ground. Gord regained his own balance and pinned his new prisoner to the wet grass. Started yelling for the locals.

CHAPTER 51

Doc walked through the door from the parking lot to the cop shop at seven forty-five the next morning. First person he saw inside was Stush. "Your close personal friend Chuck Simon's here."

"When'd he come in?"

"Snyder brought him around ten-thirty. We put him up for the night as a material witness."

"When's the lineup?"

"Hudak's lawyer can't get here till ten. You still have a couple hours to get ready."

Doc usually grabbed a cop or a guard from the jail to fill in his lineups. Today he had to contend with the fact that Chuck Simon had spent time in the jail himself and seen quite a few officers and court employees. Took Doc his entire two hours and then some to find a suitable array of city workers, school bus drivers, and day laborers with the proper body type, hair color, and age range to provide a valid comparison.

Hudak's lawyer a young woman Doc had seen around the courthouse. A little heavy, a little mousy, but presented herself well and pulled off the rare lawyer feat of not letting the police push her or her client around without being an arrogant asshole about it. Wendy Truver asked if she could take a look at the fillers before the main event. So the cops wouldn't have to worry she'd tell a judge they put her client in with two black guys, two

Asians, and a midget.

Doc scratched his head. He'd heard stories of lawyers who might try to pull something. Never seen it himself, of course, but it rarely paid to take chances. "You wouldn't be thinking of running me around gathering panels all day, would you, Ms. Truver?"

"Come on, Dougherty. I don't want to spend all day on this any more than you do. I'm looking to cover us both here."

Doc considered his options. Thought of calling Sally Gwinn and letting the lawyers wrangle it out. That could take all day, he'd probably have to gather up another panel, and Simon was already a less than cooperative witness. "How about some ground rules first?"

"Such as?"

"Your client is five-foot-eleven, medium body type. Has an— I don't know, average?—complexion. Light brown hair cut relatively short, no facial hair or scars, no visible tattoos. If I bring you in five guys between five-nine and six-one that meet the other characteristics you won't give me a hard time because you don't like one's nose or eyebrows. Fair enough?"

"Fair enough."

Doc told Ray McKillop at the jail to keep Hudak in his cell and bring in the fillers. Stood with Wendy Truver in the video room to watch through the two-way glass as the five filed in.

"You do nice work," she said.

"I live for your approval. We ready?"

She was. Doc explained the procedure. Sent McKillop with the fillers to the jail area under the courtrooms so they could all come back together. Dispatched Neuschwander to bring Simon from the maximum-security cell where he'd slept so he and Hudak would have no contact. Shooting the breeze with Wendy Truver when the phone rang in the observation booth. Ray McKillop had a problem.

"What's wrong?"

"The suspect has a sleeve missing from his shirt. It was like that when he came in."

"I know. So what?"

"I'm not trying to tell you your business, but isn't your witness the guy that's supposed to've shot him?"

Doc's patience not endless this close to a resolution. "Yeah. And?"

"Well, the suspect has a freshly dressed wound on his left arm. Won't that kind of hose the lineup?"

Doc felt the near miss as it passed. "Holy shit. Thanks, Ray. Can we get him a shirt?"

"Yeah, probably. That's not all, though."

"What now?"

"He's wearing a uniform. From where he works, I guess. We give him a civilian shirt and he has on uniform pants, won't that look suspicious?"

Doc glanced over his shoulder at Wendy Truver perusing some papers. Looked down the hall to see Neuschwander approaching with their star witness. "Can you get him pants?"

"Not just lying around."

Fuck. Fuck fuck fuckety fuck fuck fuck. "Can you round up a pair of pants from someone's locker? Tell them it's worth twenty bucks. I'm good for it. They'll have them back in half an hour."

"No one the right size comes to mind. Listen. What about a county jumpsuit?"

"Good idea. Send him in with a sign that says 'Pick Me' while you're at it."

McKillop made an audible display of patience. "I'm talking about putting them all in jumpsuits. We have them cold weather ones with the long sleeves. Give me fifteen or twenty minutes to round some up and get these guys changed."

"Wait on." Gestured to Wendy Truver. Explained the situation. She nodded. "Okay, get them changed and bring them up. Shit, wait. One more thing. We took Hudak's shoelaces, didn't we?"

"And his belt. It's SOP."

"Take all their shoelaces while you're at it. Apologize for me, but we can't have some dipshit thing like that screw us over later. Oh, and Ray?"

"Yeah?"

"Lunch is on me."

The light was adjusted to shine more or less in the eyes of the exhibits. Doc had done hundreds of these, still reminded himself not to give any sign when the guest of honor entered. Proud of the fact he'd never participated in an invalid lineup. The witness didn't always pick the right guy—if they picked anyone at all—but that was how it went sometimes.

His self-discipline came in handy when Chris Hudak entered as Number 5 and Doc saw the outline of the bandage on Hudak's left arm under the sleeve of his jumpsuit. Forced himself not to react, nor glance in Wendy Truver's direction to see if she noticed. Let it pass and hope he'd seen it because he was looking for it.

"We're in no hurry, Mr. Simon. They're going to step forward one at a time, turn each way, then step back. You recognize the man you saw shoot those people, point him out. He can't see us or hear us. Just tell me the number." Looked to Wendy Truver, who nodded.

Doc pressed a button near the window and told Ray McKillop to begin the pageant. "Number 1, step forward...Turn left... Turn right...Face front...Step back. Number 2, step forward..."

Doc preferred it when the suspect was either Number 1 or 2. Get it over with. Ray was scrupulously fair. Kept a die in his desk and rolled it to decide where the suspect stood. Doc watched Simon to see if his eyes moved ahead and took even more care not to give anything away.

Number 6 stepped back. Simon looked as if he'd spent half the day in an interrogation. Worse, since Doc had seen Simon after half a day of interrogation. "Mr. Simon, you see him in there?"

"Uh …could Number 5 step out of line again?"

Doc pressed the button. "Number 5, step forward." Hudak did, visibly shaken.

Simon gave a long look and Doc knew—body language, instinct, gut, whatever—how this would end. "No. He's not there."

Doc's voice was tight. "He's not there or you're not sure?"

Wendy Truver already moving for the door. "We're done here."

Doc turned to Neuschwander standing in the entry. "Tell Ray to turn the fillers loose. And shut the door while you're at it."

Simon turned to leave. "Hold on," Doc said. "We're not done here yet."

"What did you want me to do? I didn't see him."

Doc maintained his decorum. "You didn't have any trouble doing what you thought was the right thing when you killed Nicole Sobotka." Held a thumb and forefinger half an inch apart. "I'll give you this much credit. You took a second look. I'd like to think you were making up your mind whether to step up and not just breaking my balls when you did that."

"I honest to God didn't recognize anyone. I would've said so if I did."

"You're a lying sack of shit and a coward to boot."

"You can't call me a coward after what I done that day. Standing up how I did."

"Shut the fuck up. I've been doing this a long time. I saw all the signs. Eyes a tad wider. Shallower breathing. A little sweaty. You recognized him."

"I swear to God I didn't. Which one was he?"

"You mean to tell me you didn't notice your handiwork? The end result of your coolness under fire, giving him a flesh wound and shooting the Sobotka women straight through the spine?"

"It was Number 5, then. That's why I asked to see him again. Then, when he was closer, I just couldn't be sure. Whoever did this is going to jail forever. I had to be sure."

Doc moved within inches of Simon. "Here's something you can be sure of. You killed Nicole Sobotka. They'll never try you for it and the family probably can't even sue you, but make no mistake. She's on you."

"I've had about enough of this bullshit."

"Shut up. There was no way for him to see you or hear you today. Three cops between you, two of them armed, and you shit the bed again. You probably haven't paid for a drink since this happened. I'll bet the story gets more hair-raising every time you tell it. Here's my parting gift to you: Every time you get in bed full of free beer, right before you fall asleep, I want you to remember there are people who know what a fucking imposter and liar you are." Let it stew a second. "Any questions?"

Simon stared past Doc to the door. "Can I go now?"

"By all means." Doc stepped back to make room. Leaned on the door as Simon put his hand on the knob. "If I ever catch you playing a lottery that isn't run by the state, or buying a watch or a TV without getting a receipt, driving thirty-six in a thirty-five, or parking in a fucking loading zone, I'm going to hit you with everything the law allows. Get creative if opportunity presents." Opened the door. "Get the fuck out."

Followed Simon from six feet behind all the way to the front where Katy Jackson waited. Fine. Get all the shit over with at once.

CHAPTER 52

"What did I tell you would happen if you fucked me about going public?"

"I didn't go public."

"What did I say?"

"I'm telling you I didn't go public."

"Then how did the Stoltzes know Michael was no longer a suspect?"

Katy turned sheepish. "I told them."

"And now you're going to explain to me the fine distinction between that and going public."

They stood in the interview room the lineup had just left. Katy said, "I went to talk to them. I wanted to get a story about how it felt knowing their son hadn't killed anybody. No one else had run anything along those lines, so I thought maybe I was the first one to figure it out."

"After you promised you wouldn't go public."

"I didn't go public."

"What the hell do you call telling the Stoltzes if not going public?"

Katy stopped mid-breath to collect her thoughts. "First, 'going public' means printing a story or going on the air. If you didn't want me to tell anyone—anyone at all—you should've told me it was confidential. 'Off the record' or 'not for public consumption' or whatever other term you want to use means I can't print it. It doesn't mean I can't use it to progress the story. Besides, I assumed they already knew. I mean, who would you tell first, if not the family?"

Doc lost a little steam. He hadn't been as careful as he should have. "We thought if we told them they'd be too likely to tell someone else. Possibly a reporter." Let his gaze rest on her a bit. "We were essentially starting from scratch when you saw me that day in the parking lot. We wanted the real shooter to keep thinking he got away with it." A thought came to mind. "I didn't tell you enough to figure the rest of it out. Plus you took a while. What else happened?"

"You know I can't divulge a source."

Doc glared. Choked back his first answer. "Tell me this much, then: Did you figure it out yourself, or did someone flat out tell you?"

Calculations made. "I figured it out on my own. Nothing was being done on Michael Stoltz but there was too much activity for a closed case." A short internal debate. "I was here the day the old lady wandered off. I got a story on how the whole town mobilized to find her. I overheard someone talking about how you were normally in the middle of things like that, where were you today. Someone else said you were out of town following up leads in the Dale's case. I put that together with what you'd said and a few things that didn't sound right, and figured Michael Stoltz wasn't a suspect anymore. I really didn't know the parents weren't aware. Honest to God I didn't."

A thought occurred to Doc. "This is big news. How come I heard about it from the Stoltzes and not every news source in the country?

"No one knows but me." Doc's expression invited more of an answer. "I needed two sources before I could turn in anything with authority. You were about half of one and I would've come back if the Stoltzes had confirmed. When they didn't, I had to keep looking but I didn't have a lot of options."

Doc sat. Rested an elbow on the table. Cradled his chin with one hand. Gestured for Katy to sit. Tried to remember when he'd last felt this tired. "You want your exclusive now?"

"You're still willing?"

"Yeah. I'm pissed that you told them but I can't really blame you for it. I have to give you credit, waiting for a second source like you did." Moved on before the compliment took root. "Couple things first. We didn't speak today. Anyone asks, all I did was ream you for telling the Stoltzes." A complaint formed on Katy's face. "That's the price for this interview. I will tell you as much as I want to and you can ask me yes or no questions to confirm what you already think you know. I am not a source." Paused for effect. "Think of me as your own personal Deep Throat. Agreed?"

More calculations. "Okay."

Doc rested his eyes a few seconds. Opened them and gave a judiciously edited version of his past two-plus weeks. Left out names and anything that would lead her directly to CSI and Chris Hudak, though he had little doubt she'd end up there. Confirmed a few things Katy already knew.

She asked if there was a suspect in custody. "No comment." She threw him a look. "It's an ongoing investigation. The DA will let you know if they have anything to announce."

"But you made an arrest."

A pause, then, "Yes."

"And there is a suspect in custody."

A pause, a face, then, "Yes."

"And that's all you're going to tell me."

Doc wanted to tell her about Simon and the lineup. How hard it would be to get Sally to charge a case she wasn't a thousand percent sure of winning. Burned out and hungry was no condition to make such subtle and potentially long-lasting decisions. Chose to give Sally a chance to do the right thing. "I honestly don't know what they're going to charge. Like I said, it's an active investigation." His only lie. The file was closed. Any further investigating would be at Sally's behest. "Go next door. Ask for Sally Gwinn."

Katy Jackson had her hand on the doorknob when Doc spoke. "What if you'd been wrong?"

"What if I'd been wrong about what?"

"About Michael Stoltz being in the clear. You didn't know what I was looking for at Pocono Springs that day. You tell the parents, get their hopes up, they start telling everyone they know. Then it turns out you made a mistake. He did do it. How are they gonna feel then?"

"I wasn't wrong."

"That's not what I asked you."

Katy looked at her feet. Said, "I wasn't wrong."

Doc's head still rested on one hand. "This time. I don't think you meant them any malice, but you wanted a story and couldn't leave well enough alone. First Amendment, journalistic ethics. Doesn't matter. These are people. This is without doubt the worst thing's ever happened to them or ever will. You could've made it worse. For a story you still would've had in a day or two."

"I held it back when they didn't confirm."

"But you told them not knowing you were right. What if you'd been wrong?"

"I wasn't wrong."

"Go see Sally."

CHAPTER 53

Gord McFetridge insisted on paying for at least one round of drinks. He'd leave in the morning to escort Jacques Lelievre back to what Sean Sisler kept referring to as "Canuckistan."

"All right, Jimmy," Doc hollered to Fat Jimmy behind the bar. "Let him pay. But only fill them eighty percent full."

The attendees at McFetridge's going-away soiree already at least that close to overflowing. The brothers Dougherty, Sisler, and Teresa Shimp. All cops except for Drew, a fact not unnoticed by the rest of Fat Jimmy's clientele.

Doc regaled the assemblage with tales of how he used to manhandle Drew when they were kids. "My weekly beatings made him the man he is today."

"You make it sound like you won every fight," Drew said.

"Damn near. My record's gotta be at least a hundred and fifty and two."

"That's because when I started winning you stopped fighting me."

"Did I mention I was smarter than him, too?" Doc said.

Shimp asked if McFetridge had any siblings. He held up two fingers, his mouth full of beer. "A sister and a brother. The sister's a school teacher. My brother's a writer."

Sisler an avid reader. "What's he write?"

"Crime stories. He's pretty good, except the cops never catch anyone. I asked him why once. He said he wanted the stories to

265

be realistic."

Doc noted McFetridge's imminent departure. "I guess your boy didn't fight extradition."

"I didn't think he would. He has his code and we caught him fair and square. That doesn't mean he won't try to escape again. Besides, if he fought extradition he ran the chance you'd charge him for the robberies. I think he'd rather do his time in Canada."

Sisler turned to Shimp. "Sally didn't change him at all?"

"She filed the paperwork. Told his lawyer she wouldn't move on it if he was gone within a week."

"Plea bargaining a guy out of the country. That's got to be some kind of record, even for Sally."

Drew asked McFetridge if Canadian prisons were that much nicer than American. The Mountie shrugged. "All I know of your prisons is what I read and see on television and movies. He'll get a shorter sentence in Canada, even with the escape. He'll also have his family handy. He's close with his brother." Turned to Doc. "Speaking of charges, what's going to happen with your mass shooter?"

"Public pressure's forcing Sally to charge him with something. She may take Stush's idea and set one shooting aside for now so she can come back if she craps out. It'll be tough for her to get any kind of plea. A good defense attorney will have a field day with some of the holes we still have unless we get a witness that places Hudak at the scene. We get that, he goes down, no question. Without? Hudak's lawyer has no incentive to negotiate."

"What about your second shooter? The one who said he winged the killer. He couldn't make an ID?"

"Fuck him and his whole family. I might even be willing to talk to Sally about dropping his charges if he'd stand up and identify Hudak, but she's giving him a pass anyway."

"No charge at all?"

Doc took a long drink. "At first she tried to argue he had a Good Samaritan exception, but that's only supposed to apply for CPR and moving spinal cases and shit like that. Then she tried for Stand Your Ground. I argued that should only apply if he kills the threat, not some innocent bystander happens to get hit." Finished his beer. Pushed the glass across the bar for a refill. "I don't know what it's like in Canada, but cops rarely win arguments with prosecutors here."

Doc's phone buzzed. Caller ID read "Wilver Faison." Almost excused himself. Decided the kid could keep for an hour. It wouldn't do to seem too much like an employee.

McFetridge tapped a finger on the rim of his glass. "You really have nothing that ties him to the scene?"

"Not that'll hold up in court. Barring a witness—excuse me, a reliable witness—we're going to have to find something physical. Drop of blood or something. Problem is we already tore the place apart. It's been open for business. The crime scene's thoroughly compromised. We're fucked."

Sisler said, "What about Canuckistan? You have stand your ground laws?"

"People have the right to use lethal force, but you'll be arrested and face a charge while we sort things out. Some of the Crown prosecutors are real pricks, but unless you go over the line, you'll get off. Cost you some money, though."

"What about a guy like Simon?"

"You mean shooting a civilian by mistake? I've never heard of it happening, but all the prosecutors I know would take a dim view. I'm not sure how well he'd do in front of a jury, either. Canadians have a more restrictive concept of collateral damage than you Americans."

"Well, fuck him, then. And fuck Hudak. We all know what happened at Dale's." Sisler tipped his glass, found it empty. "It's on Sally if she can't make the case."

McFetridge checked his watch. "I hate to be the old maid here, but I have a long day tomorrow. I need to get back to the hotel."

Doc put a hand on the Mountie's forearm. "Not just yet. Jimmy!" Drunk as he'd been in a long time and not minding it.

"Where's my package?"

"How the fuck would I know where your package is, Dougherty? It's so fucking small you can't reach down and find it yourself? Oh, wait. You mean this?" Jimmy placed a paper-wrapped parcel that was clearly a bottle on the bar.

"Gord, you see we spared all expense wrapping this, and we're not letting you leave until we all drink a toast from it, but this is for you, our new friend from the vast and featureless frozen northlands."

McFetridge tore open the paper to find a bottle of Jameson Gold Reserve. "You give this to me now, after I've had too much beer to appreciate it? Bloody Yanks." Gave the bottle an admiring glance. "Well, we'd better have some glasses, then. One for yourself, too, Jimmy. You've been the perfect host."

Glasses dispensed. Shots poured. Doc raised his glass. "It seems a shame to throw back such fine whiskey, but here goes. To Staff Sergeant Gord McFetridge of the Royal Canadian Mounted Police. Dogged investigator, raconteur, blue-eyed and square-jawed and everything a Mountie should be down to that Dudley Do-Right cleft in his chin. We're better cops and men for having known—" Shimp coughed, "better men and women for having crossed paths with you. Slàinte."

"Wait!" From Sisler.

"What?"

"This is a celebration, right?" Sisler's pronunciation of "celebration" suggested Doc would have an overnight house guest.

"Yeah."

Sisler sat back on his stool. Looked at everyone in turn with eyes held open through force of will. "Depth charges?"

Silence for a second. Then Doc and Drew and Jimmy broke up. Shimp and McFetridge looked at each other in confusion.

Shimp had the nerve to ask. "What's a depth charge?"

Doc pointed to Jimmy, who showed his shot glass like a magician making sure the audience knew there was no false bottom in the box where he'd saw the woman in half. Dropped the full shot into the Pilsner glass with his beer and drank the whole thing down without coming up for air. Finished, set down the glass. Made a ball with his hands in front of his stomach. Pulled them apart with sound effects. "Bwoouussshhhh."

Doc, Drew, and Sisler looked expectantly at McFetridge and Shimp. "Noooo," Teresa said. Doc and Sisler gave her looks, paused, and dropped their shots into their beers. Drew went next. McFetridge looked at them, then Shimp, gave a *what the hell* shrug and followed suit. Doc's phone buzzed again while Shimp checked her half-empty beer glass, took a deep breath, and dropped in her shot. He reached into his pocket and turned off the phone.

Everyone drank. Shimp got most of hers down.

Hands shaken and backs slapped. McFetridge said, "Before I go we need one last toast. Pour them, Jimmy. Straight up. No naval warfare, eh?" Jimmy poured. "Now give me my bottle before we get carried away." Tucked it into a jacket pocket amid much ball-breaking. "I'd like to toast the only civil servant among us who doesn't carry a weapon for protection. We wouldn't be here tonight if not for his keen eye, faultless memory, and detailed approach to his job. Even if his brother did used to kick his ass on a regular basis, here's to Drew Dougherty, a man among..." looked at the others, "a rough approximation of men. And a fine-looking woman." Nodded to Teresa Shimp. "Cheers."

Everyone threw back the final shots of the evening. Shimp gave a mild convulsion and started for the back of the room. Doc grabbed her arm. She glared at him in desperation. "You really want to put your head in that toilet?" She made it out the front door with three feet to spare.

McFetridge watched her leave. "She's a real trouper."

Wilver Faison huddled in the corner of the recess of the old bank at Fifth Avenue and Ninth Street. Hurt like a motherfucker when the bullet went in down low like it did. Now he mostly felt cold. Pookie wasn't dead, at least not yet, lying there a few yards away, wisps of steam rising from his mouth. Last time Wilver looked at Eddie would be the last time ever after he'd seen the bits of bone and brain on the wall. Heard the sirens and wondered how long it would take them to get there. He felt cold, but not uncomfortable. Maybe a little sleepy. No hurry. They'd get to him soon enough.

CHAPTER 54

Mary Pugliese tucked a strand of hair behind her left ear. Exhaled, fists on her hips. Looked out the big plate glass window at the front of the store. Snow and wind blowing so hard she couldn't see across the parking lot. Mary understood why Dale's put the summer clothes out with winter still on the calendar. Still seemed to her Mother Nature made a point of teaching patience every time Mary started the work.

She watched the snow for a minute. Wondered how bad the roads would get. Only a few miles from here to home but Moore Street between Freeport Road and her house on Leishman Avenue had a reputation as a bad hill in an area famous for them. She locked up her brakes a few years ago and slid right past Leishman, then Vine Alley, Kenneth Avenue, and Proctor Alley until coming to a gentle stop against the retaining wall that separated Constitution Avenue from the drop to the railroad tracks. That slope so steep not even Western Pennsylvania engineers dared put a road on it. Newer car and better tires now, but a memory like that has staying power.

The last thing Mary needed was for something else to go wrong. Already a shitty year, and it was only the beginning of March. Mary hadn't known Monica Albanese or Tim Cunningham any more than to say hello and bullshit in the break room. Still, they both seemed nice. Never did Mary any dirt, or anyone else she knew of. Looked like that asshole might get away with

271

it, too. Whole country was going to hell.

Then there was that shitheel Bob Gainey. Used her like some whore while he waited for money he stole in Canada to find him. At least the cops made it right after they kicked in her door. Nailed it shut for the night and got a crew from Busy Beaver out the next day. Mary never saw a bill. The cop who come by after to apologize—Dog something, big guy—was nice. Seemed sorry for real about kicking it in.

Tedious work, checking each type of garment and style against a list that told whether to mark it down for clearance or pack it up to be shipped someplace even cheaper than Dale's. Saving anything for next season would be overly optimistic. Dale's stood on the site of more failed businesses than Mary could remember. Hills, Ames, Steve and Barry's. At least one more. Business peaked for a few weeks after the shootings— morbid sons of bitches mostly—now even below the previous levels. Mary wondered what the over-under was on how long Dale's had left and what would come in next.

Something pinged off the metal rack when she swung a handful of slacks on hangers to her arm. Sometime a mis-sized ring fell off when a woman trying on a pair pushed their hands into the pockets to see how they laid. Gone forever when that happened. The woman would notice the ring missing at some point, retrace her steps, but Lost and Found wouldn't have it yet, still lying in a pile of other stuff people had tried on and not bought. Never an expensive ring, so people didn't often leave their numbers in case it turned up.

Mary ran her hands through all the pockets fast as a sorting machine after fifteen years' experience. Found a lump in the third pair. Took it out carefully in case it was fragile. A small lump of lead with what might have been nail polish on it. Mary held it to the light for a better look and knew right away what flaked off wasn't polish.

She thought of the cop—Newschwinger? Newanger?—who talked to everyone in the break room the first day they reopened.

Told them the trouble the cops had taken searching the place, but, a place like this, things got missed. What they should do if they found anything. Mary wrapped the bullet in a Kleenex and went to the Customer Service office to see if Gina Policicchio still had that cop's card. This might be something.

ACKNOWLEDGMENTS

Writing is a solitary occupation that does not exist in a vacuum. I'm not someone who shows his books around before they're finished, but there are a lot of influences that deserve credit:

Mike Dennis, with whom I share several bonds. Mike's a good guy, the kind of person who can disagree without being disagreeable, and who will always shoot straight with you.

Western Pennsylvania, for providing such rich fodder. The anecdotes in this book weren't quite ripped from the headlines, but they all had their origins in the back pages.

Eric Campbell, Lance Wright and everyone at Down & Out Books for their continued confidence and patience.

Eric Beetner for yet another cover that exceeds my already considerable expectations.

Chris Rhatigan, an editor who makes me reconsider things I should have considered one more time in the first place. He made *Pushing Water* a better book. As usual.

The Sole Heir™, who provided the medical insights needed.

The Sole Sibling™, who provides not only a brother for Doc but a rich cast of friends once removed, in addition to being as good a brother as anyone could ask for.

And, of course, The Beloved Spouse™, the perfect first and last audience, who unfailingly keeps these books, and their author, from going off the rails.

DANA KING writes the Penns River series of novels, of which *Pushing Water* is the fifth. His Nick Forte private investigator series has earned two Shamus Award nominations from the Private Eye Writers of America, for *A Small Sacrifice* and *The Man in the Window*. His work has appeared in the anthologies *The Black Car Business, Unloaded 2, The Shamus Sampler 2*, and *Blood, Guts, and Whiskey*. He is a member of the International Thriller Writers, Private Eye Writers of America, and Sisters in Crime.

DanaKingAuthor.com

On the following pages are a few
more great titles from the
Down & Out Books publishing family.

For a complete list of books and to
sign up for our newsletter,
go to DownAndOutBooks.com.

Coldwater
Tom Pitts

Down & Out Books
May 2020
978-1-64396-081-4

A young couple move from San Francisco to the Sacramento suburbs to restart their lives. When the vacant house across the street is taken over by who they think are squatters, they're pulled into a battle neither of them bargained for. The gang of unruly drug addicts who've infested their block have a dark and secret history that reaches beyond their neighborhood and all the way to the most powerful and wealthy men in California.

L.A. fixer Calper Dennings is sent by a private party to quell the trouble before it affects his employer. But before he can finish the job, he too is pulled into the violent dark world of a man with endless resources to destroy anyone around him.

Catawba Point
A Jim Grant Thriller
Colin Campbell

Down & Out Books
June 2020
978-1-64396-105-7

When Jim Grant's flight home to give evidence about Snake Pass is cancelled he is diverted via Charlotte NC where he is forced to spend a 3-day layover at a seedy motel on the outskirts of town.

All Grant wants is a good night's sleep, but with a skinny hooker and her pimp causing trouble along the hall that isn't going to happen. Maybe throwing the pimp over the balcony wasn't such a good idea but that's just the start of Grant's problems, which lead him to a gang of white supremacists and their training camp at Catawba Point.

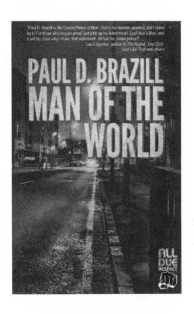

Man of the World
Paul D. Brazill

All Due Respect, an imprint of
Down & Out Books
April 2020
978-1-64396-099-9

Ageing hit-man Tommy Bennett left London and returned to his hometown of Seatown, hoping for respite from the ghosts of the violent past that haunted him. However, things don't go to plan and trouble and violence soon follow Tommy to Seatown.

Tommy is soon embroiled in Seatown's underworld and his hopes of a peaceful retirement are dashed. Tommy deliberates whether or not to leave Seatown and return to London. Or even leave Great Britain altogether. So, he heads back to London where violence and mayhem await him.

Coal Black: Stories
Chris McGinley

Shotgun Honey, an imprint of
Down & Out Books
December 2019
978-1-64396-058-6

Set in the hills of eastern Kentucky, these tales lay bare the dark realities of the region. Sometimes the backdrop is the opioid epidemic and all the human detritus and bloodshed that comes with it. Other times it's poachers or petty thieves who take center stage, people whose wild desperation invite danger everywhere they go. High in the hills the action takes place, alongside the rarely seen animals who hunt up there, and sometimes alongside the "haints" and spirits of popular folklore.

Coal Black is a collection of gritty crime stories—cleverly drawn tales with sometimes savage surprise endings.